Born into a service family in 1941, Garry Kilworth had attended more than twenty schools by the age of fifteen. He admits to having played truant a lot, especially while in Aden, where he spent a considerable time fishing for catfish and getting lost in the Hadhramaut desert. He left school before his fifteenth birthday with no qualifications, and signed up with the RAF for fifteen years. Stationed all over the world in such exotic locations as the Maldives and Singapore, Garry started to write. In 1974 his winning of the Gollancz/Sunday Times short story competition coincided with his leaving of the RAF. He took an English degree from King's College, London, and started to write seriously. He has now published fourteen novels, eighty short stories, six children's books and some poetry. He has been married to Annette for thirty years, and has two grown-up children. He now lives in Essex.

D1080625

GARRY KILWORTH

In the Country of
Tattooed Men

Grafton
An Imprint of HarperCollins*Publishers*

PG	PA
PI	PB
PR	PK
PS	PH
PV	PO 8/98
PY	PL
PZ	PW
PHH	PP

For Jane Johnson,
editor and friend

Grafton
An Imprint of HarperCollins*Publishers*
77–85 Fulham Palace Road,
Hammersmith, London W6 8JB

A Grafton Original 1993
9 8 7 6 5 4 3 2 1

05682861 ISBN 0 586 21498 4

Set in Photina

Printed in Great Britain by
HarperCollinsManufacturing Glasgow

CONTENTS

ACKNOWLEDGEMENTS

'Truman Capote's Trilby: The Facts' was first published in
BBR, 1990.

'In the Country of Tattooed Men' was first published in
Omni Magazine, 1989.

'Triptych' was first published in *Other Edens* (Unwin
Hyman Ltd), 1987.

'The Men's Room' was first published in *Interzone*, 1987.

'Usurper' was first published in *Dark Fantasies*, (Century
Hutchinson Ltd), 1989.

'Hobblythick Lane' was first published in *The Magazine of
Fantasy and Science Fiction*, 1986.

'Beyond Byzantium' was first published in *The World
Fantasy Convention* programme book, 1988.

'Spiral Sands' was first published (as 'Spiral Winds') in
Interzone, 1985.

'The Wall' was first published by *Novacon 18 Committee*,
1988.

'On the Watchtower at Plataea' was first published in *Other
Edens II* (Unwin Hyman Ltd), 1988.

'x-Calibre' was first published in *Zenith 2*, 1990.

'Bronze Casket for a Mummified Shrew-mouse' was first
published in *Digital Dreams* (New English Library), 1990.

'Surfing, Spanish Style' was first published in *The Gate*, 1990.

'Dop*elgan*er' was first published in *Interzone*, 1987.

'Networks' was first published in *Fantasy Tales*, 1990.

'Memories of the Flying Ball Bike Shop' was first published in
Isaac Asimov's Magazine, 1992.

INTRODUCTION

The chapter that requires the most effort in a novel is probably the first one. During that chapter the reader is making a special effort to come to terms with the setting, period, character and a dozen other aspects, and by the second chapter has a general feel about the work and is 'inside' the world created by the author. Thereafter, the reader can relax a little and, to a certain extent, be carried along by the flow.

When a reader tries a collection of short stories he or she has to reach this initial level of concentration time and time again, because every story is like a first chapter. Visual entertainment requires less effort than a novel and most of us just wish to be 'entertained' and therefore prefer to watch television than read a novel. Short stories demand more attention than a novel, so I do not find it surprising that volumes of short fiction are, along with books of poems, one of the least popular types of entertainment. Poems are out on their own, because there is also an oral tradition associated with poetry which has never fully died out. Poets read their works to audiences in pubs, libraries and town halls and the listeners are almost in the same position as television watchers, in that they can sit back and be entertained. The short story is stuck betwixt and between and remains the entertainment of devotees.

There is no adverse criticism intended in the above. People should be free to choose their own form of entertainment without being attacked by culture snobs. Sneering is a dangerous game anyway: the person who enjoys cowboy films may also be an avid reader of medieval poetry. Anyone who criticizes my

enjoyment of Western movies gets a lecture on the chivalric
code of the Old West and the comparisons and contrasts between
John Wayne's role in *True Grit* and Gawain in *Sir Gawain and
The Green Knight*.

I think what I am trying to say is that special effort is required
of any reader who tackles a whole volume of short stories. It
therefore follows that the author should have invested special
effort in the writing of those tales in order not to disappoint
such application. The stories in this book have been selected
from a greater number I have had published in magazines and
anthologies. These are, I believe, the best of those. I hope they
satisfy.

Garry Kilworth

TRUMAN CAPOTE'S TRILBY:
THE FACTS

I have never been a great lover of hats. For one thing, they tend
to crush one's hair and leave it looking like sweaty straw. For
another, individual hats are never thoroughly in fashion these
days and wearers are considered faintly eccentric. Even in the
city they draw the occasional amused smile or nudge, unless
seen on the head of someone stepping out of a Rolls-Royce. Of
course, there are places where a hat is completely acceptable,
such as at sporting events – Ascot, or the boat race – but for
people like me, on a modest income, buying a hat for a single
occasion is an extravagance. Finally, I think my head is the
wrong shape for most hats. It supports headgear which moulds
itself to the skull, like a ski hat, but tends to reshape less
obsequious millinery into something almost grotesque in out-
ward appearance.

It was, therefore, with some surprise that I found myself
staring at the trilby in the window of Dunn's in Oxford Street.

Purchasing a trilby requires special nerve and should really
only be undertaken by a person with a charisma impossible to
influence, like Bogart or the Orson Welles of *The Third Man*. The
trilby has a personality, an ego, all of its own. If the wearer is
not strong enough to resist alteration, it is better to steer clear
of such forceful, dominant items, the demi-gods and despots of
hatlands and the high country.

In any case, the trilby has a dubious history which is difficult
to deny. It flaunts an ancestry which most of us would prefer
to keep locked in a cupboard with all the other skeletons:

forefathers that witnessed – let's not mince words – *took part in* such infamous deeds as the St Valentine's Day Massacre, and later attended the funerals without so much as a droop of the brim. The 'roaring twenties' and the trilby are inseparable. A gangster's hat. Philip Marlowe gave it back some fictional respectability, but the taint remains. Of course, women too have worn the trilby, but since women tend to be promiscuous in the use of headwear we can assume that any honour regained from that quarter is open to question. In the 'forties, again, its reputation sank to a very dark level when the Gestapo adopted it (along with its constant companion, the trench coat) as part of their uniform, not to mention its sinister association with Papa Doc's Haitian secret police, the terrible *Tontons Macoute*. So, the trilby is not exactly a gentleman's hat, its motives are questionable to say the least, and it often ends its days perched on the back of an Australian head in some sweltering outback creek, keeping off the flies.

It is a hat given to swaggering gestures and sloping cuteness, famed for its slouch.

Consequently, when I saw this particular trilby in the shop window, and felt a strong urge to buy it, I tried to allow my intellect to govern my emotions. I was shocked by the strength of those emotions. They produced fantasies: the kind I used to have in my youth. I saw myself travelling on the Paris metro, men staring at me in envy and women attempting to attract my attention. These pretty pictures used to proceed a lot of purchases as a young man. Apparently they were still powerful enough to rule my head because I found myself in the shop, self-consciously trying on the trilby. I left the place wearing it.

The effect on the city's populace was not startling, but I felt rather good just the same. The hat seemed a natural part of me and I wondered, even after those first few paces along the pavement, how I had ever managed without it. Confidence entered my bones: my step was light. I passed a group of Italians, sitting outside the Café München drinking beer. One of them pointed with his chin, the way Latins do, and the others looked and nodded gravely. They approved. Italians are known to have good dress sense, so this increased my feeling of well-being.

Once on the tube, if the women did not exactly jostle each other for a better view of my new hat, they certainly gave it second glances. My self-consciousness evaporated almost completely. In the shop, the sales assistant had placed the hat on my head in a conventional position. I now tipped it at a rakish angle, emphasizing, I was sure, my angular jaw. The world grew lighter.

Back at my two-roomed flat, I took the trilby and placed it where I could see it, on the dresser which also served as a desk. This piece of furniture stood exactly opposite the doorway between my kitchen-diner and the bedroom, and I made a meal then sat and studied the article from my position at the table. It was grey, with a dark-grey band. Although not immediately exciting in its aspect, there was a certain charm which gave me a possessive glow of satisfaction. This was *my* hat: no one else's. Also, there was an independence about this trilby which enhanced my feeling of ownership. This self-possessed hat had chosen *me*.

That evening I took the hat to see Harrison Ford's rugged-looking trilby in *Raiders of the Lost Ark*. We both admired the way it managed to remain on Ford's head, even during the most frantic stunts. Towards the end of the performance we were asked to leave because a woman sitting behind us could not see the screen, but by that time most of the best scenes were over.

The next morning I wore it to work. The journey was delightful, but on reaching the office in Theobald's Road, I arrived at the same time as Jason Rachman, one of the company's high-fliers.

'Nice lid,' he said with a smirk, as we went through the double-doors together.

'It's a trilby,' I said, 'not a *lid*.'

He stopped, looking taken aback. I had never spoken to him as firmly as that before, and I think he was shocked at my assertiveness. He looked slightly confused for a moment, then said, 'No, no – I'm serious. It suits you. I've often thought of buying a trilby myself – never had the nerve. Perhaps now that you've got one, I'll have a go. So long as you don't mind me copying . . .'

I was feeling magnanimous.

'Not at all,' and I gave him the address of the shop. No one has ever asked me such things before.

At first, I placed the hat on my desk, within reach, but one of the managers passed by and told me to put it on the hat rack at the entrance to the office. I had no choice.

The following Saturday I made a terrible mistake. I don't know what made me do it. I suppose, after one has taken a tremendous new step, a giant stride, the temptation to go much further is very strong. I remember as a younger man I went on a youth hostel tour of the Scottish Highlands, and it was so successful I considered a trip to Tibet. Of course, the latter would have been a disaster. I'm not equipped, mentally or physically, for scaling the Himalayas, but the bug had got me and I felt that I could take on anything that mountain ranges had to offer. Fortunately, finances prevented me from making a complete idiot of myself.

Not so on Saturday. On Saturday I went the whole hog. I bought a fresh band for the crown of my trilby, a Big White Hunter thing that screamed at people from fifty yards away. A leopardskin band. How crass. How *stupid*! How kitsch. Who did I think I was? Hemingway?

The hat hated it of course. I wore the band for one morning only and then replaced it with the old grey ribbon. The leopardskin attracted the wrong sort of attention and made me feel vulnerable once more. After that experience, I never tried changing the hat again and accepted it for what it was.

We settled into certain behaviour patterns, the trilby and I. One thing I learned was that it needed to be treated with respect and care. It was not a hat to be skimmed, James Stewart style, across the room, aimed at a peg or chair. Such undignified methods of removal were not to its liking, and I had not the lean grace of Mr Stewart to enable me to bring the action off with the same aplomb. Also, contrary to Gene Kelly's doctrine, it did not improve for being danced through the streets in a downpour. Neither did it enjoy being crushed in a Cagney grip, nor being battered into a shape reminiscent of Bogart's face. It preferred to be placed, not tossed or jammed. It liked light, airy spaces, not dark corners. It enjoyed attention, but only for itself, not because of the angle at which it was worn, or how much of my brow showed beneath the brim.

We got on fine together for several months. So well in fact that I began to take it for granted.

We made lots of new friends who would call at the flat or telephone to arrange an evening out: friends of both sexes. Although no really special relationship developed, these new-comers in my life became important to me.

There was Tag, a West Indian with a stylish beret, and Jake, a young Lancastrian who sported one of those colourful knitted caps. Then, of course, there was Beatrice who always wore nice curled-brim bowlers: the kind of hat you often see on Cheltenham young ladies. Finally, there was Mona. Mona had seen *Annie Hall* six times and had consequently purchased a hat the twin of that cute, lopsided affair worn in the film by Diane Keaton.

Mona was my favourite. We once spent the night together and she put her Annie Hall hat under my trilby so that they fitted snugly, one in the other.

'For company,' she said.

Following in my footsteps, so to speak, Jason Rachman bought a trilby, too, which he wore to the office, but I felt it was inferior to my own hat. It lacked refinement. Oh, it had a little panache and a certain sardonic humour, but its charm could not make up for its lack of sophistication, and it was really a rather shallow piece of headgear. Jason knew this, but he defended his trilby with a shrug and a smile, which was only right and proper.

As I said before, I began to take my trilby for granted, and that's when things started to go wrong between us.

Looking back on it, I suppose it was my fault. Things began to get pretty hectic at the office, especially after my promotion. I hardly had a minute to myself. My social life also was a whirl of activity. Everything was done at a run, and, to my eternal shame, I forgot my trilby one evening, leaving it behind at the office.

The following morning I remembered it at about ten o'clock, but it was gone from its usual place on the rack. It eventually turned up behind someone's desk, dusty and covered in fluff. Anyway, it was in a sorry state. I sent it to the cleaners and what with one thing and another was unable to retrieve it for two weeks.

Then I left it at home, several days running, simply forgetting to wear it. Unforgivable, but there it is: you don't realize the importance of these things at the time. Finally, the last straw was when I took Jason's trilby in mistake for my own. The next day, when we exchanged, correcting the error, I could see the experience had clearly upset my trilby quite badly. Jason had gone downhill a little since he had been passed over on the promotion ladder and tended to frequent bars and dives until the early hours of the morning. There were small stains on the brim and crown of my trilby and it had lost its shape in some steamy atmosphere.

That same evening, as I stepped out of the tube station at Tottenham Court Road, the hat blew off my head, sailed along Charing Cross Road, and was swept by a side-draught down Denmark Street. I ran after it, past the music shops and a rather sinister-looking bookshop, but it had disappeared from the scene. I stood there for a while, by the small church on the corner, searching crannies and railings, but my hat had gone.

At first, I tried to shrug it off. After all, it was only a hat, and there were plenty more of those to be had. Not that I actually *wanted* another hat (I told myself) since I seemed to have outgrown the need. I was more mature, more self-assured, and no longer concerned by the world and its ways. There were plenty of friends to visit and go out with, to the cinema or theatre. In fact a hat was rather an encumbrance. One had to find places to put it, or carry it in one's hand. Being without it was a kind of freedom. It had done me a favour, blowing away like that. I was free to go where I wished, with whom I wished, whether they were bare-headed or not. Liberty is a heady tranquillizer, after a loss.

Unfortunately, my new friends did not turn out to be the kind of people I had previously thought. There were excuses and evasions, and they fell away from me with mumbled apologies. Even Mona. She told me one evening that we had better not see one another again, since she did not (after all) feel we were suited.

'It was fun,' she said, 'but our worlds are too far apart.'

I think she felt embarrassed, walking along the Strand with a hatless man, because she remained a good two feet away and kept glancing down at the pavement, as if afraid of being recognized by someone she knew. She refused the offer to take her for a drink, saying she was on the wagon, and later that week I saw her in the company of a flat-capped fellow with a plebeian brow. She cut me dead in the street.

Anyway, all my so-called new friends went the same way: towards the exit. I can't say it didn't upset me because it did. I was terribly depressed. It was all so unfair.

There were problems at work, too. Some Japanese business-men visited the firm and they were left in my hands. I was so distracted by the decline of my social life, however, that I unwittingly neglected them and the result was a reprimand from one of our directors.

'And do something about your appearance,' said my boss afterwards. 'You seem to have gone to seed lately. This company depends upon smart executives to give it a good image. A haircut would make a difference . . .'

After a week of sleepless nights, I reluctantly went looking for my lost trilby. I suppose I had hoped it would turn up on its own, without effort on my part. Although I hadn't marked the leather headband, I had written my name and address on a piece of paper and tucked it inside. I scoured the found ads and rang various lost property offices, without success. Finally, I took to wandering the streets after work, searching the alleys. Once, I snatched the headgear off an old tramp, thinking it was my trilby, but I had made a mistake and had to apologize while the old fellow remonstrated with me, using the most obnoxious language. It took five pounds to get rid of him.

There was a period when I saw the trilby everywhere: on the tube, outside a cinema, going to work. But always, on closer inspection, it turned out to be a stranger which just happened to resemble my trilby superficially. Having once made an error of recognition, I was most careful not to handle these look-alikes, but the wearers often resented my staring, even from a distance, hurrying away into the crowd or turning to glare at me.

Shortly after this period I lost my job through non-attendance at work. I didn't care any more. I began to hit the bottle.

Miserably, as the weeks went by, I toured the London streets, extending my area of search, and growing more despondent, and, yes, more resentful towards my erstwhile headwear. There were several million hats in London. What chance did I stand of finding one particular hat? The weeks crept into months, and gradually my frustration turned to anger, my anger to hatred. I convinced myself that my trilby was deliberately avoiding me. There were still times when I got morose and maudlin – when I missed it dreadfully – but many hours were spent over a glass bitterly regretting wasted dreams and shattered hopes. It seemed so silly – one breeze, one single breeze, and we had parted forever. My hatred bred a rage within me which was beyond my control. I told myself I would not be responsible for my actions, should I ever lay hands on that hat again. I bought myself another, a Sherlock Holmes deerstalker, and though we were not entirely compatible we were tolerant with one another, hoping to grow closer together as the relationship matured.

One day in October, when I was least expecting an encounter, I finally saw my old trilby plastered against a fence by the wind.

I knew it instantly, though it had aged dramatically since I had last seen it. I went to it, picked it up, dusted it off – and rammed it into the nearest waste bin amongst some discarded Coke cans and cigarette packets! Remembering I had the trilby's replacement on my head, I tipped my new deerstalker contemptuously at my ex, and hoped the humiliation was complete. I went home, determined to forget our association.

Six nights later the police came to my flat.

They questioned me concerning my whereabouts on an evening two nights previously. Eventually, they took me away, and in the presence of a lawyer, charged me with the murder of a woman whose corpse had been found near the Thames, close to Waterloo Bridge. A trilby – my hat, with name and address still inside the band – had been found pinned beneath her body. They later produced this item of clothing in court. Since it was associated with me it had gained the same sort of notoriety and attention from the gutter press as myself. However, it was its role as principal witness for the prosecution that seemed to suit it best. Like I said earlier, the trilby has a bad track record: you can't trust a trilby. When the prosecuting counsel pushed it in front of me, his accusations tying me in knots, it didn't help my case any when I threw lighter fuel on the brim and tried to set light to it.

However, at the last hour my own counsel called a witness to the stand who had seen the woman earlier the same evening that she died, and he stated that she 'had the face of a suicide'. (This remark was subsequently stricken from the record, but not from the minds of the jury.) Coupled with this was a statement from a medical consultant who had independently examined the body. In his professional opinion the police doctor was mistaken. He himself was convinced that the dead woman could have sustained such injuries as a result of a fall, say from a bridge parapet on to concrete.

Despite the controversy which raged in the press, I was acquitted and walked from the courts 'a sadder but wiser man', though not without a stain on my character. There were those who were still convinced of my guilt, not least amongst them the police.

I never saw my hat again. The last I heard, it went on the stage. Someone had written a play around my court case, and the exhibit used in the actual court room where the trial took place was considered the main crowd puller at the theatre. My ex was a box office success, right from opening night.

Since then a certain tabloid has fostered the tale that the hat was privately purchased by Truman Capote, shortly before his death: that it attended wild New York parties and was passed around superstars and celebrities. This is an extravagant claim to which I give little credence. To my knowledge, Mr Capote preferred a more flamboyant form of headwear, such as a panama – certainly not second-hand grey trilbies, no matter how colourful their histories. Nevertheless, to most people my hat has become 'Truman Capote's trilby', for which unlikely title I should be grateful. My connection with the item has almost been forgotten: overshadowed by the charismatic influence of the famous author's name.

Good luck to it. I know one thing. I shall never trust a trilby again, as long as I live. They're not worth it. They use you up and then they blow away. And when they've had enough of the street life, they have the audacity to expect to be taken back again, no questions asked. They want the magic to last forever, and as everyone knows, things don't work out like that. Magical relationships grow into ordinary lives, sooner or later.

IN THE COUNTRY OF
TATTOOED MEN

The letter was sent on to me at my home in California by the publishers of my war photograph books. It suggested we meet at his apartment in New York, since it was not possible for him to travel at that time. It stated that he was undergoing a strange experience, that I should record these 'changes' for the future. What I hoped to get out of it was a good story, if there was any truth in it of course. He would not be the first Nam vet to go crazy. At first, I was inclined to ignore the letter, but if Asia does nothing else for you, it permanently primes your curiosity. I took a flight to the east coast the following Wednesday.

I checked in at The Roosevelt, which has an old-world colonial charm about it that makes an expatriate Englishman like myself feel a little more at home in otherwise intimidating New York architecture. I feel swallowed in New York, as I move beneath giant buildings that seem to touch each other at their peaks, closing off the sky. I sense my insignificance more amongst the skyscrapers of that city than I do when contemplating distances between the stars. It doesn't help to know there are lawns and fruit trees on the tops of some of those dizzying buildings: it makes them appear to have grown overnight, carrying the turf with them, leaving us fragile mortals deep in the depths of their chasms.

The Roosevelt's decor has a European feel, with ornate brass bedside lamps bearing leafglass shades, and marble-topped cabinets. I feel more confident with such furnishings around me. I feel less insecure.

'I'm *really* gonna look after this for you, sir,' said the man who took my dirty laundry away to be cleaned. He paused in the doorway until I recognized the hidden language and gave him the two dollars which would ensure the safety of my soiled shirts.

When the door had closed, I picked up the copy of the *New York Times* which lay on my bed. The front-page story concerned the killing of a rapist in Central Park. It appeared to be a vigilante thing, and though the rest of the street gang had witnessed their leader's death, none of them was quite sure what they had seen. The woman who was being assaulted also denied that she had seen the killer, though quite understandably she blessed his intervention. Neither of these statements would have been surprising had the rapist been shot by a high-powered rifle or even a handgun. He had, however, been strangled. The police pathologist stated that from the bruise on the dead man's throat it could be deduced that the perpetrator had used a nylon cord or wire garrotte.

Beneath this article was a smaller one, dealing with the newly elected President's statement about the need to send military advisers to Asia to assist a certain country in its war against an aggressor.

Only in the Western world would a story about a vigilante take precedence over the possibility of America involving itself in another Asian war.

The first tattoo appeared one morning at the end of summer. He had been out the night before, celebrating in one of his favourite bars. There had been a lot of 'celebrating' in the past few years. The first excuse was his safe return from Vietnam, then Phil's death, then his own divorce, then . . . then any good or bad news, big or small. He was good at celebrating.

The symbol, for that was what it was, rather than a picture or word, was not even in a conventional place on his anatomy. Not for an American anyway. It was just below his left armpit and if anything resembled a Sanskrit character, or perhaps

Chinese? *Japanese?* No, not even like any of those. It was simply a symbol, a whorl ending in a sharp, angled line which went back in on itself to create a tiny maze. When he studied it in the mirror he was astounded at the fine detail, the artistry involved. The tattoo was like a world in itself: the world of a closely-inspected flower or leaf. The *inscape* of a microscopic organism.

'What in Jesus . . . how the *hell* did I get that!' he said, looking round his poorly furnished apartment, hoping to find evidence of the previous night's movements. Where had he been the night before? He remembered Stacey's Bar, then the night club on – what street was it? But a tattoo parlour? They used to be in Chinatown but he had read somewhere that they had all been closed down. Tattoos were not easy things to get rid of – plastic surgery was expensive. Lucky it was in a place only his intimates would get to see. Lucky it wasn't something crass, like a copy of last month's *Playboy* centrefold. Lucky, lucky, lucky . . . he slammed his fist into the wall above the mirror. Someone shouted a complaint from the next apartment and he yelled back, 'Go to hell!' before washing his hurt knuckles under cold running water.

Outside, the Brooklyn traffic was just reaching its nine o'clock crescendo. He pulled his slacks on over his shorts. He should have been at work an hour ago. Next thing, he would be losing his job.

Three days later, after his next binge, the second tattoo appeared. This time it was on his elbow. He called his ex-wife and spoke to her for a while, not telling her, but gaining a little strength from the sound of her voice. Then he called his son and talked about football and vacations. Jamie was full of life, told his father he missed him and that the three of them should get together soon, once college was over. Jamie was a romantic, always matchmaking, hoping that his parents would get to-gether again, even remarry. By the time he put down the phone, he was feeling better. He made a vow not to drink for a week.

Twenty-four hours later, there was a third symbol.

'I'm sleep-walking,' he said to himself. 'I'm in some sort of trance. Some bastard's got to me.' He glanced around the apartment as if he expected to see someone hiding in the closet, or under the bed. He studied his eyes in the mirror and saw fear in them. He touched his sallow cheek and his hand shook. 'Some bastard's getting to me.' He couldn't have been more afraid if the tattoos were not just coloured symbols but bodily disfigurations indicating that some deadly disease had found its way into his blood.

He was as scared as he had ever been, even in Nam. In fact, he thought, it was the *same* scared. He recognized the fear the way other people recognize the smell or taste of an unusual spice. There were various types of terror and this was definitely the jungle-death fear. It was because there was something very Asian about the tattoos: something oriental in the design. Suddenly the nights seemed even more hollow than before. Out there, in the dark, something was getting at him. He was back in Vietnam, looking at a wall of jungle, inside that wall and walking beneath giant trees whose roots had to be climbed like hills. He was an insignificant mortal in a place of no understanding. His mind was running far ahead of his body or dragging way behind it. He began starting at shadows again, swallowing fear faster than the booze. The jungle had followed him back, into the streets of New York. The little men whom you never saw were hiding in the alleys. He was too scared to drink: too scared not to drink. His fright was getting him up late in the night, sending him down to the bars to get some of the stuff that would rid him of his fear and add to it at the same time. He was caught in an ugly paradox that was driving him as crazy as he had once thought he was.

'What the fuck's happening?' he cried, as he stood on the sidewalk outside a bar, the neon splashing over him. 'Someone tell me what the fuck's happening . . .' But the passers-by, if they glanced at him at all, were not prepared to discuss philosophical questions with nuts, vets or drunks. Especially not with a man who appeared to be all three.

*   *   *

I left the Roosevelt and took a cab to Central Park. There, I wandered around looking at the map in the *Times*, trying to locate the position where the killing had taken place. When I thought I had it, I took a few pictures. I don't know why, they didn't show anything. I just like to have something on a new roll of film, to get me started. In Vietnam, first thing after waking up, I used to reach for my camera and take a shot of the other end of my body: toes, feet, knees. Just to get me started.

I suppose I was a pretty weird kid in those days, anyway. I had left home at the age of seventeen, hiked across Europe with a Pentax in my rucksack, bound for the East. There was a determination in me to become a war photographer. I set out to photograph the Arab–Israeli conflict of '67. It took me a week to get there. The war had only lasted six days. I shrugged off my disappointment and went further down, to Aden, where terrorist action against the British withdrawal from the colony was warming up. The authorities wouldn't let me in: they wanted to send me home to my parents. I set out east, heading for Vietnam, but paused in India losing my objectivity for a while in a cloud of opium, in the notes of a sitar. I finally got to Nam in time for the Battle of Khe Sanh.

My first pictures were lousy and nobody wanted them (until later, after the first book) but I was too eager to stop. I took more, got better, learned from American contemporaries. By the time My Lai hit the papers, I was good and my pictures sought after.

It was around that time that I saw the tattooed man. I was in country with one of the long-range reconnaissance patrols, when the nervous point man opened up at shadows with his M-16. 'I saw somethin' move,' he said. 'I saw the ferns twitch.' We checked the area and found a blood trail which led to a cave just to the side of a waterfall. The patrol only had two fragmentation grenades between them, which they lobbed one after another, but still no one wanted to go inside. I didn't blame them. The cave looked like a rock mouth waiting to swallow boonierats. The roar of the silver-toothed water didn't help our psychological state. I was glad I was just there to take pictures. They called for assistance and later a Huey dropped the patrol a flame-thrower and they scoured the interior with it. Then a single soldier went in carrying a .45. He came out backwards, dragging the corpse of a naked man. Most of the dead man's skin had gone, leaving only his left arm intact, and part of his chest. He must have been lying face down, with his arm underneath him, when the flames licked out his hidy-hole. The bits of skin that were left were covered in tattoos, and had a weird effect on the eyes: the same kind of effect that one gets when looking at closely printed zig-zag lines, black on white.

As the tattoos got tighter, more closely knit, he began to wonder if they were some kind of message. He stared at them in the mirror until he was giddy, trying to see some pattern which might be a language. He even tried moving, walking about in front of the glass, to see if the message might be more evident in the rippling muscles of his hard, lean body, in the actions of his limbs and torso. Nothing came to him.

He had spent sleepless nights touring – not the bars, but Chinatown, asking about anyone who might do tattoos. Finally, a taxi driver took him to a sleazy basement where there was supposed to be an illicit parlour. When the door was answered he knew he had the right place.

'You come for one more?' the guy said.

He explained to the artist that he had no recollection of his previous visits, saying that he had been stoned on all occasions and had not known what he was doing.

The artist looked stiff-faced and shook his head.

'Sure, you know,' he said, in the accents of a new immigrant.

Suddenly, there was the chilling thought that perhaps the tattooist was not Chinese, but Vietnamese? Had they tracked him across the ocean? Were they getting to him, in his own country?

He shook his head to clear it of the paranoia.

'See here, fella, I don't want any more. No more, understand? If I come here drunk or sober, you send me away again – don't give me any more tattoos. Okay.'

'Not okay.' A further shake of the head. 'You no want come here. You want go some other place. I make good tattoo. You come here, I make good tattoo . . .'

He threatened to tell the cops about the underground parlour, but the tattooist gave him an infuriating Asian smile.

'You not go policeman.'

That very night he collected another tattoo and on its discovery in the morning returned to beat the shit out of the artist, only to be met with an equal fury from the artist.

'You got flies in head. You crazy. Why you come here night and say, "Make me tattoo," then come in day, all angry? I do how you say. You not want tattoo, you no come here, you stupid crazyman.'

Relatives and friends of the tattooist seemed to come out of the woodwork of the basement, standing in the shadows behind the man, with their arms folded. The vet knew that if he caused trouble, they would be all over him in a few seconds, maybe with knives.

'You fuckers must be hypnotizing me or something,' he said. 'Why in Christ do I keep coming back? I don't understand it. What the hell's going on?'

The tattooist shrugged.

'Well, where do you get these marks from? I've never seen marks like these before in my whole life.'

The artist rummaged in a drawer at his elbow, coming out with a wad of paper. Carefully drawn on each piece was a symbol resembling the tattoos. He stared at them, uncomprehending, until the Asian explained, 'You draw. You draw them. All time you coming here, taking piece of paper, draw picture.'

'I don't believe you,' he said, appalled.

'Don't give one shit,' came the reply.

He went home after that and stared at the wall. Gradually, he recalled the incident: dredged it from the back of his mind, where he had tried to bury it, along with all the other nightmares from the jungle. The VC he had burned, in the cave. The corpse had had tattoos on the arm, like those that were appearing on his own body. Little squiggles and shapes that looked as if they had been copied from the decorations on some pillar in a snake temple. Phil had been with him on that patrol. They had talked about it, amongst themselves. Phil had guessed they were some kind of religious markings – symbols as ancient as Vietnam itself.

'Used to be called The Country of Tattooed Men,' Phil had said.

'What did?'

'This place – Nam. Three thousand years ago it was the Kingdom of Van Tang, The Country of Tattooed Men . . .'

Phil had been his lieutenant. Phil was his best friend. They had gone to college together and he had rejected a commission, just so they wouldn't be split up. They had got through their year of hell, they had come home together. Phil had let him stay in his apartment while he looked around for a place of his own. Only three weeks after they had been back, Phil was murdered, stabbed to death on the subway by a person or persons unknown. They had stolen his watch and rings and three dollars from his wallet. A whole year in Vietnam, with shit flying through the air cutting down American soldiers here, there, everywhere, and Phil had made it through, alive. Made it through to be carved like a piece of meat on the subway by some bastard who wasn't satisfied with a war in Asia, he had to start one in New York.

After walking around the park, staying out of the trees (I always stay out of the trees these days), I took a cab to Brooklyn, to the address on the letter he had sent me. I went up the back stairs of some sleazy building, to knock on a door. He let me in.

'You remember me?' he said.

'I remember the time and place, the event,' I said. 'If you say you were there, I believe you.'

'I was one of the patrol – me and Phil – only Phil's dead now. They're probably all dead, except you and me.'

I stared at him. He was wearing boots, combat jacket and a longshoreman's hat which covered even the back of his neck. Only his hands and face were visible. Even on these parts the tattoos covered every square centimetre of skin. His coat collar was up and buttoned. The woollen hat had been tugged right down, covering his ears. On his cheeks, nose and around his mouth and eyes, were strange markings: centripetals, whorls, spirals. The individual lines seemed to follow the natural contours of his features, but when you looked more closely, deviated sharply in places and broke the basic structure into shapes and shadows which might have resembled leaves, blades of grass, pieces of tree bark. It was like looking into a still pool that reflected the light and shade thrown by overhanging foliage.

'You remind me of a picture I once saw,' I said, to break what was becoming an embarrassing silence. 'An artist's impression of Queeqeg – from *Moby Dick*. The tattooed cheeks – ' I believe my attempt at lighthearted banter fell flat. I recognized no change of expression in the eyes. The eyes were my only link with reality, as the rest of his features shimmered and broke, scattered and re-formed.

'I'm bald underneath this,' he remarked, meaning his hat. 'Bald and tattooed. I don't shave it. I pull 'em out, like the Indians used to. It hurts but it means I don't have to do so much.' He paused, then added, 'I told you about these, in the letter.'

'You said you had collected tattoos, like the corpse we saw in Nam.' I wasn't sure what he had meant by *collected*.

'Yeah. You – you bring the photo?'

I nodded, removing an envelope from my pocket. He grabbed it eagerly and extracted the photograph. It was the picture I had taken of the burned Vietnamese at the cave – one of the pictures.

'Yeah, that's him,' he said in a satisfied tone. 'Hey, look,' he pulled up his sleeve to reveal an arm covered in coloured-ink symbols. It swam before my eyes. 'Look, I got it right. Can you beat that? I did it from somewhere in here.' He tapped his head. 'Got them exactly right, without even thinking.'

He had indeed copied the symbols accurately. They must have been printed indelibly on his subconscious. Something had triggered him into transferring those characters from his mind to paper, and thence to his body. You could say he had been tattooed a long time ago, internally, and the marks had only just worked their way through to his skin.

'Where did the rest of them come from?' I asked.

'Eh?'

'Well, you only had an arm and part of a chest. What did you cover the rest of your body with?'

'It's a pattern,' he replied, looking up from the photograph. 'It repeats.'

'Oh.'

'You ready now?'

'Let's go,' I said. His letter had explained: he wanted me to take photographs of him against a background of grass or trees or rock, some natural environment.

We took a cab to Central Park. On the way, careless of the inquisitive cab driver who continually glanced in the rear-view mirror, there was talk of the discovery.

'It came to me one night,' he said, 'in the early hours. The point man was a trigger-happy Cajun with eyes like an eagle. He shot at mist, ferns waving in a breeze, a leaf falling from the sky, but I never knew him to be wrong. We always got a body count when that guy pulled the trigger. What was he firing at that day? was what I asked myself. I remembered we asked the question at the time, and he said, "Smell – I smelled this shadow." This guy was used to hunting in the half-light of the bayous, back home. He was the best point man I ever knew. "Did you see anything?" we asked, and he shook his head. I thought to myself, man, if that Cajun didn't see him, then the gook must have been hiding inside a tree. Then it came to me . . .'

We arrived at the park and sent the cab driver on his way. It was coming on evening by that time and most office workers were on their way home. There were people in the park, but he managed to find a spot in the trees where we were alone. It scared the hell out of me. It was the same area where the vigilante killing had taken place. I wanted to get it done, get it over, and go back to the Roosevelt.

He began to undress and as he did, he talked, while I took pictures.

'The perfect camouflage,' he said. 'Those guys in ancient Nam, they had it all worked out. They must have spent a lot of time – I mean a *lot* of time – getting this right. Perception. That's what it's all about. Perception. You look, it's there, but you don't see. That VC we burned – he must have found it in some old book, or maybe a picture on a cave or temple wall.'

'Maybe he wasn't even NVA?' I said, the camera clicking rapidly.

'Could be, could be. Anyway, he had the secret – the secret of perfect camouflage. Early on in history, rulers of those ancient kingdoms – they must have used such men – assassins. And now me, I know ... I think it only works if the *whole* body is covered – a piece of it, an arm or a leg, well, there's an *effect*, but not the complete camouflage, not the blending into the background so perfectly that the tattooed man is no longer visible to the naked eye. You remember some of those snakes in Nam? How you wouldn't see them before you trod on them, even though you were staring right at them? Well, this is even *more* effective. It disguises movement too. The artists who invented this must have perfected it over centuries, maybe even thousands of years. They must have studied the creatures of the forest, made a science of light and shade, the delicate balance between mark and space ... hell, they were geniuses. Can you see them? those Stone Age people, distilling the dyes out of flowers and leaves and scouring the rivers for different coloured clays, testing this and that, until one day, *bingo*, the perfect hunter ...'

By the time he had finished talking, he was just a disembodied voice, somewhere in the trees ahead of me. His clothes lay on the ground in crumpled heaps. I took photographs, of nothing but trees. My skin was crawling, and when a twig cracked, somewhere to my left, I almost screamed. As it was, I jumped back about two feet, scared out of my wits.

'Are you still there?' I don't know why I whispered it, but I did.

There was no answer. I tried to watch the lengthening shadows, for signs of movement amongst them. He couldn't change the laws of light and darkness, that much was for sure. I watched for a flicker, the dark shape of a man on fallen leaves, but could not be sure of anything. Then something caught the corner of my eye, making me jump again, but it seemed to be the wind running over the grass. My heart was racing so hard, pumping my blood so fast, if I wasn't careful I would start to see things that *weren't* there.

I recalled the rest of the article about the vigilante who had killed the rapist in this park, perhaps on this very ground. None of the witnesses had seen the assailant, not even the woman who had been rescued. There had been a presence, but sensed rather than seen. A wraith, a phantom, visible only as a fleeting shadow moving through the evening.

It suddenly occurred to me at that moment that perhaps there were only two people left alive who had witnessed the incident involving the tattooed man at that Vietnamese cave. Surely, if I was the only one who knew, then I was a danger to him? Just then I felt warm air on my cheek. I could smell someone's stale breath. I turned and ran from the place, yelling like a maniac at the top of my voice, *'Don't do it, don't do it, don't do it . . .'*

When he joined me again, on the edge of the park, fully dressed, I had recovered my composure.

'That was a stupid thing to do,' he said, but with a twisted smile on his face, as if it was the first amusing thing to have come out of all this.

'Let's put it this way,' I answered, feeling foolish. 'I've got a good excuse. It doesn't matter whether the cause is scientific or supernatural, I'm not used to seeing men disappear before my eyes.'

He grunted, then reached inside his combat jacket and produced a notebook. He handed it to me.

'What's this?' I asked.

His eyes looked black and cold.

'It's my diary – you'll find all you need in there, when you come to write the article.'

'The – article?'

'Yes, but leave it for a month, before you submit anything. It'll be a bigger story by then.'

'I see,' I said.

'No you don't,' he snapped. 'Not yet, you don't.'

We walked out of the park, into the river of humanity on the sidewalk. Before he left me there, he took my arm in a strong grip. The New York traffic flowed past us, the noise and bustle of the city was all around. People began to jostle us as we blocked their way.

'Listen,' he said, 'what do you think of the new President's idea – the military advisers for Thailand?'

'What do *you* think of it?'

He stared upwards, to where the buildings fought for light and space in the dying sky.

'I've got an eighteen-year-old son at college,' he said.

Feeling more secure amongst buildings, with people around me, I threw in my accusation.

'So you're going to kill the President, like you did that rapist?'

His reply was completely unexpected.

'We've decided that probably won't be necessary,' he said. Then he was gone, hurrying along the sidewalk, his hands thrust deep into his pockets. I watched the knitted hat until it was out of sight, then took a cab back to my hotel.

When I got back to my room in the Roosevelt, I took out the diary he had given me. It told me very little I didn't already know. It certainly didn't expand on that shocking plural he had

thrown at me as a parting shot. 'We've decided . . .' Who the
hell was WE?

That night I went out and got drunk.

The next morning I hired a darkroom and developed the
photographs I had taken in the park. I stared at the prints, for
hours afterwards, in all kinds of light, and of course found
nothing but trees, grass and shadow. Plenty of shadow. He was
in there somewhere, but I couldn't see him and I doubted
anyone else could either. I suppose he wanted me to publish
them, along with the article I had promised him, but how the
hell can you prove you've taken pictures of an invisible man?
The whole thing was ludicrous. Just vanity on his part. You
could see him in his half-dressed state, a tattooed man climbing
out of his clothes, but once they were all off, he was gone. I
suppose it's a bit like putting a red scarf around a tiger's neck
and have him standing in his natural environment. The piece
of cloth helps you locate the beast and you can perceive its
shape, even against a background of shadows and foliage. It's
when you don't know precisely where to look and what shape
to look for (upright, prone, supine, curled, crouched?) that the
camouflage works its magic.

And this was not nature's attempt at camouflage – like the
tiger's or, better still, the woodcock's markings – this was the
result of a science, or perhaps an art, perfected by man. The
vet's tattoos were to a tiger's stripes, as rocket engines are to
seagull's wings.

I packed my bags, intending to return to my home in
California as soon as possible. Or perhaps I would go back to
Britain for a while? Anywhere that was a long way away from
Washington.

I thought about ringing the police but changed my mind. The
police may or may not have believed me, but certainly the media
would then get hold of the story, and they weren't so fussy.
They loved such stories: tattooed men, invisible assassins,
vigilante killers, threats against the President. Putting aside fears
for my own life, if it became public, there was the possibility of

the story becoming stretched to include such things as *the presence of Vietnamese agents in New York* – and – *hypnotized veterans triggered to kill*. I could see the headlines: MAN-CHURIAN CANDIDATE LIVES. The President would have his proof and anyone with Asiatic features would be unable to walk the streets.

I was going to have to forget what I'd seen, or rather, what I had *not* seen, and go back on my promise of publicity. The arguments I used to defend my position were really quite flimsy. I was a photographer. I recorded events, I did not interfere. I did not take sides. I was like a priest, or a lawyer, or a doctor. I maintained client confidentiality.

I had been stupid to come. He had been stupid to ask me. I suppose the Vietnam bond was still strong, or he never would have, and neither would I. His idea of reality must have undergone severe alteration in the past few months and perhaps he had needed to test its authority, on someone who had been there, experienced the same incident? My own idea of reality was now crumbling. Something was beginning to seep through its layers: the thought that perhaps he was not the only one. It was a long war, with many untold incidents. Maybe our experience was not unique? In any case, there was nothing to stop him passing on his secret. '*We've decided that probably won't be necessary . . .*'

I don't know how many of them *are* out there, moving silently, unseen through the forests and fields, the hills and valleys. Perhaps only one, possibly a thousand. More. It could be that there are so many they have taken over the areas outside the towns and cities, within the parks, that the open land has become a subworld beyond our control. There's no way of knowing. To take the extreme, it might no longer be a case of saying that there are tattooed men in the country, but rather the reverse – that *we*, we are in the country of tattooed men.

Something happened yesterday – something momentous, extra-ordinary. I haven't seen a newspaper now for several weeks, or heard the radio, or watched television – not since I left New York. I know something happened because it's in the air, like the buzzing of a million flies. The footsteps outside have an urgency about them. The people in the streets are hurrying, faster than usual, as if they should be somewhere else. There are cries reaching out for my ears, that are never quite heard. I have no plans to investigate this phenomenon.

SURFING, SPANISH STYLE

AN EXPERIMENT ON A BIRD
IN THE AIR PUMP

A picture in oils by Joseph Wright, of Derby
(Jos. Wright Pinxt 1768)

The air has been pumped out of the glass bowl
suffocating the bird, and proving the existence of a
vacuum.   (National Gallery, London)

No, I'm not worried. Lost most of my teeth, anyway. It
doesn't hurt much now. You get used to it, except when they
use the boot, then it hurts, but when there's lots of other
passengers around like now, in the rush hour, then they just
use the fist. I'll be all right. My nose isn't broken, that was done
months ago. Why do we do it? Well, what else is there? Is that
switched on? Do I get any money? Okay. Name's Frazz, with
two z's.

Yeah, when we started out, there was seven of us. Batey,
Rack, Split, Hotwire, Blindboy, Flyer, an' me. Yeah, seven of us.
Sixteen, all of us. The red bandana's our badge. I'm the only
one that wears it now. We just left school and we surfed down
to London, looking for work. Well, there was nothing for us in
York. The place was so dead it stank. It was rotten from having
nothing to do but just lie around looking at its own belly deflate.
Just like my dad, staring at the place where he used to have a

fire when he was a kid, only there's a cold radiator there now, and muttering away to himself about the time the pubs were still open and at least you could get a pint, but now you couldn't even drown yourself. Mum? She was just as bad. Anyway, she pissed off about three months before I left school. Dunno where she went, but I think it was south. Well, where else is there any work?

Anyway, I'm telling you about the club. No, not a gang, *club*. We take surfing seriously. It's nothing like a street gang, guarding its turf. Surfing is an art and a science. Look, we were all bright lads – except maybe Rack, who was a bit of a retard – we came out of school with a handful of exams each, but what can you do with them, except hang 'em on the wall? There wasn't a job going that wasn't filled before it was advertised. Oh yeah, they put some of them in the paper, but you need to know somebody, an uncle or something, to get one of them. We didn't know anybody.

The club's called *The Windjammers* after a club I read about in Guatemala. That's where surfing first came from. Yeah, of course I know where Guatemala is. I told you, I'm not ignorant. They call it *Spanish Style* because it came from a Spanish-speaking country, not because it came from Spain. Guatemala's in South America – *central* South America. In the magazine it said that the kids do surfing there because there's nothing else for them to do and that's the same here now. Why do you think surfing's so popular? Because the kids are *wild*? Or crazy? I hear those old men and women saying, look at them, their poor parents must be going out of their minds with worry, you'd think they would get a sense of responsibility at their age, wouldn't you? Yak, yak. They don't know what they're talking about. Responsibility for *what*? We haven't got anything to be responsible for. They think we wear these rags to look different, or what? This is all I've got: one dirty T-shirt and a pair of jeans. My track shoes wore out and I haven't been able to get another pair yet. *Find* another pair . . . all right, steal the bloody things, if I get the chance. What would you do? The fucking winter's coming. All right, all right I know you can't broadcast words like that. I'll keep it down.

Well London *is* just as bad as Guatemala City. That's not being unpatriotic, it's fact when you're looking at it from down here. We can't all be reporters, can we. You're the lucky one, lady. Just lose your job and then you'll see what kind of . . . join the *police force?* You must be living in a fantasy world. Like I just said, if you haven't got a brother or an uncle in a job like that, you can forget it. Nepotism? What's . . . oh, yeah. Well those sorts of things happen when places become as desperate as Britain is. I had a home, at least. Some of those robber children that you see swarming down by Tower Bridge, nicking things off tourists – they probably never saw the inside of a house. I was *lucky*. At least we had four walls and food sometimes.

I knew one of those robber children once. He was eight years old and he lived inside an oil drum under the bank of the river. I think he froze to death, last winter. You know, these things happen, don't they? I've seen them eating cabbage stalks out of the gutter. Eaten them myself, sometimes. All that money the government spends on defending the country. What for? We'd be better off under a foreign power, wouldn't we? The people that treat us like shit are here already.

Anyway, I was telling you about us and how we came to London. We surfed down. Not all the way, but most of it. Oh yeah, it's easy enough to get *on* it. You can get aboard in the yards, and there are bridges where you can drop down on the trains, where they go slow enough. It's getting off's the problem. The railway police are waiting for you in the stations and they work you over. Well, I suppose we piss them off, we get away with it a lot of the time. That's how Split got killed. She kept spitting in their faces and swearing at them, saying things like, your mother screwed a warthog to get you, that sort of thing. They just used their fists at first, but then when she started spitting blood on their trousers they got mad and kicked her head from side to side. I saw it. I was shitting my pants because they were going to do me next and I was cursing Split for getting them to lose their snouts. When it came to it they were out of breath and they knew they'd given Split her last haircut – you could see stuff on the platform – so they went a bit easy on me. What? I don't think they knew she was a girl. Would it have made any difference? Maybe. I dunno.

No, the first of us to go was Rack, on our way down. He went on one of the corners. Well, what you do is use the carriage roof like a surfboard, see. You know, you stand like this – this is the stance, see. It's a matter of balance. My hero's Jesus Garcia Cordobes – JC, same as the real JC except for the Garcia. Well, we saw a video once showing these kids surfing in Guatemala, and one of them was JC. Some American reporter made the film for television and he chose JC to follow around, because he was the *best*, JC I mean. I copied his stance and I still use it now. JC's dead but he kept going three years. That's a long time for a surfer, especially over there. What? Oh, it was on the video, at the end, when the credits come up. It said, *Jesus Garcia Cordobes died on the wires a month after this film was made*. Something like that.

On the wires? Well, you see you've got two choices when you feel yourself going, when you lose your balance. You can go with the throw, or you can hang the wires. Look, let me explain how Blindboy went. Yes, he really was blind. We used to show him where to stand and all that. It's a wonder he lasted as long as he did, but he had the *feel*, you know what I mean? That's more important than seeing, than vision. Rack could *see*, but he didn't have the feel and he went first.

The wires, yes. Well, we were surfing down to Southend one day when we came to one of those low bridges. Local kids were playing tenpin with us. That's when they swing these lumps of paving stones on ropes and try to knock us off the train, like skittles. Sure, we would have killed 'em if we caught them, but how could we? I can see their point, too. They've got nothing either, so that's the way they fill their days. Most of them aren't more than ten years old and if we get the chance we yank the ropes and try to pull them off the parapet of the bridge. That's the way of the play.

So, we saw this tenpin club, and I yelled at Blindboy to sway left, without thinking that this right-curving bend was coming up. The prick with the brick missed him, but Blindboy had gone too far over. He knew he was going to groove gravel and I heard him shout, *Do I flap my arms now?* Great kidder, Blindboy. I miss him.

I'm coming to that, I'm coming to that. Now, at this point Blindboy had a choice. He could either fall from the train and kill himself on the bank – we were doing at least seventy-five – or he could grab the overhead electric cables, the ones the train uses for its power. What happens? What happens is you smoke, of course. If there's enough to drive a train at eighty, there's enough to make charcoal.

I knew Blindboy didn't want to go downstairs and get broken up, but when you hang on the wires the train usually grinds to a halt. You short the circuit, of course, what do you think? All right, okay, I know, but your audience must be as thick as ... anyway, he didn't. Hang the wires, I mean. He knew we would have been stuck halfway between London and Southend, because we would have had to run, and there wouldn't have been any chance of getting another surfboard back to London, not with the speeds the trains do out there between stations.

So he did a fledgling, hit a telegraph pole face on. Left his mirror-shades buried in the wood. No more Blindboy. That's it. That's all in the sport. Yes I call it a *sport*. It's as good as anything else, isn't it? Good as riding bloody horses or driving racing cars? Why not a sport? They should have it in the Olympics. I'd be a champion. Last week I walked into one of these offices and asked them for a sponsorship, said I'd wear their logo on my T-shirt. I did it for a joke, but one of the men said, why don't we listen to the kid, he might have something, but the other one told him not to be so stupid.

Of course I'm good. I'm alive, aren't I? I'm seventeen and a half and I've been surfing for nearly two years, and I'm alive.

The last one. Well, the last one except for Flyer, who can't surf now, with only one leg. What? It got sliced off on the Northampton run. I dunno, we had to leave him there. I'm *assuming* he's still alive. They wouldn't let him bleed to death I suppose. Funny, they'll cave your head in when they're in the mood, but they won't let you die when you're all broken up and lying by the tracks with your bones sticking through your skin in a dozen places. They get all solicitous. Yeah, good word that, isn't it? Lady, you really know how to patronize people. I keep telling you, I'm not thick. I had a good education. It's a little raw now, because of the company I keep. I live down on the bank with the robber kids at the moment. Anyway, they get *solicitous*. Like when Flyer lost his leg. We went looking for it, back down the track, but never did find it. We told the cops someone had stolen it. They thought that was funny.

So, yes, I'm a solid surfer. I ride the roof better than anyone else I know. The *Rollers?* Yeah, I've heard of them, but they haven't got one surfer that can match me. Not for style, not for guile. Shit, they've only been going for seven months, maybe eight. Hotwire? He nutted a bridge at seventy. I don't suppose he felt anything. I often think about that now – how it's going to feel? Of course, it's going to happen one day. What do you think? I can't be lucky for ever. Yes, you need *skill*, but you need luck, too. Everybody needs luck.

You see, there's *nothing* like surfing. Swaying with the rhythm of the train. You're up there, on top of the world, with the wind rushing up your nostrils. On your *feet*. It's oxygen, pure oxygen. I can feel my blood going electric, just talking about it. *You* never felt anything like it. The closest you're going to get is doing ninety in your open-top with your boyfriend screwing you while you take the bends: even then you won't come close to it. You see, there's nothing up there but you. You and the wind. Scared? Sometimes, before I go up, even when I'm up there. Sometimes I'm so scared I can't catch my breath. But it's an exhilarating kind of fear. Probably other sportsmen get it – skydivers, people like that. There's times when I think my feet are glued to the roof and *nothing* can throw me off. Then there's times when I think every kink, every curve in the rail is my enemy and I'm not going to live for another surf.

Me? I think I'd hang the wire. I'd rather flash than smash. But I'm not going yet, not yet. I'm all-city. I've surfed from every mainline station in London. That's what all-city means. Only J-J Thompson out from Tottenham has done more lines than me. I think J-J's coming to the end, though. He slipped the other day, slid a quarter of a carriage length, but managed to stay on. Lucky. Bit the end off his tongue, so I heard. No, I've never met him. We don't surf the same trains at the same time. We're rivals, not friends. There's an element of competition, but it's long term. There's no need for us to get together, to sort it out. It's simply the one who lives the longest. Like Russian roulette.

The Windjammers? The old red bandanas? Just me left now.

Oh, I'll keep going, till I go. Go till I go. You keep asking me that, but really I dunno. I've always felt like we were part of an experiment, by them, you know who I mean. Seems like bit by bit we've had everything taken out of our reach, until now there's nothing. No chance of a job, no money since they stopped the dole, no hope for anything. If I didn't surf I wouldn't be able to breathe, because there's nothing else. It's all I've got. So I'll go until I go. There's some kids who go out looking for trouble, the street gangs and that, and there's some who rob, some who break into houses, some who drug-and-drink. Everybody's got to do something to breathe, otherwise you might just as well lay down and die, like my dad. Well, it's the same thing, staring at a cold radiator all day long. I reckon death's probably *better* than that, if you ask me. Might as well be a polystyrene tile stuck to some bloody ceiling, the wrong way up, as be a human being in this country. Unless you surf, of course.

Can I have that bloody money now? I'm hungry. I haven't eaten since yesterday. Thanks. I can still say *thanks*, which is amazing. It must have been my mother. She told me, be polite whatever happens. So when they kick me in the gut, I say, thank you officer, thank you sir, I'd like some more of that tomorrow. Indoctrination. My mum also taught me how to use the cutlery at a seven-course meal, just in case I should ever be invited anywhere and so I wouldn't embarrass everyone, especially her. Can you see me at a banquet? Me neither. Still, she taught us, me and my brothers, just in case. Well, we didn't actually have the mug and irons there, on the table. She just told us if we ever found ourselves sitting down at such a meal to start from the outside and work inwards, that way we won't get into any trouble.

Into any trouble . . . I got to go. Catching the eleven forty-five from Paddington. Got the best seat on the train, up top, first class. No, not today I won't. I feel good today, despite the way those buggers worked me over just now. That was tame. They must be feeling out of sorts. It's not them I worry about so much as the sneaky bastards – the ones who stretch cheesewire across the track. It's not kids who do that, it's . . . well, you wouldn't believe me anyway.

Nice to have met you. Gotta go. My board's waiting.

(Thirteen days after this documentary was first broadcast, John 'Frazz' Davies was struck by a bullet from a .22 rifle, fired by a person unknown. Frazz was between Bethnal Green and Mile End stations and witnesses say he instinctively grabbed for the overhead power lines. His rival J-J Thompson later visited the spot where Frazz died and hung a red bandana on a post nearby. To the knowledge of Eastland Television Company, J-J Thompson is still alive and surfing, Spanish style.)

TRIPTYCH

The Black Wedding

He was looking out of the window at the fragile day. It seemed too still, too delicate to be real. At any second it might shatter before his eyes into crisp, thin flakes of mirror glass and he would turn from the window to exclaim to Celia, only to find that the day was behind him, hiding at the back of the room, and what he had been studying was a reflection, a looking-glass image of the morning.

A bird flew past as he watched, appearing out of nowhere. A unique spectacle. Where had it learned to do that? Fly? It had to be an omen, but whether good or bad, he was unsure. It would be unwise to mention it to Celia. Her superstition was invariably negative in its bias. War, famine, pestilence. That would be her response. He felt utterly depressed by the whole business.

Guthrie moved from the window to the table where the wedding presents were displayed. An array of trivia. He picked up an object like two knives riveted together. The blades opened and closed when he worked the handles.

'What's this?' he asked.

Celia glanced across and then continued with her make-up. 'It's a pair of secateurs – yes, I'm sure that's what Alec called them. They're for cutting the heads off flowers or something.'

Guthrie held the instrument with its little curved blades gingerly between two fingers. Horror and disgust fought for control of his feelings. A device for murdering flowers? God, that was really ugly. What sort of warped mind would stoop to such an evil invention?

'You're not going to keep them, are you?'

'What? Oh, I see what you mean. No, not permanently. We'll get rid of them after the wedding.'

'Amazing, the way some minds work. Who sent them?'

'One of Alec's aunts.'

Guthrie was impressed. 'Aunts? He has more than one?'

'Two in fact.' She began to clamber into her wedding dress.

'Hmm. Nice to be wealthy. Most people are satisfied with just the one.'

Celia gave him a superior smile.

'You're just envious, Guthrie. No, really, he does have two. One lives in Brighton – the other in Bath.'

'Well, I still think it's decadent. I can't think why you want to marry such a man.'

Celia gave a patient sigh. 'Because he needs a wife. Now help me on with my track suit, or I'll never be ready in time.' She began pulling on the black silk wedding outfit, trying not to crush the folds. Reluctantly, he went to give her assistance. He really couldn't forgive her for ruining his Thursday. Why did she have to marry *every* man she met? That, in itself, seemed decadent.

He made sure his hand did not touch her skin and she looked at him pointedly, her voice taking on a prim tone.

'I can't think why you always have to be so obscene, Guthrie. It's only *me*, after all.'

'Just put it down to my low upbringing,' he said, angrily. Hell, their relationship was uncomplicated enough without all this sort of thing.

'Why can't we just have a quiet evening indoors,' he grumbled.

She was tempted. He could tell by her silence. Then just as he thought he had won, the clock lurched heavily and she shook her head.

'No. I promised him. This is the only Thursday he has free

for a month. I don't want to disappoint him.'

Guthrie bit his lip. Well, it had been worth a try. She might just have fallen for the idea. He strolled over to the wedding presents again, scanning them in a desultory fashion. Suddenly, something caught his interest.

'Who sent the ash-tray?'

'No idea. Why?'

'Why? Because it's going to be bloody useful. Don't forget we're going to Cyprus for our holidays.'

Celia paused in the act of pulling on her running shoes.

'I must admit it had slipped my mind. How thoughtful. It can't be someone who knows us very well.'

'We'll work it out later. I do hope it is a stranger.' He couldn't keep the acid out of his tone, though he could have bitten his tongue off afterwards.

'It's bound to be. God, don't you trust me after all this time? How long have we been together?'

Guthrie decided it was time for them to thrash it out.

'Yes, only . . .'

'Only *what*?'

'Only I haven't seen you with anyone I don't know lately, that's all.' There, it was said.

She rounded on him, her face suffused with anger.

'Look, just because you're too idle to follow me when I go out in the evenings, doesn't mean I'm being faithful. Sometimes I wonder about you, Guthrie. Sometimes I wonder if you're paranoid at all.'

He was incensed by this accusation.

'Of course I'm paranoid. What on earth do you take me for? An insensitive brute? Why do you torture me like this? You want to get me to stay with you, don't you?'

They stood there, glaring at one another for a long while. He knew he was being unfair. She wanted his suicide as much as he did himself, but they both had a touch of the sadist in them. Neither would give in.

Celia turned away from him.

'Guthrie, I'm sorry. I suppose I'm just bored that's all. It is my wedding day, after all.'

He was still a little stiff and formal. He was damned if he was going to please her.

'No, no, it's my fault,' he said, claiming the victory. He consulted his watch. 'Good Lord. It's five past already. You'd better start running – they'll all be at the church.'

She took her mark by the door.

'Stopwatch?' she reminded him.

'Yep. Ready. Ste-ady. *Go!*'

And she was off, out of the room, the house, and running up the hill towards the little church. A few minutes later he heard the cheer and he knew she had broken the tape. Spitefully, he let the watch run on for a few more seconds. He had still not completely forgiven her for being alive this morning.

Then he himself made his way slowly towards the church, knowing they could not start without him. Impatience makes the heart grow fonder, he thought. *How trite*. At the edge of the highway a badger was sleeping. The event was causing a traffic jam with a two-mile tailback, as motorists leaned out of their windows to look. Some people have all the luck, thought Guthrie bitterly. Only it wasn't people. It was an animal. Still, he was jealous.

At the gate to the church he paused. A shudder went through him. One more night. Perhaps one more night. Oh, please . . .

Inside the church the organ was in full flood. Strangers smiled at him as he walked to the front pew and took his place. Twenty minutes. It wasn't a record, but it was a respectable delay. He wasn't out to impress, he told himself. A quiet, simple life – that's all he wanted. Just then, right on cue, two penguins entered the church and began to waddle down the aisle. Perfect. He hadn't guessed. New twists, new turns. That was the way things were meant to be.

The vicar nodded at the pair, before calling, 'Is the bride present?' His voice was muffled from inside his suit of armour.

'Here,' shouted Celia, from the back row of pews.

'And the groom?'

'Yes. Er, here.'

This must be Alec, standing right next to him. On his left. On his left? Guthrie broke out into a cold sweat. This wasn't right. Both men looked at each other and knew instantly. Hastily, they changed places before the horror built up to a pitch in one of them and the screaming started. Nameless terror. Things not being *right*, when right was not known, only *felt*. They gave each other a nervous smile. The panic began subsiding. It seemed okay now. They both avoided physical contact of any kind, though Guthrie was itching to hold somebody's hand, just for a shred of comfort.

Finally the vicar said, 'Do you, penguin female, take the other to be your lawfully wedded husband?'

'I do,' cried Celia from the back of the church.

The process was repeated with the other penguin and Alec answered, 'I do.'

Then, said the vicar, smiling, 'I pronounce you – man and wife.'

Someone moved forward and put a paper cup on each of the hallowed penguin's heads.

'It's supposed to hypnotize them,' the person whispered to Guthrie.

'Good.'

It seemed good. It *was* good. He turned to Alec, who hadn't disappeared.

'Congratulations, old man.'

Alec blushed, shyly. 'Thanks.'

Then the other man had to leave. The penguins had been hired for the event from the local zoo. But Guthrie was pleased he had made the gesture. It had made Alec light-headed enough to tear off his watch and throw it in the font on his way out.

Guthrie was feeling aroused when he raced Celia back to the house, but nothing could spoil the fact that the wedding had gone well. They both undressed and lay between the sheets, waiting. Nothing happened of course.

'Why don't you go and do it, Guthrie. I won't mind.'

She was sweet, but he just couldn't. It wasn't fair of her to ask him to. She should be the one. What a pity it was that they loved each other so much. Other couples they knew had gone long ago. *You first. No, after you.*

'We could do it together,' he suggested.

But that wasn't the answer. One of them would be bound to go first, if only by a split second. They just had to wait, and hope. There would have been five murders already in the city. The night was well advanced. Surely there was a possibility, however remote, that their turn would come soon?

By two o'clock he was as wide awake as ever. Celia was snoring loudly, but he knew she was faking it. There was only one way they would ever get any sleep and that was permanent: the big one. He looked forward to that.

In the meantime, dawn was a thousand years away.

Murderers Walk

Place

There is a city-state, lying between two large countries, where killers take refuge from the law, but not from justice. Justice finds its own way.

A long street, not much wider than an alley, cuts through the middle of the city. The street is called Murderers Walk and over its cobbles, slick even on dry days, tread the malefactors who have run to its shadows to escape the rope.

The houses are old and overhang the walk, keeping it permanently in the shade. Along its cobbles it is not unusual to see a man or woman being dragged, or driven, or forcibly carried. Sometimes they are screaming; sometimes they are stiff with fear.

Rope

There are many reminders of rope in Murderers Walk. The limbs of those lounging in apathy against crumbling window-sills are knotted and sinuous; the washing over the street is crowded on to short lines and consequently hangs narrow and long; the shadows that ripple in the poorly-fashioned windows tend to be thin and twisted due to the warping of the glass. A walk along the street on any day will bring you into contact with men and women who know death first-hand: they have dealt with it directly; they stand on the brink of death themselves. You see them waiting in shop doorways, wearing hollows in the wood with restless shoulders. No one knows what or who they are waiting for – not even those who wait. There is no expectancy in the air.

The Game

They play a game in the inns along Murderers Walk, which newcomers shun when they first arrive. Newcomers are detached and need nothing but themselves. They are either elated or relieved at having escaped the law in their own countries, and for a time this is sufficient to sustain them. The game is played in groups of nine, called 'scaffolds'.

The Rules

Each player draws cards from the pack containing two jokers, until none remains. The players look at their hands and the one holding the ace of spades must commit suicide, by hanging, twenty-four hours later, on the stroke of eight A.M. It is a simple game, with simple rules, but the winning players recharge those feelings of elation and relief that they felt on first arriving in Murderers Walk. They have beaten death yet again.

The Victim

The players keep all their cards secret until the time arrives to take account. They gather at the inn where the game took place. One of the players will be missing and he or she will hold the ace of spades. The other players then go to the victim's rooms to witness the self-inflicted execution. Victims who are not ready at the appointed time are hunted down by the scaffold and the deed is done for them.

Alternative

There is an alternative to suicide. The victims can leave the city-state and the sanctuary of Murderers Walk to take their chances with the law on the outside. Not many do. It is not fear of death that is responsible but terror of dying in the hands of strangers: a ritual death conceived by a morality since rejected. It is a repulsion stronger than the fear of suicide.

Reprieve

There is, however, another possibility of escaping death. If a player, other than the victim, holds both jokers – those wild cards of Fortune – in one hand, these may be displayed at the last moment before the hanging. The game is then declared void and the victim is reprieved.

Murderers

Only confessed murderers are admitted to a scaffold. Membership is permanent and quarterly games mandatory for all members. As a new murderer in the walk, you survey the faces of the established population with scorn. 'I shall never become like them,' you tell yourself, as you stroll down the street, studying the apathy, the suppressed desperation. Yet, gradually, over the course of time your contempt dissolves into that same desperation. Inside you, the ghost of your victim begins its slow, insidious possession of your soul. You may relive, time and time again, those moments when you killed, especially if your victim was a former loved one. If you are without guilt, there is the bitterness of discovery and consequent flight. Eventually, you sink into the same morass as your fellow malefactors and are drawn into the game out of despair.

Play

You begin the walk along the narrow street to your first game. Eventually, you arrive at the inn where you are to play for your life. The faces of the other players register vague anticipation. The cards are dealt. The faces turn to stone.

You play the game perhaps once a quarter at first – then more frequently as the drug takes hold. As one of the eight winners, you feel the exhilaration of defeating the spectre of death. The group changes as new members are taken on in place of those who have drawn the death card. The more you win, the more you come to believe in a charmed existence, a superior destiny fashioned partly from luck and partly from the essential ingredient of a special *self*. You are not like the others. You move on a higher plane, god-like in your ability to thwart the noose.

Time

But eventually there comes a time when you draw the death card. At first the ace fails to register. It is tucked partly behind an innocent card. Then, suddenly, you see it. Inside you a silent scream begins. All the moisture leaves your mouth and your brain ferments with terror. You are sure all the other members know already, for how can such inner turmoil not show on your face? You put your own cards in your pocket, managing a smile, and call for a round of drinks. Then you slip away, after the first sip of ale, which tastes like vinegar, out into the night air. You begin running, you run north along the street, pausing only to puke. You run to the edge of the city-state, where the border guards of the neighbouring country stand ready. You turn and run in the opposite direction, to find them waiting there too. Then east. Then west. Finally, you trudge back to your lodgings in order to think, to formulate plans.

Twenty-four hours

There is only one thing worse than not knowing when you are going to die – that is, *knowing*. You sit on the edge of your bed and stare around your room. You envy the cockroach that moves across the floor: you envy its lack of imagination. One minute your hands are dry, the next, damp. The weight of guilt has gone. You are about to atone. You try to tell yourself that what you feel is remorse, but you know that it is only regret for the deed that cannot be undone, the act that placed you in this uncompromising position. Your head turns over a thousand thoughts, but none of them leads to escape. Suddenly you understand why this sanctuary exists. It is a prison as secure as any with high walls and guards. In Murderers Walk, the prisoners try each other, and sentence each other to death.

Death

You wonder what the feel of the rope will be like against your neck. You touch your throat with your fingers. Will the spine break or will you expire slowly? Perhaps your lungs will burst? You try to imagine the pallor of your distended face: purple perhaps? Your eyes, huge balls easing out of their sockets? Your tongue hanging long between blue lips? You weep. Your mind goes numb. Your eyes are dry. You head is full of a thousand active thoughts, each one a nightmare.

Void Game

There is, of course, the possibility of a void game. It is not so unusual. But the closer the time comes, the surer you are that you will not be granted a reprieve. You have taken life and deserve no mercy. The hours pass quickly, and slowly; time races and stands still, depending on whether it is the pain of life, or death, that occupies you. One thing you are sure of: you cannot hope.

Absence

It is three minutes to the appointed hour. The other players will gather together with their cards. They will know by your absence that you are the victim. They will be feeling high, victorious, excited. They will be talking in quick voices. Their eyes will be bright.

Eight A.M.

You drag the chair beneath the beam as the others arrive. You hear their feet on the wooden stairs. These are sounds to treasure: every creak, every hollow footfall. They open the door and enter. Their faces are as ashen as yours had been on witnessing other deaths. The elation has been put aside for the moment but it has to be done, for without a death there is no game, and without the game there is no life. This is as much an ordeal for them as it is for you – only the standpoint is different.

One of them hands you the rope. You stand on the chair hoping your legs will support you for just a few moments longer. You tie the rope to the beam. Your hands are unsteady. *Then – suddenly – you are ready to die.* In that moment all the terror has gone. You may still tremble, or wince, or blanch, but you are *ready*. It is not the moment of death that is so terrible, it is the preparation leading up to that moment. You are ready. You are ready. Just a moment longer . . .

End

One of the party steps forward and waves two jokers in your face. 'Void game,' he cries. 'You live to play again.' They pull you from the chair and jostle you towards the door, down the stairs and out into the street. Inside you the fear erupts again, and that precious moment, the moment when you were ready to die, has gone. They have stolen your death from you and you know you cannot retrieve that state of mind again, without reliving another twenty-four hours of terror.

That is when you dig your heels into the unyielding cobbles and grip a passing window-sill with fingers that would squeeze a rock to powder. That is when your mind flies open like a sprung trapdoor. That is when they drag you along the street, kicking and screaming, like a man being led to his execution.

Hogfoot Right and Bird-hands

There lived, high above the empty streets in a tall building, an old woman whose pet cat had recently died. In those days cats were rare and the old woman had not the means to purchase another. So she called for the machine whose duty it was to look after the welfare of lost and lonely people.

The welfare machine came to her apartment in the middle of the night, and when she explained her plight it suggested that the old woman replace her cat with a pet fashioned from a part of her body. It said it could remove and modify one of her feet to resemble a piglet, and the old woman agreed to this scheme. Since she spent all her time in the mobile bed-chair that saw to all her needs, she did not require the use of her feet, or any other part of her body for that matter, apart from her brain, to which the bed-chair and other appliances were connected. The old woman was not sick, unless apathy and idleness be looked upon as an illness, but she had no desire to take part in any physical activity of any sort. She merely went from one grey day to the next, sleeping, eating, and watching a device called wallscreen, on which she could witness the lives of others, long since dead, over and over again.

Thus, her right foot was removed and roughly shaped and given a life of its own. This appendage she called Hogfoot Right, and it gave her much pleasure to see the creature scuttling around the floor and nosing in the corners of the rooms the way such creations did. However, Hogfoot Right was not one of those pets that liked to be stroked and fussed over, the way the old woman's cat had been when it was alive, and eventually she grew tired of its company, wanting something more. Watching the creature grub around the carpet was interesting enough at first, but when she had seen it done once or twice the novelty began to pall. So she called her welfare machine again and had her other foot removed. This one she called Basil, in the hope that giving it a proper name would make it more affectionate towards its mistress.

Basil turned out to be such a sweet creature. He would sit on the old woman's lap and let her stroke him for hours, his little hog nose twitching in ecstasy as she ran her hands over his dozing form.

Hogfoot Right, however, was moody and irritable and would skulk around in the darker corners of the house and cower away from the old woman when she approached him. He did not actually hiss or spit at her, but his bad temper was evident in the expression on his blunted face and in the sour line of his crudely fashioned mouth.

However, Hogfoot Right was Basil's good companion and in that respect the old woman had no complaint. He served his brother well, snuggling up with him at night and making sure he did not get too excited when something happened to amuse him. Sometimes even Hogfoot Right would join in with his brother's antics, and the two of them would butt each other's rumps and roll around the carpet like six-month-old piglets. Then suddenly, Hogfoot Right would become resentful of something and would sidle away to frequent the edges of the room, glowering at both his brother and the old woman if they tried to entice him to play again. The old woman despaired of this temperamental pet and eventually gave up on the beast.

It was because of her great success with Basil that she decided to increase her menagerie. The welfare machine called one day to see how she was faring and she asked for more surgery. She told it she wanted to lose her hands and her ears. Her bed-chair responded to brain impulses, and she said she could not see what use both these sets of her appendages were to her any more.

The welfare machine was all in favour of the idea. The ears were fused together to make a moth, and the hands became a beautiful pale bird-like creature that soared gracefully around the room and was really the most delicate, delightful pet the old woman had ever set eyes on. She loved it from the first moment she saw it. It would perch on the back of the bed-chair and flutter its fingerfeathers with more dignity than a fantailed dove, and though it remained aloof from the other creatures in the room it would often sit and watch their games from a suitable place above their heads.

Moth-ears was a bit of a disappointment. She fluttered here and there occasionally and was best seen floating past the window with the light shining through her translucent form, but mostly she hung from the old woman's collar with her wings closed. It was almost as if she were trying to get back to her original positions on the old woman's head. She was nervous and shy and tended to start at sudden, loud noises and was really quite useless as a pet. Yet the old woman was happy to keep her, seeing in her an aspect of her own personality.

Bird-hands liked to perch on the light fittings or sit on the window-sill with folded wings, looking out at the sky. She would watch the house martins – the way they swooped before alighting on the outer sill, and she would copy their flight patterns. Since the old woman could not fondle her pets any more, Bird-hands would stroke her instead, running her fingerwings along the old woman's shoulders and down her neck. At night she nestled in her warm lap while the others slept. The old woman loved her dearly.

Bird-hands seemed the most contented of the group of creatures. There was a musical instrument in the apartment which could be played manually if required, and this the creature would do, running her fingerwings over the keys and producing the most delightful melodies. Occasionally she would switch the instrument to automatic and fly to the rhythm of the tune, adding that extra dimension to the unfolding of the notes with her graceful motion.

The group prospered. Even when Snake-arm came along the harmony remained, though at times the sinuous movements alarmed the old woman when she caught sight of it suddenly out of the corner of her eye.

Thus, they all lived together in a harmonious group, apart from the unsociable Hogfoot Right. The old woman could not thank the welfare machine enough, pouring praises on its mechanical parts whenever it came to see how she was getting along. Sometimes the machine would sit with Bird-hands and squeak at it in its high-pitched language, always ending in a rattling laugh. Once, it brought a pair of satin gloves, white, with lace around the cuffs, which Bird-hands wore to fly around the room while the old woman exclaimed upon the beauty of the creature.

Another time, the welfare machine brought an old leather boot, and forced Hogfoot Right to wear it, making the foot clump around the room while the old woman sniggered at such a humorous sight. The welfare machine carefully watched her heartbeat monitor at times like these, intently observant for any variation in its pace and strength.

It was a very happy time for the old woman.

Until, one night, it all went wrong.

A terrible noise woke the old woman. It was the sound of crashing furniture and struggling bodies. A glass ornament smashed against a wall, spraying her legs with fragments. There was a life-and-death struggle going on somewhere in the room. A standard lamp fell across a table and shattered the ceramic stem. The old woman was too frightened even to turn on the light. She was sure that an android had entered her apartment: a rogue machine whose brain had suffered a malfunction and was on the rampage. All she could do was quietly guide her bed-chair to the corner of the room and stay there until the ruckus was over.

The fighting, she was sure, was between her pets and the intruder, and since there was little she could do she had to await the outcome without interfering.

Finally, after a long while, there was silence, and she ordered the light switch on. The scene that met her eyes was horrific.

In the centre of the room were Bird-hands and Hogfoot Right, obviously squaring up to one another. Around them, bleeding, broken and bruised, were the other pets. Moth-ears had been torn and crushed and was obviously dead. Snake-arm had been pierced by a long ceramic splinter which protruded from its head. It, too, was deathly still. Basil was black with bruises, having been beaten, fatally it seemed.

The old woman had not the slightest doubt that Hogfoot Right had gone berserk. There was no sign of any android intruder, and Hogfoot Right looked as though he were now about to attack Bird-hands.

The two combatants fell upon one another. There was a frenzied scrambling and clawing. The old woman began yelling like crazy for Bird-hands, telling her to dig her claws in, while the seemingly mad hog was butting her round and round the walls with its heel-hard head.

It was a vicious battle.

Furniture was scattered this way and that, and twice the old woman had to move her bed-chair to get out of their path as they rolled across the floor, locked in a tight ball. Once, she thought Hogfoot had had enough, as he backed away into a corner, but again he went forward, just when Bird-hands was trying to recover.

Finally, Bird-hands picked him up by the hindquarters and flung him at the exposed end of the standard lamp. It was bristling with live contacts. With a bouncing arc of his body he twisted in agony as the shock went through him. He lay broken and still, across the sputtering wires.

Bird-hands fluttered to the middle of the room.

'Well done,' cried the old woman. 'Well fought.'

Bird-hands just sat there, her thumb-head turned towards the window, through which the dawn was just beginning to emerge. Then suddenly the creature launched herself into the air and began throwing her body at the glass panes in a seemingly desperate attempt to smash her way through, like a wild bird that is trapped in a closed room.

Then the old woman understood. It had not been Hogfoot Right, but Bird-hands. She had seen the martins cutting through the blue sky outside and she wanted to be free too. She wanted to be out amongst those of her own kind. Maybe she had run amok amongst the others because they refused or were unable to understand her desire for escape? Perhaps she had tried to get them to open the window – something only the old woman could do with a brain command – only to find they could not help her? Anyway, she had killed them all. Even little Moth-ears. And Hogfoot Right, the bad-tempered one, had given her the toughest opposition of all.

Poor Hogfoot, misjudged right to the end.

Now Bird-hands sat on the ledge, her nails dripping with blood. She seemed to be waiting for the old woman to open the window, which could only be done by direct order. There came, in the silence, the sound of real birds chirruping outside, and Bird-hands displayed restlessness. The old woman, still in a state of shock, refused to respond.

Bird-hands carefully wiped the gore from her fingerwings on one of the curtains. By this time the old woman had recovered a little but she had much of the stubbornness of her erstwhile right foot and she made it obvious that she was not going to comply.

Finally, Bird-hands flew from the ledge and settled on the old woman's neck. The creature began to stroke the withered throat sensuously, hoping perhaps to persuade her mistress to do what she wished. The woman sat rigidly still, grim-faced. Gradually the stroking became firmer. At the last, the fingerwings tightened and squeezed, slowly but effectively. There were a few minutes during which the old woman convulsed. Then the body went slack.

Bird-hands, after a long while, released her grip and fluttered down to the floor. She crabbed her way amongst the dead creatures, inspecting them for signs of life. Then she came to Hogfoot Right, lying across the electrified strands of the light socket. Bird-hands observed her victim with seeming dispassion. She inched forward, close to the hog's head, looking down.

Suddenly there was a jerk from Hogfoot Right, as his head flashed out and his jaws clamped on a little finger. A brilliant shower of blue-white sparks rained around the pair, and then the stillness in the room was complete.

Later, the welfare machine came to call and surveyed the scene with mechanical surprise. It made a careful note of all the damage and recorded a verdict of suicide. Just as it was about to leave, it sensed some vibrations coming from somewhere in the room. One of the creatures had stirred. Suddenly something snapped at its metal leg and then went careering through the open doorway and along the corridor . . .

(For Lisa)

THE MEN'S ROOM

The past is not what it used to be.

Such a provocative statement cannot but help grab your attention, but the fact is, the past has changed. It can be different the second time around: something to do with retravelling the two-way stretch of time between adulthood and . . . listen, have you seen that stage magician's trick? The magician calls to her assistant, and he skips on to the stage wearing one of those skimpy costumes cut high at the thigh, black fishnet tights and high-heeled shoes: all so *obviously* designed to keep the attention of the women away from the magician's hands. He passes her a piece of blue ribbon. The magician takes the ribbon and runs her fingers along it. While her hand travels from left to right, the blue ribbon stays blue, but when she runs her fingers in the opposite direction the ribbon becomes red. Well, that's what can happen to time: it can change colour, from blue to red – or rather, blue to pink.

I suppose I had better explain.

Without going into too many details, let me just say that in the forty-third year of my previous life I was an electronics engineer involved in communications research. Actually, that word *engineer* has rather a heavy sound to it for the delicate work I used to carry out: tiny circuits and components constructed with tools the largest of which was no bigger than a nail file. I was considered to be one of the best in the field. I came from a very modest home background – my father was a farm labourer – through grammar school and redbrick university, and by the age of forty was one of the most respected men in my profession. I owed a lot to my parents, of course, who (once they understood what was required of them) used all the resources available to them to put me on the right track. There was only one other child, my sister Angela, who, though she followed me through grammar school, at eighteen went and married a farmer and raised children and chickens. At the time, I thought it a terrible waste of an education. She could have gone on to do great things as a veterinary surgeon, if she had only got better exam results. Of course, she did not have the private tutors that our parents made available to me ... however, that's all past history. (Or rather, future history, the future that was . . .)

Anyway, in my forty-third year I invented something, partly by accident, which was potentially social dynamite. Something that would change everything. Without going into too much technical detail – which few of you men reading this will understand because you have been socialized into believing that such things are 'above your head' and therefore have developed blind spots – it was a kind of time travelling device. It could send someone one way only: back to the past.

The method involves using a series of symbols flashed from a screen. The messages are subliminal triggers which enable the human subject's non-physical aspects – the mind and spirit – to enter a universal time-field. The physical world, which includes the subject's body, remains in the future. The mind and spirit are able to travel back to an earlier physical world.

So, I could return to an earlier version of my body. I could effectively relive the years between childhood and middle age, and if I wished, still retain the knowledge, the wisdom, and anything else I had gathered during those years. I would be a child with a man's brain. Had I wanted to, I could have refined the material that was sent back. For instance, I could damp down or even obliterate memories of the life I had lived so far. In other words, I could send 'myself' back and start completely anew, without reference to my former life. For obvious reasons, I elected not to do this but to return to earlier years with all my faculties intact.

I have simplified this explanation to what amounts to a flavour of the whole for two reasons. One, the complete and accurate explanation would be meaningless to those who are not specialists in my field, and two, to protect my discovery from those who are.

Now, you will be asking yourselves, why didn't I announce my discovery to the world, become rich and famous, become history incarnate? The answer is, how do you prove such an invention works? *I* was quite certain of its worth, but then I had faith in my theories. I couldn't expect everyone to believe in me the way I did, even given that I was supposed to be brilliant. They have a habit of putting brilliant people away when their ideas seem to have overtaken *known* laws. Look at what they did to Galileo.

The only thing to do was to experiment on myself. In that way I could prepare the world for my invention, before 'discovering' it again. At first, I thought I would send myself back to my early twenties, but I allowed my heart to rule my head. When I sat down and thought hard about it, I ached to return to my boyhood: the gang going down to the river to swim on a hot summer's day; climbing the apple trees in the orchard; playing football on the village green; looking for birds' eggs; shooting at water rats with my catapult. I had been raised in the country and it was a wonderful childhood, full of golden days of skinned knees and cheeks smeared with plum juice.

So, with nostalgia pushing me hard in the back, I called my ex-wife and bid her a fond(ish) farewell and said I was leaving for South America and that I was going for good. She did not seem at all displeased and thought I was making the right decision. I caught a hint of relief in her tone. We had not had a *terrible* marriage, and indeed were still reasonably good friends, but I had certain – certain ways, certain *desires* I suppose you would call them, which when she discovered them were upsetting to her. However, that done and with my heart thumping, I went to my laboratory.

I awoke in my old bed in the tied cottage, surprised at how lumpy it felt. I thought that perhaps I should prepare myself for a few shocks: that age had coloured my vision of childhood to such an extent that I had idealized the past. However, the sunlight flowed through the ill-fitting flowery curtains on to the whitewashed walls in the way that I remembered it. The bed might have been lumpy, but it was warm, with a thick layer of blankets. I could smell the breakfast mum was cooking in the kitchen below: fried bacon and tomatoes. From the yard outside came other smells: cherry blossom, Jo the yard dog's kennel straw, the baked earth and chicken shit, the remains of an old bonfire which was still smouldering (which I had probably lit the night before – *last* night).

I jumped out of bed, very excited, expecting to find my young body difficult to deal with, psychologically. It wasn't. (It was then I realized I had *always* been twelve years old, in my mind, right up to the age of forty-three . . .')

I took a quick look out of the window at the world I had once known and was not disappointed. Then I looked for my clothes but couldn't find them, so I ventured down the old wooden staircase that led to the scullery and kitchen. The year, by the way, was 1953. It was my favourite childhood year. I was to receive many shocks which I will attempt to convey in the style, rather than the content, of this document.

Standing over the gas stove was my mother – no, my *father* – yes, my father, standing over the gas stove, cooking, standing over . . . my father, wearing, my *father* wearing a faded blue dress, his hair pinned back to stop it falling in his eyes, my father wearing sensible brogues, my father with an apron on, the one covered in primroses. He looked up.

'Go upstairs and get changed out of your nightie, child. You'll catch your death.'

I looked down at myself. Not pyjamas, but a pink nightdress

with a torn hem. I felt a flush of shame creeping over my face.
I tugged at the nightdress.

'There's only Angela's clothes up there,' I said.

Dad took the frying pan off the stove and pushed past me,
climbing the stairs, his teeth clicking.

'If that girl's playing games again . . .' he was muttering. I
followed him up, wondering if I had got my sister a hiding. It
would make a change. The first time around, it was always her
getting me a licking. By the time I got to the top of the stairs
my father was holding up Angela's frock.

'What's this?' he said.

'A frock,' I replied.

'Get it on, my boy, and no more silliness,' he snapped. 'I've
had enough today with your mother complaining about cheese
sandwiches again. I don't know how she expects me to give her
ham on the money she brings home.'

I went red and defiant. My father might want to wear dresses,
for whatever reason, but I didn't see why I had to follow his
bad example.

'I'm not wearing *that*.'

Father looked thunderous. 'You'll do as you're told. How *dare*
you speak to me like that? I shall certainly tell your mother
when she comes home, playing me up like this. What do you
want? Your red dress, I suppose? I've told you a thousand times,
that's for best. It's your church and party dress, and not for
play.'

He stormed out of the bedroom with a swish of his blue frock,
and descended the stairs again, leaving me feeling bewildered
and aggrieved. What the hell was happening here? Had the
whole household gone mad? Why couldn't I wear my ordinary
clothes? Why did I have to dress up? I tried to cast my mind
back, to a time when we had some kind of folk festival, or a
country fair which required us to change clothes with the
females for a day, and came up with nothing.

With a strange, uncomfortable feeling I put on my sister's
clothes and went down to the scullery. I felt very foolish,

especially since my sister Angela was now at the pinewood table eating cornflakes. She scowled at me as I entered, but didn't let loose the expected jibe or shrill giggle. Perhaps it was because she was wearing my trousers and braces, socks and shoes, shirt and pullover . . .

'Get my things off,' I said, hotly.

She gaped at me for a moment, then said, 'Shut yer gob.'

Father came in with the frying pan at that moment. He clipped Angela around the ear with his free hand.

'That's not the way to talk at the breakfast table, young lady, or anywhere for that matter.'

'What's wrong with "gob"?' said Angela. 'Julia says it and her mother's a doctor. A doctor must know what a mouth's called.'

'If you're not careful, you'll find out what *my* mouth's for – and my hand. Now get on with your breakfast. What are you doing today?'

'Gonna play footer,' said Angela. I noticed how short and raggy her hair was. She used to have plaits. I reached up and found the pigtails had been transferred to my head. 'Julie and Sue are comin' round.'

'Julia and Susan. I'm sure their fathers don't approve of such nicknames, coming from such nice families as they do. You're lucky to have such friends. Most farm girls aren't . . .'

'I know, I know,' scowled Angela. She shovelled down her cornflakes and then began wading into some bacon and tomatoes, leaving me the smallest piece.

I was too stunned to say much until now, but thought it was time to assert myself a little.

'I'm going to play football too.'

Angela's mouth dropped open again, then she smirked.

'Don't be *stooo*pid all yer life. Boys don't play football.'

I was about to protest, when dad said, 'I want you to stay and help me with the housework. I look forward to the holidays, when you're home. Afterwards, you can play with Jimmie next door.'

'Play what?' I gasped.

'Dolls, or nurses – whatever it is you play at your age. And stay away from those girls in the recreation ground.'

There was another smirk from Angela.

'I saw you the other day. Showin' your knickers to the girls. He was on the swings, dad.'

'That's enough, Angela. Now, Charles, if you want to read or draw or something, you can take your friend James up to your bedroom. You're too old for things like park swings.'

'I *want* to play football. I *want* to swim in the creek. I *want* . . .' Angela kicked me under the table with her football boots. I yelled. Father cracked her round her head. She jumped up from the table, shouting, 'Don't care,' and clumped for the door. I followed her outside, where she turned and faced me.

'Fuck off,' she snarled. 'We don't want no sissy boys, see!' And then she punched me hard on the arm before running off down the street. I couldn't help myself. I sat down on the pavement and cried. Father came out a moment later and put his arm around my shoulders, his long greying hair falling over my face, smelling of Lifebuoy soap.

'There, there. That girl's getting out of hand – far too rough. Just wait until her mother comes home . . .' But I knew from my own experience, having been in her shoes, that nothing would happen to Angela. Mother (if she was anything like my father) would shake her head and say, 'Girls will be girls. The trouble is, she's left to run wild. I'll take her on the rabbit shoot tomorrow, at back of the farm. She'll enjoy that. Like to fire a twelve-bore shotgun, eh, Angie?'

'Oh, wow, thanks, mum. You bet. Tomorrow? Promise?' 'I promise,' mum would say, ruffling Angela's hair with cracked, dirty fingers fresh from the plough, smiling with a weather-beaten face full of wind creases and tiny sundrawn veins. Then she would call, 'Where's my dinner, man?' to my father, who would be in the kitchen hidden in a cloud of steam. 'Nearly ready, dear,' my dad would reply. 'Just mashing the potatoes.' Mum would mutter, 'A woman likes her meal on the table when she comes in,' then stuff her pipe while she was waiting, ignoring me altogether. It would be no good me asking whether I could go shooting too. I would be told my dress would get dirty.

I had heard it all before.

What had I got myself into? My ex-wife and I used to argue about the nurture-nature thing. Deliah, like a lot of women of the 'eighties, maintained that she had been socialized into an inferior role. She said her upbringing had been responsible for conditioning her behaviour. I always used my sister as an example which refuted this argument. I pointed out that Angela and I had had the same kind of upbringing, yet I had gone on to do – well, let's face it – great things, while she had fallen into the old traditional role of housewife. 'As far as I can remember,' I said, 'mum and dad treated both of us in the same way. In fact I used to get far more hidings than she did. Angela used to get away with murder.' The funny thing is, I really believed we had been treated alike as children.

So, here I was, on the other side. What the hell had happened? I've thought a lot about that since then, and can only conclude that some kind of twist in the ribbon of time is responsible. Who the hell cares, actually, what was responsible. The important question was, could I do something about it?

Anyway, halfway through that day, after dad and I had been shopping and I had seen the rest of the world and its madness – we were not unique – I went up to my room and lay on my bed thinking. I had already checked my body thoroughly and found no changes there. I was still a male with all the masculine appendages. Anyway, Angela's breasts had been visible under her shirt at breakfast. That much remained the same. It was the rest of it that was wrong. I mean, men are physically *stronger* than girls. Why were we doing housework, washing, cooking? I knew why. I had helped my dad during the morning, lugging in the coal for the fire, getting the copper boiler going to wash the clothes in, carrying the shopping from the town. My arms were aching like hell. You needed to be tough for housework.

There had to be some answer to it all.

I remembered that when I was a young boy I used to keep my treasures in a biscuit tin hidden at the back of the wardrobe.

I pulled the old, darkwood wardrobe away from the wall. There were spiders' webs joining the untreated plywood back to the wall itself. I flinched, as I pushed my hand behind the tall piece of furniture, and found . . . yes, the tin box. A spider ran over the back of my hand as I pulled out my container of secrets. I blew it off with a little shudder, finding myself suppressing a scream which I knew would be expected of me in female company.

I took the tin to the bed and opened it. Inside was a variety of objects, but none that I recognized. My penknife had gone and so had the lump of galena I had pinched from a local lead mine. Instead there was a soppy letter from a girl (the spelling was appalling), a porcelain figure of a ballet dancer (a twelfth birthday present, according to the soppy letter, which I was to tell NO ONE about, even my best friend James), a magazine picture of a border collie, and one or two other things of little interest to me. One of the items *did* capture my attention, however. A photograph. It was one of my parents, taken probably in their early twenties, which would be just after they got married. They were dressed in their *proper* clothes.

'Shit!' I cried, delighted at the discovery.

'WHAT DID YOU SAY?' My father was in the doorway to the bedroom.

I thought fast, wanting to keep him calm for the next few minutes while I confronted him with the photo.

'Ship,' I said. 'Wasn't this picture taken on a ship – when you and mum went on holiday that time, to Southend?'

The black look disappeared and he took the photo, studying it for a moment. A little frown appeared on his brow, below the blue dust cap that most housewives – househusbands – wore in this part of the country.

Then the frown was replaced by a wistful smile.

'Ah, I remember this. Yes, your mum and I went to stay with

Uncle James. No, it wasn't on a boat. It was just before a party. We had a lot of fun in those days . . .' he sighed.

'Yes,' I said slyly, smoothing down my skirt, 'but what about the suit? You're wearing a suit, dad – and mum's got a dress on.'

'Fancy dress,' he mused in that funny, faraway voice, as if recalling the happy times of his marriage. 'Your mother and I were invited to a fancy dress party . . .' The little frown reappeared. 'I remember worrying about your mother that night. She seemed to like wearing those stockings and suspender belt a little *too* much – anyway,' his voice rallied quickly, as if he had just remembered he was talking to one of his children, 'it was a long time ago. Now will you come down and help me peel the carrots? I've been calling you for the last ten minutes. Your mother'll be in for her dinner, and it won't be ready. You know how upset she gets if her dinner's late.'

I was dreadfully disappointed.

'I couldn't care less,' I said.

'Now, now,' dad remonstrated. 'Your mother works hard to keep the wolf from the door. The least we can do is see that her dinner is ready for her . . .'

'Screw her and bloody dinner,' I shouted. 'I've had enough of this. I'm getting out.'

I ran from the bedroom with my father gaping after me. Down the stairs and out of the front door, into the street. I didn't care whether I got beaten black and blue when I went back home. I was going to do all those things I did as a boy. I *was* a boy. I was entitled to do boys' things. Hell, that's one of the reasons I came back, to indulge in all those old pastimes.

I ran up the lane, over the back fields, and down to the tidal river of the creeklands. When I got there, all those old smells, of cockleshells, and river mud, and grain-filled longboats, all of them were there. I went behind the sea wall, where the saltwort grew amongst patches of sea lavender, and stripped off. Happily, the tide was in and it was deep enough to swim. I waded out on the mud and entered the water that had been warmed by

almost a day of sunshine. It was beautiful. The murky water of
the creeks swirled round me as I swam – it was just like the old
days – it *was* the old days. I stayed in for over half an hour
before striking out for the bank. When I got to the shallows
there were three girls waiting, holding up my clothes.

'Put those down,' I snarled, covering my genitals with my
hands.

They moved closer to me, smiling, and I could see that the
oldest one was about fifteen. She wore an old greasy flat cap
on her tousled hair, and her jacket was smeared with dried snot
on the sleeve. The baggy trousers had holes in the knees and
she wore no socks on her feet: just a thick pair of laced-up boots.
One of the other two took out a packet of Woodbines and lit a
cigarette, puffing away like a veteran.

'You better shut it, boysee,' said the eldest, 'or we might fink
of frowin' this lot in the river.'

'What do you want?' I said, beginning to shiver now, and
tired of covering my manhood, or rather, boyhood.

She went a little red then.

'Want to come in the bushes, just for a while?'

Panic surged through me then. I looked along the sea wall
but there was no one in sight. A Thames barge was cruising
out in the middle of the river, but too far away to attract any
attention. I thought about making a dash for the grain mills,
but then remembered I was naked.

'You give me my clothes,' I gasped. 'I'll . . .'

She pushed her face up to mine.

'You'll what, boysee? Scratch me eyes out?'

They all laughed. Then, encouraged by the biggest one, they
crowded round me and began touching me, while I whimpered
in humiliation. Then someone came, walking his dog, and I
screamed. The girls ran off. One of them still had my knickers.
She had them on her head, like a hat, and was laughing so
much she could hardly run. I choked back my shame, remembering their filthy hands on my privates.

I dressed quickly and then ran home. Mother was waiting for

me. She gave me a walloping with her belt (thank God she didn't look under my dress) and sent me up to bed without any supper. Hell, was that bitch strong. She had muscles like iron hoops. My ridged backside testified to that.

I sobbed to myself in my bed, even after father had come up quietly (while mum was down at the pub) to stroke my hair and give me some sorely-needed comfort. 'Your mother's just worried about you, son,' he said. 'She doesn't want anything to happen to you.'

Afterwards I planned what I had to do. I could see what the future held for me. Any spare money in the house would go into Angela's education, she being the 'important' one. All the encouragement to 'get ahead' would be levelled at her. Men didn't *need* a good education, the way women did. So, what I had to do was change the world, change people's thinking, before I could even begin to get into a laboratory and get my hands on the right equipment, in order that I could send myself forward again. I had to get my hands on a lot of money, or into a job where the expensive equipment I needed could be made available to me.

What I had to do was start the Men's Movement.

That was twelve years ago. I am now twenty-four and am considered a radical because I advocate such things as equal job opportunities for men. It's a difficult, uphill process, which involves raising the level of awareness of men: making them see they are entitled to want things for themselves, not just for their families, but them*selves*. Many of them don't like what I'm doing. Sometimes I feel my confidence ebbing.

Well, hell, it's difficult having confidence in yourself when you're a man living in a world that's never heard of Leonardo da Vinci, Michelangelo or William Shakespeare. Sure they lived, but da Vinci spent his life doing watercolours for his grandfather and inventing crochet patterns for his uncle. (In *my* world these were important people in the arts!) Who won the Battle of Waterloo? Why, the Duchess of Wellington, Lady Wellesley! Everyone knows that, don't they? Who of the Antarctic? Why,

Jane Scott, of course. Last week I went to see a film called *Queen Quong* about a giant ape that climbs the Empire State Building in New York. (I seem to remember a different title.)

It's difficult having confidence in yourself, in a world where most, almost all, the important people in history have been women. You begin to believe that males are less capable than females, if you're not careful. When Rita Bannister ran the four-minute mile, I cursed. Whenever I see Winifred Churchill on the news, I swear. When it was announced that Olga Gagarin was the first woman in space, I laughed hysterically. I have difficulty coping in a world where the Lady's Prayer begins with 'Our Mother, which art in Heaven ...' and Mary's son Jesus trailed around after his divine mother, helping her perform miracles until she died on the cross. I think – I think –

– I think, what the hell, at least I can wear bloody trousers again, without being pointed at in the street and called names ... some of my friends seem satisfied with that. Satisfied with small steps and to leave the leaps to our sons, the next generation.

'They say there might be a male prime minister of Israel soon.'

'That's a laugh. I'll believe it when I see it.'

'I'm too busy screaming at the sight of spiders these days, like men are supposed to.'

'What I really need is a strong woman to lean on.'

'I often go to the men's room to have a good cry.'

These are the defeatist remarks I hear from some of my friends in the movement, admittedly when things get low and look hopeless.

But *I'm* not out of the game yet! My work for the BBC at the moment is fairly modest. I work in the cutting room, helping to edit material to be broadcast. I fought like hell to get this job and I'm obviously here for my own reasons. My next intention is to take a course at a university, in my spare time, in order to get inside a laboratory containing the equipment I need to make a time-travelling device. *That's* not going to be easy. The kind of course I'm talking about is full of women at this time and it'll take some determination to break into the sexist world of the engineer. Even if I make it, the course members will try to drive me out with ridicule and obscenities. I have to do it though, because once I have my contraption, I'm home and dry. I already have access to television programme material.

What do I intend doing? Well, I'm certainly not going to send myself back again in the hope that it will reverse-field, putting the men back on top. You see, after a lot of deep thinking I have an inkling why there was a reversal the first time. What if . . . what if this action, this time travel, were personal to each human subject? I mean, what if there were something in *myself* which determined the state of the past to which I was sending myself? What if I secretly envied the world of women and wanted to be part of it? There are proportions of both genders in all of us: what if the quantities are so close in most cases that inquisitiveness is enough to tip the balance? I wonder what it's like to be a . . . and there you are. Even trivial, unimportant gestures, like trying on small items of clothing, might be enough to send someone back on the other side? I don't really know. I just have suspicions and a lot of questions. Unanswered questions. Therefore, I do not intend experimenting on myself again.

It is estimated that a certain soap opera is watched by seventy per cent of the viewing public. I help edit that programme. When I have my device I'm going to send millions of people back, not to childhood since that would deplete the population of adults, but just ten years. I intend refining the subliminal triggers, to fuzz the part of the memory which deals with expectation. A female subject who finds male dresses and lingerie in her wardrobe, will suffer only a vague twinge of concern, shrug her shoulders and put them on. Likewise, the man who finds a shirt, suit and tie at the bottom of his bed will be puzzled for a moment by some obscure disquiet in his breast, but soon dismiss it. There will, of course, be those who remain with the same garments they took off the night before. In both cases, there will be little expectation of others. What the hell will happen to all the other sex roles, at home or at work, is anybody's guess. Dammit, I haven't got all the answers. This is the first time it's been done on such a large scale.

If my suspicions are confirmed, the result will be a carnival. I'll confuse the roles so much that it won't be a case of socialization according to sex, but according to individuals. In other words, wearing certain clothes, playing certain sports, following certain careers, all those sorts of things will be as personal as whether one takes coffee with sugar or tea without, and all the other combinations in between. What it will do to the history of the world is anybody's guess. Maybe it will be a wonderful chaos. My *own* belief is that men and women will share heroic figures between them. There will be women artists as great as Raphael was in my first history; there will be men explorers as great as Marcia Polo is in the present history. Gender will not bury greatness, or have prevented it from flourishing. Only such attributes as talent, fortitude, determination, diligence, stamina, courage – the list is long – will determine greatness. Whether a man or a woman carries them within will not matter. There will still be those who do great things but remain unrecognized, of course (me, for one), but it will be due to factors other than sex.

I've got to get into that laboratory. The interview for North East Polytechnic entrants is next Tuesday. I notice from the pamphlet that *all* the interviewers for the engineering course are females (what else!) and I intend to present a suitable image, while at the same time using a little male charm. A grey two-piece pinstripe, I think, with a cream blouse and string tie. I'll wear the skirt above the knee, so that the nylons show my legs to their best advantage. Black leather shoes, with short heels . . . I'll do that *accidental* little trip as I walk into the room, that always gets them halfway out of their seats. It has them feeling slightly protective towards me, but as long as I don't *fall over* completely I won't be dismissed as just another silly male. Not too much make-up, but enough to put aside any thoughts that I might be butch. I listen attentively, ask sensible questions, but do not appear to be as clever as most women. I must be acceptable, but not dangerous. I must make them believe that having a token man on the course will remain an exception, all down to their personal feminine magnanimity. Finally, I'll make some vague promises with my body language which are open to interpretation. I mean, if you've got it, why not use it?

DOP*ELGAN*ER

In 1838, Ambrosia de Magdalana wrote: 'Provided psychological resistance to the incredible is overmastered by the strength of need, the effect of directing applied concentration towards a desired entity is to call that entity into existence.'

Of course, Ambrosia was primarily concerned with deities and apparitions – we first experience the need and then provide whatever satisfies that desire – but certainly a very diluted form of the antithesis of that statement has some truth in the modern world, where unwanted objects suddenly proliferate. For instance, if you purchase an unusual second-hand car, a type which you have not seen before, you will not be driving it for very long before you notice dozens of the same model and year of manufacture. You will see them purring at every set of traffic lights, speeding past you on the motorway and parked outside supermarkets on a Friday evening. You will be piqued to find that the world and his wife seem to have acquired the car you believed to be of uncommon make, style and colour.

However, it would be more appropriate to go back to Ambrosia and his ideas on the birth of devils and gods, before I begin to unfold the nightmare which has been with me for two weeks now.

I first saw her in the library of Queen's College, Edinburgh, poring over some fusty facsimile of Hoffman's *Die Elixiere des Teufels* – no, perhaps I should start the story a few moments before that point, where I was giving a subject deep consideration.

That subject was *doppelgängers*, which as a student I was studying for the purpose of doing a tutorial on Edgar Allan Poe. I was sitting in my usual seat by the main window, where the light was good and the radiator actually worked efficiently, it being winter and drawing towards evening. I remember being delighted at finding what I believed to be a connection between Poe's *William Wilson* and James Hogg's *The Private Memoirs and Confessions of a Justified Sinner*. It said in some notes that the plot of Poe's *doppelgänger* story was suggested by Washington Irving's *Unwritten Drama of Lord Byron*, but while idling my way through the Introduction of Hogg's work I came across the names of Hogg's most outspoken critics – *William* Howith and Professor *Wilson*.

Quickly investigating the dates, I discovered that *William Wilson* was published fifteen years after Hogg's own *doppelgänger* tale. There were other factors: Poe's only story set in England; Poe regularly read *Blackwood's Magazine*, where *Justified Sinner* was reviewed; there were similarities in the authors' descriptions of their *doppelgängers*.

Clearly, to me, Poe had read Hogg's work, had seen the reviews and borrowed a Christian and a surname from each of the critics, and had given the tale a similar background to that of *Justified Sinner*. My discovery, which for all I knew was exceptional, precipitated a feeling of feverish excitement, manifesting itself in a hot flush which (I had no doubt) turned my face a brilliant scarlet.

At that point I looked up to find myself being observed by a woman three tables away, whereupon I blushed even more furiously. The reason for my embarrassment was not because I generally disliked being scrutinized, but because the woman who was looking at me so hard was my ex-girlfriend, Gillian Grovenor.

I gathered up my books and left the room. Gill and I, both in our third year at the university, had parted because of her family's strong objection to me. They believed Gill was too young to become seriously involved and in any case they disapproved of my working-class origins. Gillian, I found out, always bowed to her parents' wishes, which were to her inviolable.

The split had left me feeling miserable and wretched, still in love and unable to put distance between myself and Gill. I still saw her, quite often, at the college. Were we not thrown into each other's paths so often, I expect we would both have handled it a great deal better than we were able to at the time. More often than not, when we did meet by accident, she would turn her back on me and feign interest in the notice board or another student, until I had passed. In turn, this left me feeling frustrated and angry, and I would write some note to her about her manners, saying things that would make me wince inwardly when I recalled them later.

I revealed feelings so ambivalent in those notes that she struck back with an effective character assassination. If we did stop to speak, her efforts would be directed towards trapping me into a contradiction, which she could then fling back at me as an example of my supposed deception during the time we had been together. This, after much brooding, would precipitate more notes from me, until the whole thing became so entangled in a welter of recriminations, regrets and accusations that the facts of love were turned into an unbelievable fantasy dreamed up by the past. Somehow the truth became buried beneath layers of bad taste and unpleasant words. We dug a grave for the love we had once felt, threw it in, and shovelled earth on top. There was not even a cross to mark the spot.

It was with some surprise, therefore, that I had caught her staring at me. I had no doubt that gaze was critical and I had to get out of the library before I exploded with wrath.

Once in the corridor I breathed more easily and made slow steps towards the office in which I was to have my tutorial. On my way I passed several of the lecture rooms and glanced in as a matter of course.

Suddenly, I stopped and gaped.

To my utter astonishment, Gill was sitting in the back row of Room 17, listening intently to a lecture. She glanced up, saw me staring through the glass-panelled door, and quickly turned away again: that gesture I knew so well. *This* was Gill. There was no mistaking that angry flick of the head, on witnessing my presence. I could see her cheekbones turning red, and the cold fire in her eyes.

My first thought was to wait for her and accost her: explain my presence and attack her for misinterpreting the reasons as to why I had stopped to stare. But, on further reflection, I could see this was a mistake. Instead, I went back to the library, fascinated by the fact that Gill had a double. Was there a twin sister? She had never mentioned it.

The girl was still there. I circumnavigated the bookshelves and came up behind her. Looking over her shoulder I saw what she was reading and decided to use that as an introduction.

'Excuse me – when you've finished with the Hoffman . . .'

She looked up, startled, and once again I was shocked by her resemblance to Gill. The only difference, so far as I could see, was that her complexion was much paler than Gill's – it had a wanness to it, as if someone had brushed the bloom from her skin. Also the colour of her hair and eyes would have appeared diluted compared with those of Gill.

She gave me a wide-mouthed, big-eyed smile.

Had she been the real Gill I think I would have passed out from sheer joy.

'I'm sorry,' I managed to blurt out a few seconds later, 'I thought I knew you. There's a girl named Grovenor on my course, and . . .'

She interrupted me in a deep, throaty voice quite unlike Gill's musical tones.

'But that *is* my name.'

I was taken aback.

'What – Grovenor?'

'Yes.'

Some of the other students were beginning to glare at us and I realized we were making too much noise. I sat down in the empty seat behind her and whispered, 'Are you twins?'

'Who? Oh, no. I have no sisters. I'm an only child.'

'Oh – my name's Paul by the way.' I held out my hand and she shook it. At that precise moment I wanted Gill to come into the library and see us together – me with this Xerox copy of herself – deep in intimate conversation. And she did! She *did* come in. But the instant she saw me, she turned and immediately walked out again. For once a miracle had happened – but too fast, much too fast. (Why is nothing perfect?) She had not seen . . .

'What's your first name?' I asked.

'Gillian.' Another brilliant smile.

Something did a flip-flop in my stomach. I should have got up then and left. I should have followed my instincts and run. But we never do what we see in retrospect as sensible. We always stay just that little bit too long. Cats are supposed to die of it.

I repeated slowly, 'Gillian Grovenor? Your name is – Gillian . . .'

'. . . Grovenor,' she finished for me. 'And your name is Paul.' She touched the back of my hand with her fingertips. Then she added that she would be finished with the Hoffman in a short while. Where could she find me?

'In the refectory,' I replied, hoarsely. 'I'll be having a coffee.'

'Fine. See you then?'

I left the library on unsteady legs and made my way through corridors lined with oak, glass-fronted bookcases, my reflection keeping pace with me all the way. Gill – my Gill – was in the refectory when I arrived, but she left the minute I entered, a half-cup of steaming coffee remained on the table at which she had been sitting. I almost threw it after her in exasperation.

It was only after I had sat down myself and had slipped into a calmer sea of thought that the word *doppelgänger* actually entered my consciousness. It was immediately followed by the consideration that I might be going mad. I dismissed the idea. My obsession with Gill, over the past few months, had obviously drilled a hole deep into some forbidden and normally sealed part of my mind and hallucinations were beginning to seep through. Gill could not possibly have a double, bearing exactly the same name: things like that did not happen in the real world – not to such exactitude.

My doubts were fortified by the fact that the second Gillian never arrived. At five o'clock I gave up waiting, took a quick look in the library (there was no one in there that even remotely resembled Gill) and made my way back to my flat in St Andrew's Street. Obviously, I was very disturbed by the afternoon's events but was determined to get some rest. I then intended asking for a year's sabbatical and getting the hell away from Edinburgh and Gill while I still retained shreds of my sanity.

She was waiting for me in my room.

I stared at the new Gillian.

'Your landlady let me in,' she said, 'I hope you don't mind? I went to the refectory but couldn't see you. So I got the address from the college registry office. You *don't* mind, do you?'

I shook my head, dumbly.

She held up a ticket. 'I've reserved the Hoffman for you. They said they'd keep it until tomorrow lunchtime.'

'Thanks – look, I'm still a bit thrown by your resemblance to a girl I know – a girl of the same name. I find it difficult . . .'

She interrupted me.

'I know. I've seen her. She does look a *bit* like me, superficially. Actually, if you saw us together, you'd see we weren't very much alike at all.'

I wondered about the truth of this and had to admit I had not seen them together in order to compare them. Perhaps they weren't really that much alike? After all, Gill and I had not been in each other's company for more than a minute or two in the past few months. She was more of a fuzzy image recall than a flesh and blood person, even though I had had glimpses of her from time to time. Since we had parted, Gill had changed her hairstyle and use of cosmetics, and I carried another picture which had to be reinforced by imperfect memories. Perhaps I was superimposing my idealized Gill on this different woman, because of a coincidence of names.

Turning on the lamp I studied the new Gillian's features, trying not to be rude. There was a small mole on her pointed chin – exactly the same as Gill's – but I would have sworn that whereas Gill's had been a fraction to the left of centre, this mole favoured the right side.

'Well?' she said, 'I feel as though I'm hanging on the wall of an art gallery.'

'I'm sorry.' I threw my books on the bed. 'I've been reading too much lately. Forgive me.'

'That's okay.' She grinned. 'You know, I like you, despite your funny ways. Perhaps because of them. Would you take me for a drink?'

'Gladly,' I said. If there was one thing I wanted at that precise moment, it was a good stiff whisky.

We left the flat and went to the nearest hotel bar. I bought the first round and she the second, and so on. She talked all evening, about very little, and I noticed that her face gradually deepened in colour until it almost equalled that of her counterpart in tone. I put that down to the drink and the warmth of the atmosphere in the bar. I remember getting very drunk and being supported back to my room where, it seemed without asking one another, we crawled between the sheets together, and made love. At least, we tried. I was a little too far gone to be of much use, but I did notice the freckles on her shoulder. It was impossible to recall, given my state, whether the position of this constellation of brown stars – the left shoulder – matched with my memories of Gill's cosmography. All I can say is I did my best to navigate between them with my lips, and fell asleep halfway through the voyage.

She left before I woke. I staggered from my bed to the bathroom mirror and noted, with gloomy satisfaction, that I looked ghastly. My bristled face was a grey colour and on sticking out my tongue, saw that it was covered in a rash of white spots. I needed at least two hours more of sleep but I had a lecture to attend. I did the best I could with an already well-used razor and palsied hand, and then went to college, resolving never to drink that much again.

Gill, with the right-sided mole, was also at the lecture. Sitting behind and to the side of her, I was able to study her profile without fear of receiving one of her looks. She appeared just a little pale herself that morning, as if she too had been hitting the bottle. So far as I could make out, she was not wearing any make-up, however, and it could be that her appearance was due to a lack of cosmetics. She didn't look my way and I was glad for it. I didn't want to see anyone – anyone at all – much less her.

Without any effort on my part I managed to run into the new Gillian in the most unlikely places: in the museum, outside a cinema, while walking the battlements of the castle on a frosty morning. These chance meetings almost always ended in our going to bed together, though nothing was ever planned – at least on my part. I found, to my surprise, that I did not fall in love with her. I enjoyed being with a copy of my Gill, though we talked about very little of importance (she seemed to discourage questions about herself and in all honesty I was not that interested in her private life), but I certainly enjoyed the physical contact with someone who was, to my eyes, a replica of my beloved Gill. Without too much trouble I was able to fantasize during our frantic sessions between the sheets, that my life had not taken a backward step. I was being given a second chance.

I was horrified to learn that she stole. Not just small things – but money and expensive items. She practically stripped my flat of all my movable possessions, such as they were, and secreted something out each time she came. Of course, I challenged her, only to be met with denials and tears. I never actually caught her red-handed, but it could only have been her – no one else ever visited me. And I was desperate for her company. In the end I thought that if she needed the things

that badly, then good luck to her. So long as she left me with
a change of clothes.

There was another strange twist to events. She began to wear
clothes that I had seen on Gill. I wondered about this, lying
awake at nights, thinking, could she be stealing them? But when
questioned she replied that she was aware that I was still
carrying a torch for her namesake, and she had bought similar
clothes in order to please me. She had taken the trouble to study
what Gillian Grovenor had been wearing and had purchased
similar items to make me feel good. How close that was to the
truth – that she actually bought the things – I had no way of
knowing, but she was right about me. I did like the fact that
she copied Gill's styles and colours. It helped me nearer to my
previous position in the world: the one I had held and lost, those
year-long months ago.

The week following our first meeting was half-term and by
that time I was aware that I was looking ill. In the morning I
would get up and study myself in the mirror, hoping to see some
improvement in my colour. I felt okay inside – a little hollow
and wasted, but that had been so since Gill had left me. But my
normally ruddy complexion took on a permanent waxy look,
which seemed to worsen with each passing day.

No one commented on the alteration in my physical appearance – not my landlady or the one or two shopkeepers who
knew me by sight. The new Gillian said I looked fine – she
hadn't noticed any change in me. Perhaps I was hitting the
books too hard? It *was* half-term after all. I should be enjoying
myself a little. I accepted this quite readily. No one wants to
believe they are ill. I put my increasing lethargy down to
dispirited feelings and a general lack of enthusiasm. I tried,
thereafter, to avoid looking at myself in the mirror. I thought
perhaps that I was becoming too obsessed with my appearance
and this was influencing me psychologically, further exacer-
bating my depressed state.

I determined to study hard, to take my mind off these
problems, hoping to relieve some of the stress. However, once

the books were out and I tried to apply myself, I found my concentration slipping before I had read three sentences of Poe, and even when I switched to Hawthorne it was no better. My mind seemed full of trivia, and yet those mundane details were somehow a heavy responsibility. The decision to make a cup of tea would take half an hour of deep thought.

Dwelling on minor things, I became overtired, constantly taking to my bed to replenish the energy I burned in doing nothing. The new Gillian expressed sympathy for my condition and brought me some iron tablets.

'You're just a little run down – anaemic. The iron will pick you up.'

'Only if I take enough to bolt my spinal cord together,' I managed to joke, hoping a change of attitude would help me improve. I was aware that such conditions were often psychosomatic.

Gillian fussed over me in many ways, but it usually had one end: to get me into bed with her. She was an insatiable lover. I didn't mind that at all. It helped me forget the present and remember the past. I talked incessantly to the new Gillian about the old. It should have made her angry, but it didn't. She encouraged it, saying that I had to get it out of me, and once that was done, then perhaps my condition would improve.

'You've bottled her up inside you. Just let it come,' she would say, stroking my hair.

The truth always has to lay itself at our feet before we recognize its terrible form. Truth is an ugly creature when it confirms our nightmares.

For three days, in the middle of half-term, I did not leave the flat. Gillian brought me food from take-aways and she and I lay in bed all day playing word games. I shuffled letters around the page playing hangman with her in a desultory fashion. She seemed full of life. Her skin glowed with the ripeness of a woman in late pregnancy.

On Friday afternoon, Gillian hanged two figures before I asked her to leave me alone.

Once she had gone, I stared at the two stick characters she had drawn, dangling from their scaffolds. She had given one of them a skirt. One man, one woman, decorating two sets of gallows. Just a word game. Only a word game.

I decided to play one of my own. On a blank part of the same piece of paper I wrote down EDGAR ALLAN POE and began rearranging the letters to form an anagram. Eventually, I came up with a possibility:

À LA DOP*ELGAN*ER.

Almost, Edgar my friend, almost there. Two characters were missing – but it was close. I found that if I injected Hogg's nickname, PIG into what I already had, the result was:

À LA DOPPELGANGER.

But there was an 'I' left over. 'I' was redundant, superfluous to requirements, unnecessary. It had to be erased. 'I' had to go. *I* was no longer of any use.

Shit! What was I doing? Who was this person lying in bed waiting to drift away into the ether? I was *me*. I was . . . I was . . .

I had forgotten my own name.

I rose and ran to the bathrom to look into the mirror. I stared in anguish . . .

. . . and cried out in fear.

My hair had turned a semi-transparent white: a mass of glass-fibre filaments.

I rushed to my bed and threw myself on to the covers, sobbing in frustration. The hands that gripped the sheets were bloodless and opalescent. I think I cried myself to sleep.

When I woke it was evening. I checked the mirror again, feeling better able to withstand the shock of my appearance. A faint copy of an albino would have had more colour in his cheeks.

I threw on what clothes I still owned and went for a walk. I expected people in Princes Street, well lit as it was, to turn and stare. They did not. In fact they hardly seemed aware of me at all, brushing my shoulder as I tried to avoid collision.

I managed to muster a dim spark of anger for Gillian – the *doppelgänger* of my ex-girlfriend. I had no doubt now that I had called her into existence. The internalized desire for Gill had been so strong, albeit subliminal, that I had unwittingly created her double to take her place. What I could not understand was how Gillian was managing to rob me of my vitality. What was *she* doing to *me*, that was causing the very energy of life to drain from me? There was something which Ambrosia had written, which I tried to call to mind, but the necessary concentration was too much for my weakened powers of reasoning. Putting one foot in front of the other – walking – was a problem in itself.

I stopped and watched the strong flow of living people flood around me.

It was about ten-thirty and patrons were coming out of the cinema across the road, pouring on to the pavements and running for parked cars. No one took any notice of me and I watched couples spilling into the streets, envious of their togetherness. Then I saw a pair I recognized.

They were one of the last couples to come through the double doors, pausing on the threshold.

Of course, I noticed *her* first – my beloved Gill – but her appearance brought a lump of anguish to my throat. She was – how can I say it? – yes, she was as translucent as frosted glass. I could almost see through her. The lights of the foyer behind her revealed the bones beneath the facial flesh, and such thin, wasted bones they seemed too!

I think I let out a cry, and then *he* stepped forward, peering into the darkness. On seeing me, he grinned. A few months ago that smile would have been familiar to me, especially since it was framed by the upturned collar of my own overcoat. But I had not grinned like that, myself, for a long time. Especially not into a mirror.

Did I feel a loss of identity? Did I feel threatened? Did I feel helplessly lost?

Yes, all those, and more. But mostly I felt despair. The double trap had caught us both, sapped us both, drained us both dry

of personality, character, spirit. We had stolen each other from
each other. I recalled then Ambrosia's qualifying statement on
the creation of desired entities: 'If the unique already exists, and
a replica is elevated from the conscious or subconscious mind,
then displacement must occur.'

I waved to Gill, still standing there on the steps of the cinema,
and saw the delicate internal structure of my own hand, like a
bird flying against the sun. She tried to wave back, but even as
I watched there was a marked deterioration of her form, as it
blended with the light behind her. Then I turned away before
I had to look at that other thing again: the manifestation of my
beloved Gill's unconscious desire.

That was three hours ago. As I sit here writing, the lamp which
shines upon the paper seems to grow brighter, but that is an
illusion caused by my condition. It is me that is growing dimmer,
not the world increasing in luminescence. The fingers that hold
my pen begin to take on the consistency of air. I know that I
shall soon cease to exist, in this place, where the dispossessed
become unnoticeable, and simply fade from being . . .

1948

Before I begin this narrative, I need a name by which to call myself. I need a pseudonym, for I dare not use my real name. They are already suspicious of me. I'm followed daily from my lodgings and constantly watched. There's always at least *one* of them in every dim doorway, blue as the shadow itself, merging with the sunless interiors of alleys. Only the hard, cold eyes give them away. Yes, felt trilbies moulded out of darkness; heavy navy overcoats fashioned from shadows. I know them. They know me.

For obvious reasons I must keep my pseudonym a secret. It would be dangerous to reveal even that much about myself. They know all about everyone and they *know* the kind of false name I would choose. When someone invents an alias for himself it is commonly believed that the false name is chosen at random, out of the air, and has no connection with the real name. Not so. Our personalities, our subconscious, our characters do not allow for pure inventiveness, for absolute originality. We pluck out a name, but that name has a connection with us, somewhere in our past history. Our subliminal egos surface to produce a name by which *they*, through clever deduction, will know us.

One must hide behind legions of false fronts or they find you out, and the watching ceases, the torture begins. No, they do not kill you. Of that I am certain. Death is too final. They can't reach you beyond the grave. They can't torment and punish you, turn your mind inside out, if you're just a mouldering corpse. They keep you alive, in a room somewhere beyond the outside world, and slowly, so very slowly, pick at your brain with sharp, fine needles.

The watchers have been following me all my life. I realize that now. Of course, as an infant and adolescent I didn't notice them. Children are too engrossed in fantasy to notice what is happening in the real world. It was only after I started working at the Ministry that I became aware of them. Let me describe to you the first one I ever saw, using notes I made at the time . . .

Since he stands alone and half inside any available darkness (it is always twilight when he is most in evidence) it is difficult to guess his height. Sometimes he seems of slight stature, below the average, and at others strangely bulky and menacingly tall. His features, hidden by his upturned collar and low-brimmed hat, are barely discernible, but I am certain he is of European descent. There is something in his bearing suggestive of Continental origins – yet on occasions the sharpness of his shoulders below the muffled head have a distinctive Englishness about them. His stance is non-committal, and his overall shape melts into grey buildings, blurring the image against the background, as an Impressionist painter will form an outline from a haze of similar colour tones. Of his hands and feet I can say little. These are always hidden, in his coat pockets, in nondescript footwear. His walk is peculiar for its deliberate tread, which is soft, even and determined. I have never heard him utter a sound and if I stare too long he has this trick of merging with his environment, like a camouflaged cat.

These are the alarming details which I recorded with meticulous precision.

Before I was aware of being watched, I paid little significance to the importance of my job as a filing clerk at the Ministry of Agriculture and Fisheries. However, as I told Eric, it suddenly struck me one day that I never really read any of the papers I was told to destroy from time to time. *I wasn't obliged to.* It seems obvious to me now, now that I understand the significance of my role in that invulnerable all-powerful machine we call the State, that they could not let me walk around unmonitored.

They believed I knew too much.

Perhaps I'd better tell you a little about what I do.

Ostensibly, I'm a clerk, a filing clerk. That's the title they give me, anyway. Once upon a time, I would have called myself a minor employee but Eric does not believe in grading one's status. Everyone, he tells me, has an equal importance in running the affairs of the country, and I believe him.

My duties? Well, that of preparing and filing paperwork, making sure everything is easily accessible. This is where certain unanswered questions begin to rear their ugly heads and if you have a sixth sense, as I have, for the underhand, the surreptitious, then the hairs on the back of your neck should be lifting.

Accessible!

Sometimes you know exactly where a piece of paper *should* be, but when you look in the correct file, under the right date (we use the chronological system), that particular piece of paper has DISAPPEARED. When you fail to produce the now missing document, officials in authority begin to rave about incompetence, but this is bluster to cover up the TRUTH. Current files, archives, they're all the same. They swallow the very document that some Minister wants immediately for his meeting. You search frantically through all the likely files imagining some large oak table surrounded by irritated, impatient men with large watch chains who simply cannot proceed without the vital information which you should have at your fingertips. When it can't be produced, there is a total breakdown of information. Where do these documents, these memoranda, these data go? That's the question I have been asking myself for many years. Then, recently, the answer came to me. When a document DISAPPEARS, then TRUTH is lost. The world can never be the same again. It has changed, permanently.

When I told all this to Eric, he looked at me with knowing eyes and scribbled something down in that notebook of his.

My other duty is destroying the so-called superseded or out

of date contents of the files. While I was telling Eric, it struck
me that I only destroy what I'm told to destroy. Who makes
the decision? Well, who knows where these commands origi-
nate? Somewhere in the hierarchy to be sure, but finding the
exact source is an impossible task. The decision-makers, the
destroyers, hide themselves in the crowd. There are legions of
clerks, secretaries, officials, executives milling around in the
halls of my workplace. Apart from my close colleagues, I never
see the same faces twice. So orders move down to me under a
perfect anonymity. 'It says here, on this memorandum, that you
must burn such-and-such a file in the basement incinerator',
and when I look at the signature on the order, it is in-
decipherable, a mere scribble. *Anything* could be written on
those letters, forms, minutes, that I throw into the furnace. I
have secretly tried reading some of late but they are in code –
full of jargon and figures about herring shoals and crop yields
– obviously hiding information which could be used to control
the world. This is a brutal task; unsavoury, unpalatable. I said
as much to Eric who immediately nodded hard and made further
notes.

Eric plans to write a book about it, I'm sure.

When I told Lorna, however – Lorna was the girl to whom I
was unofficially engaged (they got to her in the end, as I knew
they would, and she was forced to terminate our relationship.
She was too afraid for her life to give me the real explanation
for her defection to the barber's assistant, insisting that we were
incompatible, that the haircutter and she were in love, but I
knew better) – anyway, Lorna just laughed. 'Don't be silly,' she
said, 'they're just old pieces of paper. They take up too much
space. The Civil Service runs on paper, my dad says, like a car
runs on petrol. It uses it up in order to keep the engine running
and the parts moving. My dad says it needs paper fuel to make
it look as if it's useful and doing something, but it's just an
engine idling away, not going anywhere . . .'

I have never been convinced by Lorna's dad's argument. I
think he was a naive man. He worked for the London docks

authority and everyone knows what dockers are like. They leave sugar out in the rain and meat out under the sun. Enough said.

Lorna refused to take the watchers seriously. I was afraid for her, afraid for us both, because we were unmarried.

Lorna used to say, 'It's not against the law, us sleeping together. What are you afraid of, you nit? Losing your reputation?'

What was I afraid of? This. Every Tuesday, when we *did it* at a flat loaned to us by a friend, one of them would be outside, watching. The flat was one of those sleazy little tenement places with a kitchen off the bedsitting-room and a curtain for a door between them. The curtain was too narrow, of course, they always are, and while we lay on the greasy sheets I could see the dirty dishes piled on the draining board through the crack. If I pulled the curtain the other way, to hide them, I could see the damp patch on the kitchen wall. It was just above the water heater, where the fungus had formed into a map of Australia. There was no way to hide from the dreary kitchen interior. It spied on us while we made love and I could never fully concentrate while those dishes were there or the furry antipodean wall chart gazed blankly at our illicit (if not illegal) activities.

Outside the flat HE would be waiting and watching. Listening. I could sense his presence. If we were only violating an unwritten social code, or church law, what was he doing there, pressed against the brickwork, his eyes on the window behind which we lay in each other's arms? Gathering information? Perhaps one day they would confront me with my (let's face it) sin. Perhaps they would fling it in my face as I sat in the chair in that bare room somewhere beyond help, beyond the reach of friends.

'FORNICATOR!'

I couldn't stand that. I would die of embarrassment. They would have me in the palms of their hands, to mould, to twist into an instrument of evil, to become their slave.

I never ever pulled back the shade to look down into the

street, having once sensed he was there. I'm too smart for that. They knew I knew he was there, but I wasn't going to prove it to them by some stupid overt act which would have had them pouncing on us, naked in our shame, while we wallowed in guilt.

Lorna said I was typical of someone with a strict Christian upbringing. I thought about that, but dismissed it. I haven't been to church since I was eighteen, though my parents are always writing to ask me and I *say* I'm attending regularly. I don't think that's hypocritical, though I realize it's a lie. I'm trying not to hurt my mother. She would be very upset if she thought I wasn't going to church. Honour thy mother.

I don't consider this dishonest in the evil sense. One has to modify the truth when dealing with innocents.

When I said as much to Eric he looked startled. Out came that little notebook of his and he scribbled away like mad.

When I first met Eric, a few years previously, I asked him what he was writing and he mumbled something about domestic livestock. Eric is a queer fellow, says the drollest things at times, and on occasion has been known to walk about dressed as a tramp. We meet at a café called The Chestnut Tree and the place is full of down-and-outs, so I suppose he wants to fit in. Most of them eat like animals.

'Look at them,' I once whispered. 'Like pigs at a trough, pushing, shoving, sticking their snouts in and gobbling away at the eggs and bacon . . .'

I remember Eric said something funny, about it being canni-balistic, pigs eating bacon, and I laughed out loud. He is very droll.

The war was on then, so people enjoyed what food they could get hold of. I didn't fight in the war because of my job and flat feet. However, those of us who stayed at home didn't have such a wonderful time of it either. There was the blitz to contend with. Bombs, bombs and more bombs. Then the doodlebugs and V2s. Yet, despite the air raids, it all seemed so remote and unreal. I never actually *saw* the enemy. Oh, I watched newsreels of the war, and planes flying overhead, and heaven knows the bombs were real enough, but I never actually came face to face with a German, Italian or Japanese soldier. I wasn't even sure who we were supposed to be fighting at any one time. Certainly, the war took our minds off food shortages and rationing. It's difficult to think about your belly while explosions are showering shrapnel over your house and rattling the window panes. It crossed my mind that I couldn't remember which came first, the war or rationing.

One day, during the war, I was on my way back to my bedsit in the Strand. The blackout was on and there was no moon so I had to feel my way along as best I could. As always, HE was behind me, my ears sensitive to the tread of soft rubber-soled shoes. Suddenly, for some inexplicable reason, a wind of fear swept over me. I didn't know what to do. It was like one of those times when you wake up from a terrible dream, soaked in sweat, with the reason for the terror still caught somewhere in the nightmare. The cause of the fear has slipped irrecoverably from memory to somewhere at the bottom of your subconscious. You are afraid, but worse than that, you don't know what of.

Instinctively, I ran out on to a bridge over the Thames – Waterloo Bridge, I think it was. I stood there, by the parapet, gulping down air like water, ready to jump if necessary into the cold river below. For a long time I stood pressed against the damp rail of the bridge, listening for something. I could feel my heart banging in my chest and then, without warning, a loud wail rent the stillness. The air raid siren. Shortly afterwards bombs began falling somewhere eastwards of me, probably the docks. Then they came nearer and an incendiary device hit a nearby house which caught fire.

In the sudden light of this bomb, a figure appeared. He was vaguely familiar. His broad face reminded me of my older brother: a big kindly man whom I hadn't seen since he left home at eighteen. My big brother had always looked after me at school, always watched over me. This man was very like him. He was scruffier than I expected, but that was obviously a disguise. His soiled garments smelled.

'Got a match, mate?' he asked.

I gave him a light for his dog-end and in the flare saw behind his weak mask, behind the watery eyes, certain aspects.

'Got the price of a cup of tea, guv?' he said.

The voice confirmed my earlier suspicions, though I didn't reveal that I had seen through his charade. He wanted me to believe he was just another destitute alcoholic, down on his luck. So thorough had his training been and so clever his skill at interpreting the role, that had I not been alert for signs I would have accepted him as an unknown tramp. His body looked wasted and brittle: his face ravaged by the excesses of drink and living rough. I decided to play along with his little game and humoured him with a sixpence.

He stared at the small silver coin in his palm and then, to my mind, overdid the part he was playing.

'Can you make it a quid? I need a meal and kip.'

I stared into those rheumy eyes and gave him a knowing look.

He said, 'Just a sheet, guv. You look gentleman enough to stand me that. Good night's kip, see? Coppers keep turning me off the park bench.'

Since we had begun acting out the farce, I decided to carry it through to the end. I took out my wallet and with a gesture that he could not mistake – one of contempt for a minion of the State – I handed him a pound note. His eyes softened and he snatched at the money eagerly.

There was something in the way he looked at me afterwards which was significant and as he was walking quickly across the bridge towards the dark alleys beyond, I felt an unmistakable wave of sympathy flowing between us. We were two human beings caught in the mesh of political intrigue: pawns in the hands of chess masters. In that aspect, there was a common bond between us.

Why had he wanted to confront me? I pondered over this

question for a long time while studying the black waters of the Thames below me. The bridge had been a perfect place to meet, of course. It was a no man's land – a place, a natural border, where two sentries from opposing armies might meet and share the common experience of being similar cogs in two big machines that they neither understood nor cared about. For a few moments in the course of a war, two enemies might find a certain kinship.

I decided that he had engineered the meeting for a reason. There had been sympathy in his eyes. He had wanted to warn me of something. What? I racked my brains for a clue: went over and over our short conversation in my mind, looking for his coded message to me. It had to be something to do with the person, the man behind it all. It had to be something to do with the big boss himself.

The watcher had been trying to pass on a name!

The ministries were full of names without faces. It had to be someone who was never seen but whose name was a byword. Someone behind the scenes who controlled it all. Mentally, I went through all the signatures I had read on documents I had filed, but none of them had that ring of recognition that I was seeking. Besides, most of the documents had a limited, even restricted, distribution. It had to be someone whose name reached the whole populace – a name that was there with us the whole time, but one we saw so often that it no longer registered. A name that would mean nothing to us if we heard it in the street, but one that was with us constantly.

I took out my wallet and went through the contents. My driver's licence? I studied it hard but nothing clicked. My library ticket? Again, it sounded no bells. There was only one other piece of paper in my wallet and as I reached for it my fingers trembled. Of course! How stupid of me. That had to be it. How many of us walk around with no money in our pockets?

Can you make it a quid, guv?

My adversary's words returned to me as I lit a match and

held the pound note up to the light. There he was. I had found my man. On every pound note there appears a signature, a man who signs the legal tender on behalf of the Bank of England.

The signature read: *O'Brien.*

This then was the man whose name controlled my destiny. The signature we should all fear, but one which we all love to have in our pockets. The man with whom we have an ambivalent relationship.

O'Brien, we love and hate you.

I hurried away to tell Eric.

On the way to The Chestnut Tree a bomb shook the buildings around me and I ducked into an alley for safety, using two dustbins as protection.

Just as I was considering that it was safe to leave, a rat ran out of the space between my feet. I think I screamed. Rats terrify me and those that have me watched are aware of that. They find these things out and use them against you. I had no doubt they had sent the rat as a warning. It was so clever, so devious of them, to send a rat after me in a place where one would *expect* to find such creatures.

When I told all this to Eric, he gave me a strange look. For the first time in our acquaintance, I felt uneasy in his company. Since I am honest, I told him so. 'But I'm just feeling a little paranoid at the moment,' I said, 'what with the rat and all.' I then explained to him a theory of mine. This: *the natural paranoia we all have within us is used against us, to create the impression that everything we see and hear out of the ordinary is attributable to mental disorder. As part of our defence system, we have paranoid tendencies, which are justified. THEY tell us that all paranoia is due to mental illness, so that when they begin to apply pressure, following us around, watching us, we dare not tell anyone in case we are considered insane.*

'So clever of them, eh? They cover their tracks in such devious ways.'

*   *   *

Recently, the full extent of their surveillance techniques has been realized by me. For the first time in my life I am beginning to understand how thorough are their methods.

The other evening I was making love to a woman I met in a cinema, painfully aware of the noise we were making. Out of the corner of my eye I caught sight of the wireless. It was one of those Napoleon-hat shaped devices, with a circular speaker and two knobs below. It looked a little like a face. There was a nefarious aspect to this seemingly innocent piece of furniture. At first, I couldn't place it, until I moved my head and the light fell on it in a particular manner.

'What's – what's the *matter*?' I heard the woman say.

'That wireless.'

'What the hell are you TALKING about?' she seemed breathless.

'That . . . *device*,' I yelled back at her.

She struggled underneath me, saying, 'This is ridiculous, I have to get home.'

'No. No, it's not. I've just realized. You see, there's a wireless in every home. If they can transmit sound *to* us, why shouldn't they also receive the sounds we're making. They're listening to us, to our illicit love-making. The clicking of the bed, our breathing, the other sounds. They can use it against us, when they take us in. Think of that, Lorna.'

'Sylvia. My name's Sylvia.'

'Yes. Think of that, Sylvia. A perfect medium for spying on people in the privacy of their homes. Under the guise of a piece of equipment which is supposed to be for our entertainment, it enables the authorities to listen to everything we say . . .' My voice dropped to a whisper.

Sylvia jumped out of bed and went to the sink, turned on the tap and began splashing cold water over her face.

'Good idea,' I whispered. 'Drown our voices with background noise. Well done. Clever of them, isn't it? They knew exactly what we were up to. Probably have transmitters in the cinema too. A whole network of listening devices.'

I crept out of bed and covered the wireless with a heavy blanket. Sylvia was dressing by this time, and quickly. I imagine she thought they would soon arrive and start breaking down the door. I tried to explain to her that they didn't work like that. That their methods were more subtle. That we could finish what we had begun, but the woman was obviously frightened out of her wits because she rushed out of the flat and I never saw her again.

I gave her half an hour's start and then slipped out the back way. I went straight to my own flat and disconnected the wireless from the electricity supply. On reflection it was probably a silly thing to do, since it would tell them I was on to their tricks, but I tend to panic sometimes.

I thought, of all people, I could trust Eric.

Things are coming to a head at last. Yesterday night I went out into the streets. As usual my footsteps were dogged by the shadowy form wearing a trilby and heavy overcoat. I found myself on Waterloo Bridge, staring down into the water. It was midnight. There wasn't a great deal happening in the world and for a while I lost myself in the lights dancing on the water, when suddenly I had an urge to strike back.

How? Radical comment? I had a piece of chalk I keep in my pockets for such times. I decided to scribble something on the parapet which would be understood by all subversives such as myself. I had just completed my mission when someone walked into the light of the lamp. Though he was dressed as a tramp, I recognized him straightaway.

'Eric,' I cried. 'You're spying on me. Have you gone over to them? How did they get to you? First, my older brother, now, my friend. Who will they recruit next, to watch me, to try to catch me out?'

He stopped and squinted.

'Smith? Is that you?'

(Of course, Smith is not my *real* name.)

'You know it is,' I cried.

He saw the chalk in my hand and then stared at the parapet

behind me. I tried to hide the words with my body but he pushed me firmly aside. He read my message and then copied it in that damned notebook of his, which will probably one day be used against me, in some small room out of reach of the world.

I looked over his shoulder. Yes, he had copied my message of hope to all revolutionaries, just as I had written it, surely for his report to his superiors. The words were clearly inscribed in huge capitals, covering the whole page:

PARANOIA IS SANITY

That was the last time I saw Eric. This is my story, written here on these sheets of paper, and one day they will reach the eyes of sympathetic readers. The TRUTH cannot be hidden forever. I am hiding the document in the heel of one of my boots. I am afraid, but defiant. *They will not grind me down.*

USURPER

As Franz Culper left the house for work that morning, he sensed that something was dreadfully wrong. He tried to think whether he had misplaced or forgotten to do anything – a telephone call? a letter that needed posting? – nothing came to mind. Some task left undone? No, it was more than that. The wrongness he felt was vague, yes, but it was also terribly fundamental: something was missing from the universe: *his* universe. Perhaps this unnatural feeling had been with him since waking, but he only recognized it the moment he left the house.

He stared up at the sky. It was a crisp, bright October day, the air before him like thin glass. The answer to what was bothering him did not lie there. Whatever it was, it was beyond his control, and he sighed before setting off towards the tube station.

Franz Culper was not a bad man. Up until now he had enjoyed a simple life with few major upheavals. He liked his wife, felt they were good companions, and tried to please her in most things. That morning, as she had kissed him goodbye, she had seemed a little distracted. In fact her kiss had not even landed on his proffered cheek, but that was not unusual, since Franz was often moving towards the door as she was forming the bow with her lips.

When he reached the entrance to the tube station, he felt inside his coat pocket for his wallet. It was empty.

'Damn,' he muttered. He must have forgotten to collect the wallet from his bedside cabinet. Not a thing he did often. In fact he could not ever remember doing such a thing before. He searched all his pockets, in case he had put either money or season ticket in one of them, but found nothing. His briefcase? He looked down at his hand. He had forgotten his briefcase, too. Amazing! Well, there were two things he could do. He could go back to his house or he could walk to work. The office was in the city centre, two miles away.

He decided to walk.

Franz Culper was a manager in a firm that imported blinds, shades and screens from the Far East, fashioned of materials ranging from silk to ricepaper. The offices were in Change Alley, close to the river. It was not the first time he had walked to work through the narrow dockland streets – it could be a very pleasant activity on a summer's day, given that he had allowed himself time – but whereas he was used to striding out, confidently, he found himself dragging his heels, sauntering past the idle wharves where the boats threw dull reflections on the murky water, and becoming easily distracted.

When he reached his offices – not an old building with charm and character, but not one of those sharp-edged modern blocks with chrome and tinted windows either – it was ten o'clock. He climbed the stone steps of the back stairs, anxious not to be seen by any of the directors, sliding his hand up the cold iron banister rail until he reached the second floor. Then he opened the fire doors to enter the corridor which ran past his room.

He stood outside his closed office door. Beyond it, the light was on and through the frosted-glass panel marked PRIVATE in black letters, he could see the silhouette of a man sitting behind a desk. *His* desk.

Franz felt something in his stomach: a hollow sensation that at once recalled his anxiousness on leaving the house that morning. He stared at the figure behind the glass: a hunched form that seemed to be dashing off work, papers, in a flurry of energy. He knew the man: at least, he recognized shape, posture, gestures – and he was frightened. Their familiarity aroused a quiet terror within him. He watched the form for some time, unable to move closer, before looking first up at the fluorescent corridor lights, then down, behind him.

There, in its negative aspect, was the reason for his previously unidentifiable concern: the cause of his nagging apprehension. He looked up, then down again, trying to make sense of a situation which in his experience had no precedent. There was no mistaking what he saw – or rather, what he did *not* see.

He had no shadow.

He looked up again, slowly, the fear having a definite form now.

His shadow, he now knew, was inside his office, doing the work that Franz should have been doing; usurping his position; taking control of his affairs. Franz was extremely shocked and mortally offended.

He stumbled along the corridor to the washroom, turned on the cold tap and splashed his face with water. The paper towels had all been used so he wiped himself on translucent panels of hard toilet paper, which scratched his skin.

Out in the corridor again he considered a confrontation, to attempt regaining his former position, but just as his courage reached its peak, his shadow straightened behind the frosted glass, glaring back at him. The dark gaze was strong, in-timidating, and Franz's bravery faded. There was an arrogance to the figure's stance which suggested that any meeting would end in humiliation for Franz. His shadow had all the psy-chological advantages: it had reached the office first; had occupied the desk like a fortress and was now waiting, pen in hand, ready to use cold contempt as a weapon.

Franz regarded the familiar shape for a while longer, unable to understand the reason for its confidence. He read meaning into its state, though, and what it said was: I can do this job better than you; I am more deserving of it; you are weak and I am strong.

I could go to one of the directors, thought Franz, and explain. I could say there is an imposter sitting in my chair, doing the things that are rightfully mine to do.

But if his shadow *were* doing it better, what would the director say? It did not matter to the firm which one of them did the job, so long as it was done, competently and efficiently. The shadow certainly appeared to be fulfilling the duties required of a manager.

Franz stumbled out through the fire doors and down the back stairs. He needed time to assess the situation, to think of a plan for regaining his lost position behind the desk.

He walked along the river bank, glancing behind him occasionally to see if his shadow had returned to its normal position, at his heels. There was never anything there, and finally he found a park bench in one of the public gardens where he sat watching others go by, and of course, they all had their faithful shadows.

The world is not a very happy place for someone whose pride has been severely impaired: it shows indifference, a distinct lack of interest that drives the spirit of a man deeper into himself, beyond any reach. Franz felt a kind of hunger that had nothing to do with food.

He decided to go to a pub for a drink and perhaps gather some courage. He retraced his steps to the office, drifting quickly past the main entrance where June, the receptionist sat engrossed in some giveaway magazine, and to the doors of the 'Harvest Moon'. It was just twelve-thirty.

Before entering, he glanced at the window that ran adjacent to the pavement. It was one of those misted windows of public houses that have the name of the brewery arcing like a silver rainbow, from one end to the other. Behind the window was a brass rail, with dulled hoops holding up a dirty red velvet half-curtain. Above and beyond this, he could see the fuzzy shapes of the patrons in the dim light of the bar, standing, talking, drinking. Phantoms.

One of them was his shadow.

Franz backed away from the doors, the anger rising to his throat. He choked on it. There must be something he could do! He saw his shadow turn away from its drinking companions and stare towards the window. This time the waves of contempt were full of brutality. *Come in here,* his shadow was saying, *and I'll knock you to the floor, stamp on your face. I'm amongst friends.*

The shadow then raised its glass in a mock salute, then turned away, presenting Franz with a broad back. Its left arm came out and rested, lightly, on the shoulder of a female companion. Franz had been dismissed.

He felt wretched. He saw the figure lean forward as if whispering, and then the dark form shook as laughter came rippling out of the pub doorway.

There was little else to do but walk on, through the streets, staring at everything and nothing. Once, a cat came out of an alley and padded over his feet, as if he did not exist. Until that morning Franz Culper had not been happy, exactly, but he had been comfortable, content. He had a home, a nice wife and a secure job. He wasn't going anywhere that he had not been to before, but that had been all right. There was nothing wrong with standing still – lots of people did the same. He saw them on the tube train every morning: pale grey faces that gradually aged over the years. They lived their lives wrapped in nonentity, with little to bother them beyond small back gardens that produced a few flowers and weeds. What was wrong with that? Did this kind of life-style justify such victimization as he was undergoing now? What had he done, or not done, to deserve being swept aside like a pile of dust, by his own shadow? It wasn't right. A shadow should not achieve more charisma than its owner, should it?

When darkness came, there was nothing to do but return to his house. Perhaps there, he would be able to formulate some plan, some scheme for regaining his lost position in the world? He walked the stretch of the river again, unimpressed by the sheen that danced on the water, or the boatmen that cleaved through its ripples. He passed figures in rags, who sat around punctured oil drums that had flames licking through the holes.

When he came to his own road, he walked through the pools cast by the street lamps until he reached his front gate. There were two bottles of milk on the step which his wife had not yet taken in. He would have to speak to her about it. Standing in front of the door with its coloured glass panels, one red, one blue, together making the shape of a Norman arch, Franz reached for his key.

Of course, his pockets were still empty. He lifted the door mat hoping that she had left her key there, even though he strictly forbade it, but there, too, was a space bearing only dust. Next, he tried the doorbell but remembered, even as he was pressing it, that it needed new batteries and was not working.

He yelled through the letter box.

'Hey! I'm home!'

Nobody came, so he rattled the flapper, loudly.

There was a shadowy movement in the lighted hall behind the glass, as if the bulb were flickering prior to going dead. Someone, or something, stood in the passage for a few moments, before the light went out and blackness formed a wall beyond the door.

Franz felt as if something were blocking his windpipe. He staggered back a couple of paces, almost falling over his own feet. *His own home!*

He went out into the street and stared at the bay windows of his living-room, at the net curtains. There were shapes behind them. He leaned forward, over the wavy concrete wall in which the builder had imbedded lumps of coke. Then the main curtains were closed and the lights went on. Through the cloth he could see two figures moving backwards and forwards, as if carrying items either in or out of the room.

Then there was the dancing light of the television screen. Franz watched and watched, the despair growing in his breast.

He ran up to the door and hammered on it with his fist, without hope. Nobody came to answer. The bushes whipped his thighs as he ran back out, into the street, just in time to see the living-room lights go out. Then the little pink bedroom lamps, with their soft rosy glow, came on. He saw the two shapes behind the curtains and the intimacy of the scene shocked him deeply. The pair came together, briefly blurring into one black velvet image for a few moments. Had they merely crossed, or were they . . . ? That was his *wife* up there.

'Not right,' he whispered. 'Not right.'

Nevertheless, he stayed, and watched. Finally, the lights went out in his house and there was a stillness within.

Shortly afterwards, when the moon came up over the rooftops, he saw his wife come to the window and look down on him through the glass. She had an expression on her face which appeared to be a mixture of sadness and triumph, and he leaned forward, his face upward, as she puckered her lips and blew him a silent fleeting kiss before the curtain fell back again, and she was gone from his sight.

Franz groaned inwardly.

There was only one place left to go – one place which might give him the help he needed. He realized now that direct confrontation with his shadow was not the answer. He needed to build his own spirit to match that of his usurper: bring it up from the depths of himself, and put new strength into it. His very soul was the place where he would find the power to conquer this pretender. A physical battle would not answer. A combat of wills was required.

He walked quickly to the nearest church, found a way in, and spent the night trying to fortify his spirit with the atmosphere of the chapel. The old grey stones and ancient wooden pews, however, remained impartial. They withheld their mysterious forces, keeping their secrets to themselves. The embossed altarcloth, the candlesticks, the stained-glass windows, none of these had anything to say to Franz.

When morning came, he realized it was all hopeless. He had let his spirit fall too far within himself, beyond recovery. Why should his wife help him when he had estranged her with petty trivialities and a lack of warmth and passion? Why should the Church help him when he only called upon it at the last moment?

He climbed the spiral stone staircase, past the arrow-loops

with their narrow rectangles of light, to the top of the church tower. He walked to the edge and climbed into a crenelle on the parapet. The ground stretched itself, a long way below him. Shadows were growing tall across the land.

All it took was a jump. He felt bitter that he had been let down and he wanted them all to suffer: especially his shadow.

At that moment, he knew he *could* win. Of course, it meant sacrificing himself, but he had intended to do that anyway. He had climbed the tower to commit suicide, but he suddenly realized he could take his shadow, his wife's lover, the trespasser, with him to the grave. This cuckoo that had thrown him from his soft, warm nest could not survive without him. *I'm the object that casts him. I'm the it that gives him shape and movement.*

Franz Culper leaned forward. Out of the corner of his eye he caught sight of his enemy, hurrying swiftly across the land like the shadow of a cloud blown by the wind. *Too late*, thought Franz. *You're too late.*

As he somersaulted through the air, the figure below stretched out its arms to catch him, but he passed through them. He landed on his back, his arms and legs splayed in the shape of a star. He felt nothing on impact, but an exhalation of air: all the breath in his body.

Lying there, unable to move, he saw the dark shape come to him, with the sun behind it. It stood at his feet, looking down on him, and though it was a silhouette in the blinding light of the morning sun, the features hidden, Franz knew it was not unsympathetic to his position. He tried to speak but no sound passed his lips. He felt thin, wasted.

Then the vertical figure turned on its heels, and as it did so the two pairs of feet became entangled. Franz was caught on the soles of the other's shoes. The usurper walked off, briskly, down the flint path towards the lychgate, dragging Franz Culper behind it. Franz's dark, flat form rippled over the uneven cobbles, through the damp mosses, almost drowning as he was pulled through the black shade of the old church tower.

NETWORKS

Ten past midnight.

The carriage, being at the tail end, swayed violently when the train rattled round the bends. Empty beer cans rolled insolently down the aisles, under the seats, and the whole place smelt of fast-food wrappers. Outside, the night rushed by, black around the business areas, yellowish around the residential streets. Out on the islands of the river estuary the catcrackers, tall gas-burning chimneys, lit eerie stretches of water with their giant candle flames.

I was alone in the carriage. Somewhere, down below, steel was talking to itself in the repetitive phrases of a bag lady. There was still over half an hour of journey left and I decided I needed to use the toilet. It was right across the aisle from my seat and I rose and tried the door.

It appeared to be locked.

I looked at the vacant/engaged plate just above the handle, thinking someone must have fallen asleep in there. Certainly, no one had gone in since I had been sitting in my seat: not that I'd noticed.

It read VACANT.

I rattled the knob. The door refused to budge an inch. This was not unusual. Toilets on commuter trains are vandalized so often they are almost permanently locked. There was usually an 'out of order' sticker on the door and I stepped back to scan the whole surface. Sure enough, there it was, just above my head.

I cursed and went to sit down in my seat when something about the notice seeped into my consciousness, something that registered retrospectively. I got up and stared at it again.

It read:

> SORRY, THIS TOILET
> IS TEMPORARILY
> INSANE

Damn, I thought. That was typical of commuter trains. Just when you were feeling desperate, you were stuck with a toilet that had lost its reason. There was no way to force the damn door open if it did not want to go.

I turned away from it quickly with a self-conscious grin on my face, caught between feelings of embarrassment and annoyance. There are those who like to observe the misfortune of others with a certain nasty satisfaction. There are those like me who are infuriated when experiencing this kind of situation from the standpoint of the victim, but are too timid to do anything but sulk. Then I remembered I was alone and had no need to worry.

I settled back uncomfortably in the hard seat, staring first at that intimidating notice, then out of the window, into the blackness. The window was a mirror. All I could see was the toilet door, standing firm. Its impertinent surface began to irritate me. I wanted to use the toilet quite badly now, the insistent pain was irritating.

I got up suddenly and gave the door a push. No response. A sharp kick? . . . but I dislike violence. The knob turned but it still held fast. This was typical of modern conveniences. I had often walked the streets of the city, looking for unlocked toilets, only to find myself wetting a wall in some trapped courtyard. The city is a maze of tortuous alleys and streets turning in on each other, a network of crazed pathways lined with trees close to lunacy: trees that never know what season is in the air. The city is itself a conglomerate god gone mad. It is a place of eternal shadows and perpetual darknesses, with obsessive and brooding corners that never see the light.

Then there were those toilets, that shut their doors against users.

I sat down again, wondering at its stubbornness.

Insane. A paranoid toilet. Wouldn't let anyone in. *Afraid* to let people in. Some of the passengers, especially at this time of night, were only intent on smashing things, breaking up the toilet, leaving the interior devastated. This toilet, like most of the toilets on the trains, had been vandalized so often that they had been battered into a defensive state of mind. They started out neat and clean, and before they were one day old they were kicked and hammered, the towel racks torn from their mountings, the paper rolls stuffed down the loo, the light smashed, the mirror screws removed, graffiti on the walls, the seat pan broken, the mirror cracked.

It happened to them, day after day, night in, night out.

The railway company is one of the top three landowners in the country, and you would think it would use its wealth to provide therapy for its trains. However, the vast tracts of land to which it holds the deeds are long and thin, and not good for very much else but the purpose to which they have already been put. The railway company cannot readily turn its assets into cash. What is needed is sympathy from the more responsible passengers, but they are pathetic cowed creatures who cram themselves into the morbid confines of the carriages. They have nothing left but pity for themselves.

Schizophrenic? If it were me I would have run berserk before now: a homicidal maniac, a psychopath intent on getting as many victims as possible before they chopped me down. But toilets are, by nature, passive. They are stationary, inanimate. That was my belief.

Suddenly, the door to the toilet swung open and began flapping in a pugnacious way with the swaying of the carriage.

Bang, bang, bang . . .

It *was* tormenting me.

I got up and gently pushed the door wide open. It was empty. The light was dim inside, as if the bulb were running down, except that bulbs don't do that. The mirror was indeed cracked. In fact it was shattered and crazed in one corner and black lightning zigzagged across its face. I could see the reflection of the towel rack, hanging on a single rivet and swaying gently from side to side. The toilet roll was on the damp floor, some of it undone and wound around the bottom of the pan. There were graffiti of all kinds covering the interior.

It looked terrible.

The smell was its least offensive aspect. The small sliding windows were open revealing a square dark mouth that gave out a hollow ooming sound. Did I dare enter, desperate as I was?

'Ticket?'

I almost left my skin. Someone had come up behind me.

'What? Oh – ' it was a ticket inspector. The last ticket inspector of the day. On his way home, I suppose, and keen.

I fumbled for my ticket, the toilet door banging and clicking again behind me.

'There,' I produced the slim piece of card. 'Okay!'

The inspector was an elderly man with very short grey hair. He looked fresh, as if he had just got out of bed after a long tiring day.

'Thankyousir.'

He began to amble away, down the aisle, when I called, 'Hey, know anything about this?'

I pointed to the sticker on the door.

'Out of order, is it?'

'No, it says . . .'

'Sorry, not my fault, sir. Kids. They got to smash everythin' these days. Know what I mean? No respect for property.'

Then he was gone, into the next carriage.

I shrugged and remembered my desperation. The toilet door had shut again. Turning the knob it felt as fast as it had been before. I couldn't shift the damn thing.

'You sod!' I cried, the indignation rising within me. 'Open!'

But it refused. In fact as I was tugging and pushing, the ENGAGED sign shot into place. The train was really rattling along now at high speed and being in an empty end carriage I felt I ought to sit down or be thrown off my feet.

I tried the end door to the carriage: the doorway through which the ticket inspector had appeared and disappeared. It was locked. The inspectors were afraid of being beaten up by thugs and almost always locked the doors to interconnecting carriages. Many of them never even bothered to leave the guard's van: not after dark.

I regained my seat, just as the train pulled into a station.

Someone got in at the other end of the carriage: a fat cat businessman by the look of him. Midnight-blue pinstripe suit and pompous air. After a few minutes he walked the length of carriage unsteadily, but whether the motion or too much drink was responsible I couldn't judge. I moved closer to the window, to be out of range just in case he was sick. He tried the door of the toilet.

'It's temporarily insane,' I said, pointing to the sticker.

He peered through bleary eyes.

'Damn,' he muttered thickly, rattling the knob. Though portly, he was a strong-looking, middle-aged man. I thought the handle would come away in his hand the way he twisted it. Then he looked down and repeated his expletive, only with more feeling.

'Damn!'

I looked at the floor. Water was pouring under the toilet door and was washing around his expensive-looking shoes. It looked none too clean.

'Did you leave a tap on? I can hear it.'

'I haven't even been in there,' I said.

'Why won't the damn door open?' he growled, thumping it. 'Says vacant.'

I stared at the sign. It had indeed gone back to being vacant again.

'It seems to open and close as it pleases,' I replied. 'I want to go, too, but the door seems jammed. At least, sometimes it opens, but not when you want it to. The notice says it's bonkers.'

He sploshed around in the swilling water.

'Ridiculous,' he muttered. 'You can never find one in its right mind these days.'

He raised a leg and by holding on to the seat behind him, was able to give the door several crashing kicks with the sole of his shoe. Nothing happened and he turned away with a snarl.

He turned back again on hearing it swing open and I shrugged at him. Then the toilet seat slammed down making a sound like a gunshot and we both jumped, visibly. The train lurched as I got to my feet and stared at the washbasin. One of the taps was pouring forth and something must have been blocking the drain hole. Water was flowing over the edge of the bowl, washing in the dirty corners and flooding through the doorway.

I didn't remember seeing water before. But then again, maybe the plumbing was shot to hell and ebbed and flowed at whim? Maybe the tap water was subject to tides and currents, the gravitational pull of the moon, the addition or subtraction of meltwater from polar regions or rain-swollen subterranean lakes and rivers? Perhaps when someone turned off a tap in Madrid, the tap in this railway carriage toilet came on? Maybe all the waters of the earth are mysteriously linked in some way? Or the whole complex plumbing network of large and small bore pipes, sluices, cisterns, boilers, stopcocks, valves, tanks, faucets, showers, baths, drains – the copper-clad streams, the lead-encased tributaries, the brick-enclosed rivers – perhaps this vast intricate maze of straight and angled piping which covered the world has its own eccentricities, its disturbed personalities?

Fat man came and stared inside.

'Look at it. Bloody mess. I'd like to wring their necks.'

'Never catch them, can you. They're like wraiths. Even when you do they'd just as soon beat the crap out of you, as the toilet.' I grinned at my own joke, but the fat man scowled.

'It's not funny. I pay a lot for my annual season.'

'Don't we all, pal?' He was beginning to irritate me.

As the door began to swing shut again, he kicked it savagely open, making it slam back against the washbasin. The tap stopped flowing immediately.

'That's the way to treat 'em,' I said, impressed.

He turned and wagged a finger.

'You mind your own business.' This came out very slurred, as if he had been holding back his drunkenness, and was unable now to maintain his dignity. His face was very pale. Then he sploshed into the toilet and shut the door, clicking the engaged sign into place.

I'm not sure what happened next. There was the sound of running water again, and then the noise of the toilet flushing, over and over. Water began to seep under the door. Then fat cat began screaming. When the door flew open of its own accord, I could see him. He was sitting on the loo, his white flabby bulk overflowing the pan, his trousers around his ankles. Then he kind of jerked, downwards, an inch or two. His eyes were wide and round, fixed on mine.

'Help me!' he croaked.

Again he jerked and quivered, as more of him disappeared into the pan.

'It's . . . it's sucking me down . . .' he whispered, as if he could not believe it himself. His flesh was rolling at the edges, twisting, sliding, the blubber vanishing slowly as it was squeezed and drawn inside. Somehow the toilet system had created a vacuum within itself and now it was drawing the flabby blockage into the inner void.

There was another great pull and fat cat's legs shot upwards, his ankles touching his shoulders as his body bent double on its travels into the ceramic mouth. His armpits and the backs of his knees were squashed against the lip: his hands were groping for a grip on the towel rack. He found it, got a hold on it, and then it came away from the wall.

I stepped forward and the door slammed shut in my face.

Despite the terrible pleas I could hear from fat cat, I could not get the door open and finally there were sounds which told me it was all over and my assistance was no longer of any use: the toilet was flushing again.

I stared out of the window. We were alongside water and I could see the cockleboats bobbing up and down, their lanterns dipping and rising. A ruined castle went by, partially floodlit on its knoll. When a famous artist had painted the ruin in the last century, it had been abutting the sea. Now imported engineering had claimed some of the estuary's land from the water and the stretch was wide enough for the railway to run between those old stones and the dyke. We were still fighting the war against the biblical flood.

I began to drift off into a doze, my loins still painful.

The train came to a juddering halt.

I sat up quickly, then got up and went back down to my old seat, curiosity having got the better of me. The toilet door had flapped back towards the inner wall and was half open. A tap was again flowing and water had drained under the door and was washing under the seats right to the end of the carriage.

The toilet looked empty. The walls were dripping, running with moisture, and the little window was now closed. While I was staring inside the toilet pan suddenly shuddered violently and let out a great emotional sucking sound.

I looked back down the carriage. There was a briefcase and an umbrella on a rack near where my travelling companion had been sitting. Were they his? We were at the end of the line now.

I put my head out of the carriage window and stared down the platform. It was empty. The guard was hanging out of his door. He indicated that I should get out, but I went back to stare into the toilet again. The mirror had a second crack now, probably due to an inherent weakness and the violent motion of the train. This jagged line ran horizontally across its face and turned up at the corners. There was also a foot-long, crescent-shaped piece missing from the bottom of the glass. This lay on the floor.

'Where is he now?' I said.

There was a pound coin on the floor, near to the washbasin stand. It was under an inch of water. I was not tempted. I closed the door, but it swung open again. The latch appeared to be broken. It would not stay shut now. Then I saw an object on the wet floor. It was a small cylinder of some kind. I hooked it out with my foot and saw that it was a can of paint spray.

Fat cat?

I looked inside the toilet again, at the walls. There were graffiti on every square inch. One giant set of initials looked fresh. I.F. Had they been there before? They looked neat and imposing and they were in the colour contained by the can of paint spray.

I went along to the briefcase and picked it up. There was a name in gold letters just above the handle.

I. FURST, M.D.

I left the case where it was and went back to my seat to get my own coat. Then I remembered I still had the paint. I leaned over the doorway and was about to put it back where I found it when the toilet flushed again, and a voice behind me said, 'You shouldn't do that while we're standing in a station, sir.'

It was the ticket inspector again.

'Do what? Oh, I didn't flush it. Seems to do itself. Look, where do I hand this lot in? There's an umbrella and case down there, and this can. Someone left them. A man called Furst. I *think* they may all belong to the same man . . . the toilet did away with him.'

'Leave them to me.'

'Right,' I said, thrusting the can into the meaty hand of the inspector. 'And don't forget the other bits . . . and the lunatic should be locked up.' I indicated the toilet.

He nodded, testing the spray against the door. There was still some paint in the can. He seemed satisfied with a 'W', but then after a moment added the letter 'C'.

'Wacky Convenience?' I questioned.

'Good night, sir.'

The ticket inspector entered the demented small room, and the door closed slowly behind him.

I walked the length of the platform and relieved myself against the fence. Then I stared at the train. I stood there for a long while, but no one emerged. Still I waited, wondering what to do. The guard and the driver were long gone: I had seen them leave the empty station before me.

There was a newspaper blowing around my legs and I thought I caught sight of some headlines which read PSY-CHIATRIC HELP FOR T . . . but the rest was hidden from me and as I bent to pick it up a gust of wind blew it down the length of the platform.

Then I left the station, quickly, and went to the telephone booth just outside. It was a two-mile walk home and my wife was waiting for my call. I hoped the car was back from the garage. It had been savagely scarred by someone with a key and had gone in for a respray.

I pulled open the door of the booth and was about to step inside when a small white sticker on the glass caught my attention. I let go of the door and took out a box of matches, since there was no light on inside the booth.

I struck one, reading the little sticker.

I thought it said something about the booth being defaced, until I read it properly.

It said:

VANDALS HAVE DERANGED
THIS TELEPHONE BOOTH

The phone dangled obscenely. Its cord had been stretched and the wires from the broken receiver licked the floor obse-quiously as it swayed back and forth. Frayed cable poked nakedly from the paybox and I could see the glint of coins jammed in the slits, rammed there by someone vicious. The booth had been robbed of all its dignity: there were wandering voices on its lines. Exchange relays were lost to it, the distant terminals unreachable. The whole interior had been violated, raped, left exposed to the cruel eyes of the world.

The match burned my fingers. I flicked it away, sucked the sore tips, and then hurried off down the road. I was anxious to be out of the way. Someone might think I had done this terrible thing. Such outrages were now so common that anyone on the midnight streets was treated with suspicion. Hardly anything had been left sane, even here on the outskirts, and no wonder with such brutality abroad.

As I approached my house something happened. Suddenly, in all the houses the telephones were ringing madly, and immediately following this shrill cacophony was the noise of toilets flushing and refilling and flushing again, and of taps in full flow. I could hear plugholes sucking and slurping as if swallowing vast quantities of thick sludge.

Messages had been sent throughout the great networks and at last there was a destructive anger amongst the sound of mind, as well as the insane.

All the streetlights went out. Darkness means confusion.

Networks. That was what the modern world was about. Kick in a telephone box in Glasgow and the word is immediately passed to every corner of the kingdom.

Synchronized movements: a simultaneous opening of valves, timed to the instant by another vast network with terminals in every home. I stopped and stared into the night. It had to be. It had to be. Everything has its threshold. Occasionally, the world must run amuck to restore an earlier sanity.

Networks. Roadways, railways, telephones, telex, electric, gas, waterworks. There is nowhere to hide. Hidden webs, overhead meshworks, underground mazes, crosscountry plexi. God is omnipresent and therefore omniscient.

Now that the signal has been heard all over the city, perhaps in all cities everywhere, and the waters flow, there will be no stopping to interrogate, no time to make distinctions. The innocent will be drowned along with the guilty. It has happened before. Except that this time the animals will not need a Noah, or indeed an ark. This time the mighty flood will be *inside* the houses, the buildings, the factories, the residences. This time the flood will be contained by the halls of the wicked.

Fat cat was probably the first victim. He had been squeezed into two-inch diameter tubing. The mad toilet's impetuosity had given me what I needed. It had been unable to wait for the signal and given me warning of what was to come. Even defiled gods choose some righteous souls to save.

I thought about my wife, but decided that now the end of the world had come, it was everyone for themself. She was probably a long worm of flesh by now. I ran down the suburban road towards open country, hoping to find safety there.

HOBBLYTHICK LANE

July. Frostfern patterns decorate the windowpanes. Mother says it used to be warm once, in July, when she was a little girl. I don't believe her. It's another tale, like the one about the man who used to come with presents in a sack. Just tales.

Yesterday I found a bottle of lemonade, buried in the rubbish at the bottom of the garden. I have drunk half already. I pour myself another glass, then plunge my face into the foam, so the bubbles go up my nose. It hurts, and tickles. I drink it down, too fast, and it pains the back of my throat; but I can't stop drinking, and although it hurts, I like it. I enjoy the pain driving away my thirst. My eyes water and it feels like crying.

'Anselm!'

Mother is calling Anselm awake. He sleeps in the shed because the third room leaks when it rains. The shed is a good thirty yards from the house, but she always tries, before having to go out and throw a brick at his door. She keeps a pile of stones ready, just outside, by the rainwater barrel.

'Anselm!'

He won't wake up. He never does. The whole of Essex County can hear Mother's screech, but not Anselm. It's so cold in his shed that thick ice forms on the inside windows, out of his breath. So he makes a pile of blankets as high as a house and crawls underneath them like a dormouse. An earthquake wouldn't wake him. It would take the world exploding to penetrate those blankets and get at his ears.

I can hear Mother crashing the breakfast crockery in the kitchen and muttering to herself.

I rub the pane and spy out through the hole I have made. I can see the river, moving in the middle where the ice is not. The day is dirty yellow, as usual, and the river shines a little, especially the thin ice at the edges. Up from the river comes our lane, Hobblythick Lane, winding about and with houses spaced apart, on either side. This is all there is. The rest is all hard fields where the winter greens grow. It is summer, but they are called winter cabbage and such. I must ask about that, if I remember.

People in Hobblythick Lane say that Mother is a Christer. That's why we have to leave here, today. I'm nine years old and I've lived here my whole life. I don't want to leave, but I have to, because Mother is a Christer – everybody says, anyway. Since Dad died, people have been writing things on our wall and calling out. Mother is getting frightened, not for herself, she says, but for us, Anselm and me. When people start that kind of thing, they don't know when to stop. (Like drinking cold lemonade, I suppose?) There's something inside, something you can't help, that makes you keep on going.

Years ago, before I was born, they had a smelling out. That's when you get someone who knows what to do, to go sniffing round the houses to see if there's any Christers or Christchuns about. Then they go on a Christer Hunt. They found some – not like Mother, she's no real Christer, or that would make me one and I don't feel any different from Porker, Maggot, or any of the other kids, even though they call me names now they never used to. No, these was positive Christers. They had a book called the Holy Bibler, which Witchley Smith found after they put stones on these people and pricked needles into them to make them tell. They prayed to someone called 'God', who is invisible. 'Creepy,' Anselm said. 'Really creepy.' He's thirteen, so he should know.

'You couldn't see this God – nothin' like that. And these Christers, they bent down on their knees like this' – and he showed me how, as if he was playing marbles, except his hands was locked together – 'then they said things called prayers, which *sound* like spells, but they're not. They're prayers . . .'

'What happened to 'em? These Christers?'

'That's for boys to know and little girls to guess,' he said.

'I'm not so little any more, and anyway, I know what happened, see. They sent them away.'

'Huh. A lot you know, 'cause they burned 'em, see. They put 'em on a bonfire, like Guy Fawkes, an' set light to it. I saw it – or I would've done, if the bedroom window was facing the right way. Anyhow, I heard 'em screaming. Worser than a rabbit with a weasel at it . . .'

'That's a big lie,' I cried, 'they wouldn't.' I felt the tears in my eyes.

'A lot you know,' he said.

But our mother's no Christer. She don't have no Holy Book and she don't do that praying. Well, only once, when Dad was dying. She made this kind of cross out of two sticks and put it over his bed. But she only did that when the spells didn't work. I know because I was there that time. Nancy Grissom came with Witchley Smith, and they tried all they could with spells and potions and herbs, but none of them worked. Anselm and me even caught a snake with a half-swallowed frog caught in its throat, which Witchley said was good, and he poured wax on the snake and lit it, but Dad kept on dying, even though the snake was writhing around and doing its best for him.

So after they'd gone, Mother made that cross out of twigs and said a few words. That don't make her a Christer. Anybody would do the same if their man was dying.

People say she said, 'Bless.' I don't remember her saying 'Bless,' and I was there, most of the time. She wouldn't say a word like that. My mother's never sworn in her life. Then the coven made us a visit and told her she'd done wrong and said she'd have to go through trial. That was last week.

'*Anselm!*'

I put on my other overcoat, on top of my sleeping one, and pull on my boots. Then I go outside, into the cold day, and bang on Anselm's door. I hear a muffled word and I know he's awake, so I walk back to the house. Down by the river I can see the pile of wood. They have been collecting it for several weeks now, and I even helped until I knew what it was for. Bits of wood, here and there. They are hard to find. When Dad was alive, we had a fire in our hearth at least once a month, but now there's only three of us to collect, it's once in almost never.

I go indoors. Mum has made some soup from greens, and I see her hunched over the cup. Her gloves have holes in them where the mice have gnawed, and her red skin, all chapped, pokes through. The soup is warm. She saved a rag to burn for this morning because we would need something warm before going out to wherever we are going.

'Eat some soup,' she says, from under the layers of scarf.

'Anselm's comin',' I tell her.

Her eyes are all red and swollen. She has been crying again. She's still upset that they buried Dad in consecrated ground, but they said he died of poisoned water and was not fit to go with others. They said he was hallowed, or something like that. She tried to dig him up, but it was too hard, the ground, and we had to leave him holy. Mother had to make do with sacrificing a stoat over the grave and hoping that the blood would wash the earth clean of church and stuff.

Anselm comes flopping into the kitchen, wearing his blankets with head-holes, over his coats. His nose is running and I look away.

'Lucifer,' he says. 'Hot soup!'

'Warm,' says Mother, 'and don't blaspheme.'

'Well, I done it already,' he says back, defiantly. Anselm is bigger than Mum now, and she has a hard time with him. We all eat breakfast in quiet, except for the wind that comes through the cracks. It's this northern wind, Dad used to say, what makes us so cold. I don't know. Me and Anselm, we don't mind so much, but Mum does. She hates it, and since Dad went, she says the nights are colder than death. I think death would be colder because you have to go into the ground like a block.

'We have a long walk to do,' Mum says, 'so eat up quickly. We should've left earlier – before dawn.'

She has told us it's thirty miles we have to walk. She tells us again.

'How are we goin' to do that?' says Anselm. 'Sis here will never make it. She's not done more than two in her life. You got to think of that.'

'We got no choice,' says Mum, softly.

'An' the marshes,' he says, as if he hasn't heard her. 'What about them? And crawlin' with Christchuns, too. They'll convert you, soon as look at you, it ain't right.' He adds quickly, 'I ain't afraid of 'em, but there's no sense in riskin' being converted, is there?' His face is a pale colour, maggot grey, and I can see he is scared stiff, which makes me scared, too.

'I don't like Christers,' I say.

Mother's lip trembles and her nose goes pinched-red the way it does before she cries. 'You'll do as I say,' she says; and Anselm stays quiet, but his face has gone the grey again. I can see his fist clenched by his plate. He's got a temper on him worse than a ferret, and I don't say anything in case he takes it out on me.

After breakfast, Mother leaves the things where they are, on the table, and packs the last few bits of food in a case. We all put on more things, and Anselm looks like a water barrel, but I don't laugh. Blodwin once laughed at Anselm and he split her lip – and she's a girl, too.

We, Mother and me, move out of the door, but Anselm, once he stands in it, stays put.

'I ain't goin', Mother. I'm stayin' here.'

His voice is low, and I look up at Mother. She is crying again, and the cold wind freezes the tears when they reach her chin. Around us the yellow sky is quiet. None of the birds are around yet. I stamp my feet as the cold comes up from the ground.

Anselm stays put. He is crying, too, now, but his face is set. I know he means it. Mother knows, too, and she knows she can't make him.

'Anselm?'

'No. I ain't done no prayin',' he says. 'I never done no wrong, see. It's you. You called upon Christ.'

Mother goes white and she bites her lip. For a long while she just stares at Anselm as though he's going to change his mind, but he's not. Then she says, 'Your father was dying.'

'It don't matter, now,' he replies his voice all soft and quiet. 'You go. I can't come. I don't want to come. I'll dig him up, if I can sometime. I promise.'

So Mother gives him a kiss, and he jerks his head away at the last minute and goes into the house. We see him looking through the window at us as we start down the hill. I can't see whether he's still crying or not, but I know he is because Mother's doing it and they always do the same thing at the same time.

At the start of Hobblythick Lane, they're waiting for us, women and men. Kids, too. Blodwin is there, and Maggot. I smile at them, but they don't smile back. I wish I had some of the lemonade to give them, but the rest was ice, even though I kept it in bed all night.

Mother slows down to a stop as I drag the suitcase past her. I stop, too, and wait. The wind is cutting through my coats, and I want to walk, because it's warmer that way.

Witchley Smith is looking hard at Mother. He is a thin man with sucked-in cheeks and eyes like lamp wicks burning low. Glowing, smoky eyes, but not warm.

'You got to come,' he says. 'They expect it.'

No one else says anything. They are all looking at Mother with a kind of eager look on their faces, as if someone had just seen the sun come out.

'Why don't you just light it?' Mother says.

'That ain't the way it's done, you know that. There's got to be a reason . . .'

Mother hunches in the wind. 'Reason enough,' she says.

'Not for this. It's the only way to hold 'em together. You're making it hard for me . . . You should've left in the night.'

'Well – I didn't.'

'No, you didn't, and here we are.'

He grabs Mother's sleeve and tries to pull her.

'You leave her alone,' I yell, and kick Witchley Smith in his legs, over and over. He bats me with his hand, and Mother shouts, 'No. Don't hurt her.'

'Send her back to the house, then . . .'

Mother stares at me with funny eyes.

'. . . We'll let them come down, afterward. They won't miss much of it. Just the first part. You could have gone, you know. You had the chance.'

Someone brings out a kind of hoop thing, made out of hawthorn twigs, and goes to put it on Mother's head, but Witchley says, 'No need for that.'

Mother says, 'Go back to the house. Stay in until someone comes. Tell Anselm you mustn't go out.'

'I don't want to,' I say.

'You must.'

I look at her face, poking out from her scarves, and she looks better than I've seen her for a long time. Her face is all quiet and smooth. Then she looks around her, at the frosty ground. 'Yes,' she said. I see her glance quickly, at the churchyard on the hill, and then she gives me a little shove. I start back up towards the house.

Mother watches me, and I see her give a smile to me when I'm almost there. Then they go off, down the lane towards the river. She is not walking slow like she was before. She's walking fast, and the others have to hurry to keep up with her.

I go indoors to Anselm. He cuddles me. I guess he's feeling cold, and I cuddle him back.

GIANT

When I was younger, perhaps eight years of age, I had long black hair – iron black – that fell straight to my ankles. I was slim and dark-eyed in those days (even the eyes have changed to a watery-red – some disease carried by the dust they tell me) and I could *run*. Oh yes, I could run, faster than a gazelle, and I thought that was to be my role in life: to be a runner, a messenger for the king. I would have liked that. I am, by nature, a quiet man, solitary. You won't find a more peaceful man in the whole of Palestine. It would have suited me to have been out on the plains, alone, with some important note from a king, to a king, in my hand.

There's something very inviting about being unencumbered by the trappings of war – the heavy armour and weapons that have plagued me throughout my life – that's good for the soul. The sandals and loin cloth of a runner allow not just your body but also your *spirit* to breathe. You feel free *inside* as well as out. Running between cities, too, somehow severs your relationship with them. I would have been as free as the animals of the dusty plains.

Runners get to meet a lot of important people. Not just their own king, but others as well. Of course, it can be a dangerous business when a royal-this insults a royal-that, and you're the one carrying the poisonous words, but what occupation is completely free of danger these days? Being a messenger can also be a rewarding job. The birth of a child, the marriage of a son or daughter, the death of a tyrant; these are all good news, entitling the bearer to all sorts of fine gifts, from baskets of figs to gold amulets.

Yes, I should like to have been a runner. I did begin as such, within the city of Gath, but as I put on weight and more height I became slower and realized that running was a career that I was growing out of, literally.

How the other children taunted me about my height! I had my hair cut because it looked so stupid – this tall, shambling creature trailing a long mane of hair. The jibes still came though, and not very original. Jokes about ice behind my ears and to be careful when eagles were about, looking for places to nest. How they wounded me, those catcalls, yet I smiled through them, good-naturedly. What else can you do? It's always supposed that a tall person is good at fighting, but that's not true. Height, even strength, do not make a good fighter. Warriors are born, not made. Those who love a battle arrive in this world with a chip of ice lodged in their heart, or fire in their guts, and they are usually naturals when it comes to weaponry. Sometimes they carry a grievance against mankind, which manifests itself in viciousness.

Anyway, they have the killer instinct, the will to win, which I do not. You've either got it, or you haven't. You can't fake it and you can't make it. It's there, or it isn't. A goatherd might have it and a king might not. That's the way it goes, and it's no use whining about it.

I was neither hot-headed nor did I hate my fellow men. Any skills at war I had to learn the hard way. I was clumsy and had no enthusiasm for ways of the sword and was consequently not very good at it. Of course, I learned a certain amount: enough to survive in battle after the first few close shaves, but anyone can do that. One thing I could not do was fight against my friends. That's why I allowed them to taunt me. Hitting a stranger is far easier than striking a companion.

Anyway, I kept on growing until I was an embarrassment, even to my mother. Of course, there's always a limit to these things, and there came a time when the insults suddenly stopped and were replaced by looks of awe and wariness. I suppose it was about the time that I reached eighteen years, when my shoulders filled out and my limbs began to thicken. I did a lot of lifting in those days: blocks of stone that went into building walls and houses. I could reach higher than most and the builders said (usually with a smile) that they found it cheaper to use me than to erect scaffolding.

I don't want you to get the idea that I was so huge I could touch the rooftops. Nothing of the sort. But I could reach first-floor windows, which none of the other workers could manage. I began to feel a certain pride in myself, for the first time in my life.

In those days I used to do a lot of drinking: building labourers do. I became acceptable to my companions once more, especially since I could drink my quota, and theirs, and carry half the drunks home with me afterwards. I think that was the happiest period in my life. I managed to save enough to buy myself a wife, less than half my size, but she made up for it in brains. She was a very clever woman and unlike many other girls I had asked out, didn't mind being seen with me in the street. She was the fiery type, Rachel. One of those small people, with the killer instinct, that I spoke of earlier. She would have made a far better warrior than me. I let her bully me a bit, which amused my friends, but they didn't understand. It wasn't necessary to brook her: she knew what was what, and I was quite happy to let her manage our affairs. It was Rachel who said that the slaves being brought into Gath would eventually put me out of work and that it might be wise to seek some other line of employment, before all of us were on the streets and there was a glut. I took her advice, of course. She was always right about these things. I joined the army. There wasn't anything else I could do.

Sure enough, that summer our Philistine commanders were more successful than they had ever been and who needs to pay workers by the week, when you can buy them outright?

I was miserable at first, in the army. No one pushed me

around any more, but I found the life hard. The fact that I was big didn't make the armour any lighter. I had to carry twice the amount that a normal man hefts around and I had to keep it clean, too. I would be polishing my breastplate and helmet long after the other soldiers had fallen asleep for the night.

The marching and drilling was loathsome and I was glad when we were sent out into the field, despite the fact that you baked during the day and the night was cold enough to freeze the water in your goatskins. At least I wasn't banging my head against a beam over a doorway, and out in the open the smells were cleaner and purer. It all seemed so much clearer out there, on the plains. I really envied the runners and the occasional shepherd we passed. They had the best of it. If only I hadn't kept on growing! I comforted myself with the idea that I was closer to the stars, and imagined I could reach out and touch them. It would have been a great pleasure to have gathered them in a net and distributed them amongst my companions.

Wishful thinking though. We sweated, and choked on the dust thrown up by the wheels of the officers' chariots as they thundered past our ranks. Only the thought of a jug of water from some distant well kept us going.

I was never promoted. Despite the fact that I was strong, they never considered me fit for command, and passed me over continually. I didn't mind that much. I'm not a great one for discipline. I'll obey orders, of course, but I'm not sure I'd enjoy giving them. You have to be a special sort of man for that. One of those with a chip of ice, because it's a lonely life as a non-commissioned officer. I was already lonely enough as it was, without adding to my troubles.

No, I was happier in the ranks – but still, I felt a twinge, just a twinge of envy, when other, younger men were offered advancement. Rachel used to nag me about my lack of ambition, but that was Rachel. I knew she was proud of me, whatever I did. It would just have been nice for her to be able to rub something in the noses of her family.

They had never approved of me – a builder's labourer and

despite the fact that my offer for Rachel (who some do not call pretty) had amounted to more than she had been expected to fetch, large bride prices do not win respect. In fact I got the impression that they despised me for overpaying, thinking it ignorant and vulgar. But as Rachel pointed out, they took the money quickly enough. That's relations for you.

What I didn't like about the army was that you had to kill people. It's a messy business. I was never much good at jabbing with a straight arm. I'm your hacking type – much more useful chopping down at the heads, rather than poking at people. Besides, I was much more likely to blind a man – the heart was a bit low for my thrust – and I would hate to think of some poor creature stumbling around in darkness, from city to city, with a begging bowl in his hands, and all because of my inept swordplay. Better to cleave a skull in twain than leave a man without his sight.

I can throw a spear, of course; quite well in fact. But that's a one-off business. If you miss, which is quite likely, because they're easy things to dodge, then that's it: you have to go in with the sword anyway. People have been known to miss with javelins in a small room, so I've got little faith in them. Spears are not very reliable in the heat of the battle either. You're just as likely to hit friend, as foe. I've got this long, heavy shaft with an iron head, which I flourish around a lot, but that's mostly for show. A lot of the time I won't even bother with it, once the fighting starts. Pretty useless things really, unless you lunge with them. Arrows and slingshot stones are much harder to avoid.

They're the things that trouble me: little whizzing bits of wood and stone flying through the air. You can't even see them, let alone know when to duck. None of us likes them. The captain said the other day that when we catch a slinger, we ought to cut his pebbles off to make him impotent. The other men laughed, but I couldn't see the joke. After all, there's nothing funny about missiles you can't see, hitting you in the eye or somewhere else just as deadly.

And what glory is there in it? Why do they bother to come to the field at all, when everyone there, even people on their own side, despises them? There's nothing noble about firing into a mêlée, hoping that your random shot will find a mark. Much of the time you can't even see if you've hit anyone, or if a soldier's merely tripped or stumbled. Half those the archers and slingers claim as definite hits get up and walk off the battlefield afterwards, dusting their thighs and complaining about loose greaves. If you're going to be in the fighting, I say, then *be* in it – not half-a-mile away, ready to run if you miss. Cowards, most of these people. They can get within thirty paces of you and still be away like rabbits. They don't wear armour, so that doesn't hold them back. Many's the time I tried to put up a chase, but it's hopeless when you're carrying a ton of brass on your back, and the little bastard in front is built like an antelope. But then, that's war for you. Anything goes. There's no rule says you can't hit and run. I've seen more Israeli bottoms than faces, and that's a fact.

I'm sixty now and getting past it. That surprises you, eh? Sixty? Well, I'm almost bald, except for a grey tuft or two poking under my helmet, and these eyes give me trouble. (I think it *must* be the dust. You can't march about for forty-odd years and not get sore eyes in these lands.) My nose has gone a funny shade of purple and people complain about my gaseous bowels, but I'm still a man to reckon with. Of course, the old bones ache of a cold morning and I have difficulty in bending these days, but *still*, not bad for an old soldier. A few wounds here and there, most of them healed cleanly, but what veteran doesn't have his battle scars to parade before the raw recruits?

Did I mention that Rachel was dead? Last year. Sad, really, since I'm about to retire. This is my last battle. The captain has told me by this time next month I'll be lying on my back in Gath, sucking grapes. (Not much else you can do, when all your teeth have gone, is there?) Rachel died of some lung complaint, poor dear. She didn't let it get her down though. Game to the last. It'll be a lonely retirement without her. We planned a little farm, but now I think I'll move in with her brother. He could use an extra hand in that vineyard of his. These old scarred hands are not good for much these days, except lifting hayricks. They once warmed a frozen sparrow back to life, but that was long ago and not worth mentioning really.

Ah! Four o'clock! The captain's calling for me. I've got to go out into the valley and bellow at the enemy. Poor devils have been cowering there amongst the rocks for days, while I shout my head off and strut around like lord muck. All show really. It was the captain's idea. I think he's bucking for promotion, and anyway, it's nice for me to go out of the army with a bit of flair. There's not been much of that in my life. Strap on the old brass and get out there with a bit of lung power. Nothing to it. Not much chance they'll send anybody down to meet me now. I've been at it for days, without a sign from them. They're enjoying the rest as much as we are.

Of course, there's always the possibility that some squirt with the killer instinct is looking for a quick way up the ladder. There's been one or two rumours lately. I expect old King Saul is having his ear bent by some impatient fool now, but that bit about 'You'll be our slaves, or we'll be your slaves' has kept him in check so far. No one wants that kind of responsibility. Clever of the captain to think of that. Only a complete egotist would risk the slavery of his nation on a single combat. I know *I* shout it, but if they'd done it first you wouldn't find me going up to the king and saying, 'Please sir, let me go down and sort him out?' I'm not a quick fellow, but I'm not that dull either. Too much responsibility can slow a man down in times of crisis.

There. That's the breastplate on. Where's that fellow that carries the shield for me? Always late. I don't blame him. Bloody boring business, if you ask me, lugging another man's shield around. Quite a new experience for an old warrior like myself, to have a shield-bearer. It would have tickled Rachel. All show. All show. Got to give the spectators something to look at, I suppose.

Ah, here we are. Well, that's it. Be back in time for evening meal. If they *do* send someone out, which is unlikely, it'll be a sweaty business until the sun goes down. It's like an oven in this stuff, and he'll be no better off. So long as it's quick and clean, either way. I shan't be sorry to go. A few clashes with the old blade will work up an appetite for one of us to satisfy. That's the stuff. He'll be quicker than me – they all are these days – but I've still got strength on my side. Sort of evens it out. Makes a fair fight of it.

At least I won't need eyes in the back of my head, looking for those wretched archers and slingers. That's something to be thankful for. Sticks and stones? Not today, I hope.

BEYOND BYZANTIUM

I believe I have come to this country through my dreams. It appears to be a Greek island, a village, but there are no people here except the widows and elderly spinsters. Only the old husbandless women sit, hunched over their lacemaking, lifting their heads to smile at me as I pass. Theirs are narrow conspiratorial smiles, from within the folds of the black shawls draped over the black dresses. They know the secret of the island, but when I ask them for explanations they merely offer enigmatic expressions, as if they do not understand.

I have nothing but contempt for their way of life. They have given up in favour of apathy. So it seems to me.

'Once, I was a man among men . . .' I begin to say, but they seem uninterested in my outpourings, and turn again to their lace. I carry on, unable to help myself. 'I was a man who could see improvement in change only when it related to something already proven. Look at the bicycle – a beautiful instrument, a wonderful invention. Cogs and wheels, gears that mesh. You don't have to feed a bicycle, like you do a horse. It needs no fuel like a car. A bicycle is an aesthetic piece of machinery. It was invented by an artist rather than a scientist. It shines, it moves elegantly. Further additions, improvements on the original machine, have only served to make it more attractive. The gears whisper and bind and make motion on gradients easier, and thus the movements of the body are more genteel, more refined. The bicycle is one of those machines, similar to clockwork timepieces, that has been invented by the heart rather than the head. It needs nothing more than a regular motion of the legs to carry its passenger speedily to a destination: no noise, no fuss, no intricate complex engine. It is an extension of the body.'

The old women look up, at odd times, and smile. Some of them have teeth, some do not. Their expressions disturb me.

'I have always been involved with bicycles,' I tell them. 'I used to think that human beings would be better off with bicycle wheels instead of legs. Legs are too slow, yet cars too fast. If we had been born with bicycle wheels instead of legs, we would have had no need to invent the internal combustion engine. We could have travelled at safe speeds and got to our destinations without the terror of potentially terrible events waiting on the road.'

Nods and smiles. Nothing more. Then back to the lace. Dusty, black dresses covering shapeless forms. They seem timeless, these women. They have sat at their work since before Homer's great grandfathers took wives into their lodges. They have witnessed waves of foreigners washing across their small islands over the centuries. Yet they are still here. Penelope still weaves her tapestry, old and quaint as she is now, while Odysseus has long been dust. Yes, still they are here. Frail, yet strong. Insubstantial, yet immovable.

Not one other person on the island but me and two dozen replicas of Whistler's Mother. *Arrangements in Grey and Black.* Why? Why me? What is it that I have in common with old women who wear faces of dried, cracked mud? I am not so *very* old. I do not wear black. *I am not a woman.*

'I have always been a strong man,' I tell them, 'not one of those given to weakness, either physical or mental. I always led, rather than followed. I treated people, especially women, with civility. I was never *familiar . . .*'

I turn and walk away. I stroll along the dry river-bed outside the village, where lizards are fired from bowstring grasses and bury themselves in oleanders. Snakes rustle quickly out of my path. Bee-eating birds curve from my line of sight as I approach.

Why do they all avoid me? Am I an unclean creature? Do the animals avoid the black widows, picking out their lacy webs on patient laps?

In the distance is a volcano. I begin to climb the long dusty path to its summit. It is hot. The midday sun burns through my straw hat and the earth bakes the soles of my feet through my sandals. Perhaps everyone else is hiding in the crater? Perhaps the god of the lava is having a celebration and omitted, an oversight perhaps, to invite me?

I reach the lip, tired and thirsty. The smell of sulphur is strong in my nostrils. It burns like a heavy inhalation of snuff. I have difficulty in breathing.

There is activity here. Gelatinous mud exhales bubbles of heat into the already oppressive atmosphere. Steam hisses through thin sulphuric mouths. I walk across the crust, listening for the others, but can hear nothing but the slow flow of viscous rock under my feet. There are no people. This place does not want me. I do not belong in the lava.

The liquefied faces of the dead having eluded me, I begin the long trek down to the village again.

Driftwood and pumice litter the beach. Bones and stones. The beach is a graveyard and I wander between high tide marks and the waves with the feeling that I am on the shores of Byzantium. But no one remains in Byzantium any more. They move on. They change and move on. I need to go further, to join the others. But how? Perhaps they left me behind on purpose, to be denied? Perhaps I am to be excluded by my fellow souls, the way children in a playground will cruelly ostracize a schoolmate in order to create an exclusive group? Without someone outside the circle, desperately wanting to get in, there can be no whispered secrets, no conspiracy.

'Bicycles have no souls,' I yell at the waves, 'that's why I like them. They're clean and efficient. They're insentient. They are without sin.'

This morning, when I first woke, I thought the world was normal. Donkeys were singing to one another in strident voices over the fields; roosters gave throat to their egotism; wild birds patterned the air with their notes. I washed and dressed and went to breakfast on yoghurt and honey, followed by coffee. I have always been a solitary person, alone and untroubled.

Here, on the beach, I am still alone, but full of anguish. The difference is that I *know* I am alone. Knowledge is only a good thing when it is linear. Once it locks itself into a cycle, it erodes the mind and leads to madness.

Walking again between the whitewashed houses that crowd the dirt streets, the sun blinding me, I see the old women. They smile again, knowingly, and I wonder whether I should fear them or accept them. What is it that binds me to them? Death? Are we both so near death that it would be pointless to take us?

I watch their crabbed fingers at work and then study my own.

My fingers, too, are thin and clawlike. Also, I remember the truth. I am not so young. In fact, I am an elderly man in the eyes of all others but my own. My shadow, walking beside me, has a gentle curve to its back. With a start I realize I have developed a stoop. Since when? A year? Two? How often do I study myself with a critical eye?

'If I were a bike,' I tell the old women, 'my crossbar would be bent.'

I laugh at my own joke and they smile with me.

One of Whistler's Mothers nods to me as if we are companions. As if we share many things. And, now I pause, and think. We are not so dissimilar. We are both old, creased and worn at the edges. The peace of approaching death has settled like dust on our shoulders. We are of a different sex – yet even that difference has faded out of use, along with passion and desire. In that respect we are like my beloved bicycle, hollow of frame.

Mentally, we share the present: days of sun and drifting memories. I *was* looking for something, but I've forgotten what it was. Perhaps it isn't important any more? Should I sit, like her? In the ancient, creased face the eyes are still bright and alive.

The heat of the afternoon is blistering, yet the flies remain active. A black shawl would keep both at bay. Something worries me about the harbour.

There is a movement amongst the old women. What is this? Has Gabriel sounded his trumpet at last? Will they all hop up on to rickety legs and follow the multitudes up the wall of the world, into the sky, while I remain – a pathetic, lonely creature, master of the earth, master of nothing?

There are waves on the ocean and one of the black widows, the black spinsters, has left. I stare at her empty chair. It looks inviting, but I am not yet ready. Then she returns.

It is evening now. The sun is a red blemish on the face of the sky. The woman hands me a black rag. It is an old garment. I pull it on and take the chair that has been left for me in the shadows. I sit beneath the window of a whitewashed room. In the swollen redness of the day's end, I am finally at peace.

I sit and wait and watch.

One of my companions stands up and hobbles towards me, features twisted with the effort. When I am reached, my face is studied and there is a nod. Then I am offered a black shawl, which hangs over an arm. I take the item and return the gesture. I drape the shawl around my head.

Now I am ready.

The youngsters come, spilling out of the houses, up from the harbour, the beach. They are singing, laughing, chattering like birds. One of them is riding a shiny new bicycle. He grins at me as he sweeps past.

The streets are suddenly full of colourful people.

They shout greetings across each other's heads.

As they pass by my chair I look up at them, and smile. Their young faces shine back.

I am an old woman, with an old man's dreams. My life is closing, but slowly, quietly. Each day now I will take my chair outside into the sunshine and watch the world pass by, until the harbour lights find twins in the dark sea. Days will be long, lengthening into dimness. I have no cause for grief.

I must find something to do with my hands.

SPIRAL SANDS

There must be the hawk with defective eyesight. There must be the Bedu tribesman who is not a crackshot: whose family is resigned to meals without meat. There must be the Ethiopian who cannot run; the clumsy mountain goat; the pigeon without a sense of direction. There must be these misfits that fail to reach the common standard of their kind. I was such a creature – a poet without the gift of fine words – a man born to a love of poetry which could not be satisfied by merely reading the works of others, but had to have some *definite* connection with the art.

I finally resigned myself to the fact that I would never write any great verse. At times I had thought that I was close to those lines. Times when I woke in the middle of the night with the faint hum of something on the edge of my brain, which, once pen and paper were to hand, eluded me and left me weeping in frustration. I had been in places – climbing a mountain; running for a bus; entertaining a lovely woman – when inspiration came upon me, sometimes like an exotic snake, sliding into my consciousness; sometimes as a beautiful bull that thundered upon my sensibility and stood there, snorting white plumes and defying captivity. Yet, when the first opportunity to put those thoughts, those dreams into words was available, they fled from me, never to be recovered. *The poem* was destined to be always just out of my grasp and I was getting older. The days were greyer and shorter than they used to be and time was slipping through my fingers faster than a dying affaire.

Consequently, when I heard of the man, I felt that there, there was my last chance to achieve immortality through my one and only love, through poetry. Admittedly, it was to be a compromise – my fame would be established through the discovery of another poet, yet the sponsor can achieve almost as much recognition as the artist if handled carefully. I had reached an age where time had blunted the edge on my pride with its swift succession of yearly blows. I needed a strong connection with the art to satisfy my yearning, my longing to *become* part of it. To have ignored the opportunity would have been to condemn myself to an unfulfilled life, a life not without purpose but without the least taste of success. I would have died empty with nothing but a gravestone to mark my passing through the temporal zone. It was Carey, the soldier of fortune, the adventurer, who gave me the first clue.

I was sitting in the corner of a pub that stands close to London Bridge, where pseudo-literary types gather seeking company in their own kind, when Carey entered with a young lady he introduced as his niece. She left us almost immediately to join some rather loud friends imitating peacocks in both dress and manner. Carey bought me a drink and I asked him where he had been. Carey was always just back from somewhere.

'The Hadhramaut, old chap. Been looking at some interesting caves there with a friend.' He saw my frown and added, 'South Yemen desert.'

'What sort of caves?' I asked, simply for the sake of conversation. 'I mean, was your interest archaeological, geological or anthropological?'

He gave me a sort of half-smile. 'One of those . . . there were some paintings which might have been interesting. Turned out that they were of more recent origin than I had hoped. However . . . can't win 'em all. What about you? Still running that magazine for little old ladies with a literary bent? Poetry, isn't it?'

I ignored the apparent sneer. 'No. I gave it up three months ago. I had hoped to discover some hitherto hidden star, as they say, but as *you* imply, the contributors were lacking in that vital ingredient – talent.'

'Pity. Great pity. What about your own work?'

I glared hard at the table, declining to answer and after a while, Carey took the hint and stopped staring at my hairline. We sat in an uncomfortable silence for a time then Carey said abruptly, 'I might have something for you.' He reached into his pocket and produced a folded piece of paper.

'What is it?' I asked, leaving the paper where it lay, amongst the beer slops on the table.

He reached across with one hand and opened it. I could see about six and a half lines of writing in what appeared to be Arabic. Beneath these lines was pencilled a translation.

'Well?' I said.

'Found it written in charcoal, on a cave wall. The rains were due and as the place was deep in a wadi, there was the possibility – well, certainty – that this would have been washed away with the flood. I thought of you and your tireless search for poetic talent. This looks like a fragment of something . . .'

I snatched it up and read the lines.

'Are you serious?' I said, after a while.

'Perfectly. I read Arabic, you see. That's my translation. Someone with more *feel* for the thing could do a better job, I've no doubt. God knows I haven't any pretensions . . .'

'I know. You once sent me a poem for my magazine. You called yourself Sybil Smith.'

He laughed at that, making heads turn and me feel foolish. The blond hair flopped over the handsome face almost obscuring his blue eyes. Carey had everything he needed for his chosen role in life – everything the potential adventurer required – good looks, contacts, a private income, a fine physique, courage, audacity, mental alertness, a touch of aristocracy – everything. It was sickening.

'All right,' I said, 'it wasn't that funny. Jameson told me it was you – after I'd made a fool of myself. How do I know this isn't a hoax?'

Immediately he leaned on the table and tried to assume a serious countenance but his eyes still betrayed an undercurrent of amusement.

'I'm sorry, Alec, but you're such a ... look, who was it who had that awful argument with me in a Chelsea pub about modern poets? I said they didn't make sense ... and you said ... Anyway, let's forget that. This is no joke. I'm not that cruel.'

'Perhaps. Let's have a look ...'

I trailed the sentence and read the fragment over again. The translation would be bland. As he had admitted, Carey was no poet.

'Can I keep this?' I asked, after a while.

He nodded. 'You can keep it but ... if you want to take it further, don't forget to give *me* a call. I've a good idea who wrote that ... people talk in the empty quarter, to pass the time, and I've heard a name ... in your own language, *like a whisper on the wind*. Give me a call.' He finished his beer and then left. The niece remained with her group in the corner. Perhaps she really was his niece?

I sought out a friend at Oxford who did a better job of the translation. The lines were, most definitely, intriguing. They had a certain depth, a quality, which was not easy to grasp. The ambiguity in the short phrases fired my imagination and I spent many hours poring over the fragment, trying to decide whether there was something of real worth there. It was difficult to tell with so short a piece but finally I took a positive stance and called Carey. 'I want you to teach me Arabic,' I said. If I were to go looking for this nomadic poet, I needed to learn his language. To translate a masterpiece into a lasting work of art was almost as rewarding as being the creator of that masterpiece. Edward Fitzgerald is as well known and respected as Omar Khayyam. I might have been chasing ghosts but what did it matter? At least I would be doing *something*.

For the next two years I studied hard. Languages have never been one of my blocks, though I have many of those, and even

Carey was surprised at my progress. I soon left him behind, and fired with a sense of purpose, I went back to Oxford and stayed there until I felt I had mastered the thing well enough to begin the search. Of course, I should have to continue with my study but I had my life's work at last. My enthusiasm was boundless. The thought that my poet might have died or stopped writing did cross my mind occasionally but I soon dismissed it. I am a great believer in fate and God would not have placed such a tempting quest before me just to snatch it back again once the hard work was done. No god could be that vindictive. Carey and I left for the Hadhramaut in October. He was almost as excited as I was but I suspected it was merely the expedition that was responsible for his frame of mind, not the purpose behind it.

The desert moves into your soul. Once you have allowed your senses to absorb its atmosphere, you can never get it out of your heart. Lawrence and Thesiger had been seduced by the desert and I was influenced by its immense powers of attraction, I am sure, as strongly as they. It is strange that a monotonous empty landscape can appear more beautiful, more exotic, than a hundred different skylines full of shape and colour. It produced a yearning in my breast that left me with a physical ache, never to be healed. The desert is magnificent in its sense of space and time, and absence of tangible presence. There is a sense of anticipation about the wasteland, as if it is waiting for some great enactment to be played out on its vast, undulating stage.

The desert barely touches life with the occasional gazelle or hawk but its odour is as intoxicating as opium and just as addictive. Once you have smelled the desert you have to return, again and again, to satisfy that created need. The privation it forces upon the traveller does not produce a hostility towards it: on the contrary, it creates a closeness, a spiritual marriage between the animate and the inanimate. One might take a handful of sand, or a basket of rocks, and say, 'This is the desert, for there is little else.' Yet, it is not the substance, the material, that fashions the desert, it is the lack of all else, the wide stretches of lonely nothingness under a furnace sun or canopy of cold stars. You do not breathe the desert, the desert breathes you, filling its void with your spirit. In the daytime, the heat is like a hammer striking the ground with dull blows and at night the frost finds fissures in the rocks with the sureness of steel chisels.

I had learned that the name of the elusive poet was Al-Qata and that he was Bedu without a family, a lone nomad. We stocked up with provisions at the village of Muraq and hired two guides and six camels – dromedaries in this part of the world. We began our quest.

At sunset, several months later, we found some strange markings in the sand beside a well. They could have been words – I was positive they were – but the wind had distorted the letters, had blown the sand away until they were barely perceptible and impossible to decypher. As we sat and ate our evening meal, I said to Carey, 'I think we're close. I feel it, strongly. Do you think we're close?'

'I think . . .' he said in measured tones, as he chewed on a roasted bird the guides had caught, 'I think there would be more meat on the wing of an emaciated bat than there is on this fowl.'

'But . . . look, Carey. This is important.'

He grunted. 'So is this bird.'

And he was right. Over the months our bodies had hardened to nomadic life in the empty quarter, and hardship had brought us closer to our environment. Without possessions, except those necessary to exist at subsistence level, we had been stripped naked of our civilized selves and had been reduced to the essence of humanity. Life only was important and our next meal, a meal necessary to survive, could not be found at the corner shop. The roast bird was the most important thing in our lives at that instant in time and the quest was merely secondary. We gnawed our respective bones in silence.

The next day, however, my anxiety had returned and I rose

before dawn and went to the highest point in the vicinity to see if I could spot smoke from any distant fire. The freezing air which had stiffened my joints during the night retreated before the rising of the sun and soon the cold rocks began to heat, expanding quickly, sometimes cracking apart with the sound of a gunshot. Lizards emerged, and skinks and small snakes, all eager for warmth. The desert swelled in size and with life. Soon the stones were hot enough to feel through my sandals and tendrils of heat rose from the ground to warp my vision of distant objects. We were close to the Yemen and I could see, far off, the city of Sanaa, perched on its plateau, rising up out of the cliff of red sandstone, the rose-coloured walls of its houses a continuation of the rock, embedded deep in its face. The natural and man-made was a single entity and it was impossible to tell where one left off and the other began. We would need to go east soon, for the Yemenis were hostile to strangers, suspicious of anyone who was not a cousin or closer in blood. The fierce Bedu families we occasionally met on the trail were contained by the desert code but not so the city dwellers. Not just xenophobic; they had their own set of ethics which did not include hospitality high on the list.

I scanned the horizon for smoke but seeing none, returned to the well. Carey was up and placing dried camel dung on the hot ashes of the previous night's fire. His face was raw and almost burned black by the sun. I wondered if anyone amongst his occidental friends, barring myself, would have recognized him. He might have been a nomad for all his life until that moment and I knew I presented a similar picture.

I checked the marks in the sand again in the full light of day. They could have been words, or they could have been the scratchings of a lizard or bird. It was impossible to tell. We continued our endless journey, turning east and into the Great Sandy Desert.

For the next few years we followed Al-Qata over the deserts and mountains and always he was tantalizingly close, yet not quite within reach. We received reports of his possible presence in this region, or that area, from fellow travellers. We never met anyone who had actually *seen* him but our informants had heard second-hand of his whereabouts. When the money ran out we let our guides go, having become accustomed to the trails ourselves and no longer being in need of them. We lived by shooting the occasional gazelle or wild goat and trading for ammunition and provisions.

Al-Qata was like a ghost, an elusive phantom who left his mark here and there on a rock or in the sand. But never enough to make me sure that this was my man, or indeed that he *was* one and not *many*, but enough to keep my curiosity primed. Once I became ill and was taken in by a local sheik but as soon as I was well enough we went back on the trail again, searching, ever searching. We read the Quran by the fire at night, myself delighting in its poetic content and Carey interested enough in the fundamental religious issues that bound it all together. We visited Mecca, once, and managed to avoid detection as European infidels. We were concerned by Carey's blue eyes but though such a deviation was rare, it was not unique. No race on earth is pure enough to escape the consequences of inter-breeding and there are red-headed Arabs, blue-eyed Arabs and Arabs with fair skins. Mecca, with its golden domes and white Arabesque architecture, was of course, beautiful, but after the desert it meant little to me. I wanted to be back amongst the rocks, out on the dust.

The quest for Al-Qata, my mysterious poet, was both an arduous and mystical experience: the days spent high on the camel chasing horizons and the nights in thankful but often interrupted rest. At all times we were lost in profound con-templation of our purpose: what were we doing there? Pursuing the unattainable in the infinite? The desert was not, of course, infinite, but it had the appearance of limitless space and while I did not believe Al-Qata was unattainable, he was as elusive as Big Foot or the Abominable Snowman: a spiral wind drifting across the dust.

There are those abstract aspects of life that have eluded most women and men from the beginning of time – fulfilment, contentment, happiness, love – especially love. We seek these intangibles up and down the days of our lives, never quite getting within grasping distance, but also never falling so far behind that we are tempted to let them go and give up the quest. They are, like Al-Qata was, always *just* out of reach. We feel if we could only stretch just that little bit more, get our fingertips to them . . . we would be there. Yet we never do quite make it and we are afraid to stand still for a moment in case they get too far ahead. But what if we did stop? And wait? Perhaps they would come to us? No. The risk is too great. We must pursue. It is in our nature. No prey ever wanders into the lazy hunter's den and climbs into his larder.

One day in June, we thought we saw a man buried up to his waist in sand, appealing for help, but as we drew close and the heat waves no longer distorted our vision, we realized it was a corpse. The man had died sitting up, with his arms reaching forward, as if grasping on to upright bars for support. How had the body remained in that position after life had finally flickered and died, leaving the carcass to dehydrate into a waxpaper husk? Why hadn't the kitehawks descended to feast on the dead flesh? There was something vaguely unnatural about the whole scene and I knew Carey was uneasy too. It was almost as if this hollow-eyed corpse, with the ants busy between its teeth, had been placed there, carefully, for us to find it. Were we being given a warning of some kind?

Yet . . . ? Yet perhaps not a warning but a *welcome*. The arms were open, ready to embrace, as if the desert had created this effigy in order to remind us that death was as close to it as life, and that we had to accept death readily, and with as much *approval* as we accepted life.

We buried the corpse in a shallow grave without straightening the limbs and continued on our way. Carey never mentioned it again, and neither did I, but the image of the sitting corpse returned with shocking frequency – sometimes as a vivid dream at night; sometimes during the day I caught sight of it out of the corner of my eye, as we crossed a ridge, or entered a low valley, making me jerk in on my mount. The images plagued me and I did not understand why. Then, one year later, we were passing the place where the corpse was buried and I crept away in the middle of the night intending to exhume it. I wanted to embrace death, place my cheek against its cold bone in order to exorcize the images, but the corpse had either been moved or I was digging in the wrong place. In any case, the dreams ceased after that night, and I was left in peace.

The horizon rippled in the distance. One day there was a half-sentence in the clay beside a well. In several years I had found enough of Al-Qata's work to cover only a few pages of my notebook. Yet I felt vaguely fulfilled. I travelled in the faint ripples which formed his wake as he moved ahead of me, leaving his barely-existent signs on rock and sand. His touch on the world was light, the traces of his coming and going as transient as desert dew. Foolishly, I began searching for even less distinguishable signs – the brush of his *jalabiya* on the flowers of a shrub; the mark of his sandal on the dunes that roll across the wasteland as surely as ocean waves, if a thousand times slower; the pattern of his rope *agal* upon an oasis palm. I was content that we shared the same moon, the same stars, the same arduous way of life. These common factors bound us together in spirit. The click of the beetle amongst the stones had been heard by him just a short time before the sound fell upon my ears. The scurry of the scorpion had attracted his notice just prior to mine. Was that his camel that I smelled on the breeze? Were the pie-dog's distant cries prompted by his presence? Was that silhouette on the far ridge, stark in the sunset, him? Al-Qata, the poet?

Carey was happy to go where my instinct took me. He drank his tea, spoke his words, and tended his camels with as much complacency as a successful businessman contemplates his material wealth. He was as happy with his hard life-style as was any millionaire with his luxury. We had found peace. We were our own breed, proud of our adopted land. We would have defended a single grain of the vast sea of dust as ferociously as if it had been a nation, clinging to it as tenaciously as a dictator clings to his autocracy. There were no classical lovers who gave themselves to each other as completely as we gave ourselves to the desert.

One evening, we made camp at Wadi Hafa.

'A long time,' said Carey, staring into the flank of the dark night. The words were comfortable.

'What's that?' I asked.

'We've been here . . . I don't know how long. Do you think you'll ever go home now . . . back to England?'

I stared into the hooded face before me. The fire fizzed and hissed as it ate through the camel dung, flaring occasionally to emphasize the dark lines on Carey's face, rather than highlighting the prominent brow and cheekbones. Behind him the rock forms whispered with desert life: beetles, spiders and scorpions, sandflies and snakes. His features were almost as rugged as the ochre rock and the cracks and creases in the rust-coloured skin appeared to contain as many hidden life-forms as the *jebel* behind him.

'No,' I replied. 'Will you?'

'I . . . no. No, I'm here for good.' There was a note of satisfaction in his voice which I found disturbing, but he continued, 'One becomes integrated, doesn't one? It's almost as if I were part of the desert now – mutable but irremovable. The desert is in me and I in it. We have fused, become a unified body.'

'Carey?' There was a question I wanted to ask him which had been on my mind for some time but I had not asked it because . . . well, I think I was afraid of what the answer would be.

'Yes, the desert is the beginning and the end of life,' he said, as if he had not heard me. 'The two polarities of evolution. Which end are we at, I wonder? The birth or the death? Are we witnessing the flowering of a new world or the fading of an old one?'

'Poetry,' I said. 'That's what I want to talk to you about. Carey, is Al-Qata real . . . ? I mean, I want the truth. Is there such a man?'

Carey leaned back, with his hands behind his head, staring up into the dark sky.

'Shooting star,' he said. 'Amazing things . . . who knows? I didn't invent him, that's for sure. I mean, I haven't been laying false trails all these years. But I did *use* him. You see, the sand found its way into my blood when I was here before. I knew I would have to come back – the call was too strong. Compulsion. It was as if all my ancestors had gathered in one place and with one unified voice, a single mental concentration, were compelling me to join them.

'I didn't want to return alone. I was afraid . . . afraid of the silence, and the space and the solitude. *The timelessness.* Those are terrible things to have to experience by oneself. The empty quarter, wasteland, the harsh, privative life, but not alone. You were different from me, someone with an appreciation of natural beauty. The ideal companion for a man of practical stamp – a man who lacks the imagination to express what he feels. Although your poetry – the way you put your feelings into words – might not be considered great art, it does things for me. You find the words, you see, where I cannot. You express my sentiments without me having to tax my brain for what is, eventually, an inadequate expression. So I told you about AlQata.' He sat up abruptly and stared at me with those incongruous blue eyes.

'So far as I know, he's a living, breathing man but I could be wrong. Maybe he's a myth – a kind of siren figure that calls people like you and me to the desert? Once here, we never get away – because we don't really want to go. Like the lotus-eaters, we have been hypnotized by the land. We no longer have a will of our own – it belongs to the desert.

'Al-Qata may be some poet of the empty quarter . . . a camel driver, a trader, a footloose dreamer. A person of flesh and blood. Or he may be a magical manifestation of the dust and rock that surrounds us and wishes to call its favourites to its breast, to hold them there until they truly become part of it, until it takes its own to itself as ashes and dust. We will drift on spiral winds, you and I. The grains of our dead bones will swell the desert, imperceptibly – but there will be more and more of us, until the desert has grown to cover the whole earth, and we will then finally be *one*. A single, unified presence.'

I stirred the fire with a twig and saw his eyes brighten in the sudden flare. Carey was right. This was our spiritual home. How we came here was of no importance. Here we were and here we would die, whether by a Bedu's bullet or of thirst or hunger . . . it did not matter. Perhaps there were more of us already? Who could tell? We looked like Arabs, we spoke like Arabs, we told our campfire stories and sang our songs of past tribal glories. We were the desert, the desert was us.

'The sand is our bed and the sky our tent,' I said. Carey nodded.

'For the rest of our natural lives,' he added.

We settled down and Carey passed me a quid of qāt grass. We did not chew the drug often but there were times when we felt the need to commit ourselves fully to insensibility. Qāt allows you to drift into a kind of timeless lethargy, where the ache in your bones melts into the sand, leaving your body drifting on the dust with the night pulsing through your veins.

I lay there, looking up at the skies, chewing slowly on the grass. After a while I focused on a single star, Sirius, and it seemed to me that this one jewel held the universe together, keeping the movements of the night in harmony with its delicate force. Hairspring constellations trembled above me. Then the night sky melted into a softer image of dew-covered webs, and suddenly I felt if Sirius were to fall, myriads would descend with it, like white rain, leaving darknesses folding into a deeper dark.

As I lay there, allowing myself to be seduced by these thoughts, I became aware that another man was sharing our fire. Visits from strangers were of course infrequent, but not unique, and the desert code provided that we shared the warmth of our fire, food and drink with those who were in need. The qāt was having its full effect on my brain and I saw him only as stark, intermittent images, as if I were observing him under a strobe light. His finely drawn features bore an inherent air of preoccupation. The bright eyes sought their own secrets in the fire and we, Carey and I, remained on some vague periphery of their attention, as if we were no more relevant to the scene than another shrub or rock. Shadows filled the hollows in his cheeks and the narrow nose emphasized the blade-like quality of his face. At times, he seemed to be merely eating and drinking, but I also had momentary visions of him with a brushwood twig in his hand as he scratched away at the dust. Shortly afterwards I fell asleep.

The following morning we rose as usual with the sun. Our guest had already left us, silently, before the first rays had stirred the camels into vocal agitation and we had crooned them back to calmness. We broke camp, neither of us mentioning the visitor, and I collected what charcoal remained from the dead fireplace. Beside the white ashes were some marks in the dust. Without pausing to study them further, I erased them with my foot – an action prompted by some deep motive which had not crystallized into any definite awareness. Immediately afterwards I was even a little appalled at my rash act and turned to speak to Carey, but he was doing something with the bedrolls, humming a tune to himself through cracked lips, and I changed my mind. He looked up at me after a while and gave me a grim smile.

'What price an April shower?' he said.

'More than you can afford,' I replied.

A few moments later, I noticed he appeared to be surreptitiously studying some faint indentations in the sand where the morning breeze was stirring dust and filling hollows. They might have been our own tracks from the previous day, or an animal's spoor, or . . . anything. They seemed to be heading, or coming from, the east, where the sun was climbing up the sky.

'Let's strike out north,' Carey said, briskly. 'Maybe he's been back to the hills again?' I nodded, and we returned to our separate tasks with deliberate and meticulous efficiency.

Two months later we met with some trouble which I believe had something to do with water rights, at a small well in the Fakhiri valley. There were three Bedu, two old men whose faces were masked by their hoods and a boy of about sixteen, a son or nephew of one of the other two, no doubt, since the Bedu almost always travelled in families. They came in as we were watering the camels, we exchanged salaams with them, but then they left without watering their own mounts, which was too unusual to ignore. There was also something rather chilling in the way they had studied our faces.

When they were three hundred yards away they turned and fired in unison. Though we had been half expecting the attack, it still had an element of surprise and the thing that remained in my memory the strongest was not the sound of the volley and its subsequent echoes down the valley, but the awful smell as my new pack-camel defecated in fright. We ran for the rocks and Carey took a shot in the chest just as we reached them. It was a flesh wound – I could see the blood underneath his armpit where the bullet had come out. Having unslung my own weapon on the run I helped him with his and we began returning the fire. After a further exchange of shots one of the saddles of their camels was empty, the beast itself careering round in tight circles. The remaining two Bedu struck out for the open desert.

We waited for several hours.

'I'm going out to look,' I told Carey. He had his hand over the stain on his chest and refused to allow me to look at it.

'Don't be long,' he said. 'I want to dress this thing again – the pad is completely soaked.'

'Shall I do it now?'

'No, no. Don't worry. I'll be all right. Be careful . . . they may be back. The other two.'

I walked slowly across the dust to the fallen Bedu, my eyes

alert for his kin. His mount was nosing around nervously about thirty yards away as I knelt down beside him. He was dead: the first man I had ever hurt, let alone killed, though I felt no remorse, just a kind of bleak emptiness. One arm was twisted underneath his back and his left foot had caught under his right knee and formed a triangle. But it was his face that startled me. I then recognized the sharp features of the man who had visited our fire two months previously. My bullet had hit him in the abdomen – not a wound that one would normally have expected to kill instantaneously but perhaps the shock had been too much for him. He was one of the two older men. I tried to drag him back with me, pulling him by his armpits, but he was heavy and eventually I abandoned the body, not really having any clear idea about what I wanted to do with it anyway. Rigor mortis had begun to set in and I left it in a sort of slouched, sitting position, the arms locked forward.

Carey was nowhere to be seen. His camel was still grazing by the well, but the man himself had gone. I rode through the outcrops calling his name and risking my life, for I was fairly certain the Bedu had circumnavigated the well and had abducted him. I have not seen him again, though I know that both Bedu have been following me ever since.

It is three years since Carey was taken away from me. The two Bedu are persistent, never giving up the chase though I manage to remain just ahead of them, just out of their reach. I am becoming more confident as the days pass and I am certain that they will never catch me. I have even been leaving messages for them in the dust – enigmatic little poetic phrases which I hope will confuse them.

I sign them with a name which I feel I have earned from the man I killed. It is a way of getting back at them for their damned persistence. Perhaps one day, when their wariness has been blunted by the length and arduousness of the pursuit, I shall have the audacity to visit their fire and confront them?

I wish I knew where Carey was though. I have this ir-repressible feeling that he may be back in England; perhaps recruiting another man to help look for me? Yet, perhaps my feelings lie to me and he still shares the desert? I shall continue searching for him, watching for a particular striding walk on my infrequent visits to a souk, or studying the set of a distant rider's shoulders at a rare encounter in some lonely wadi. When he finds me, or I find him, we can once more take to the trails together and continue looking for . . . looking for . . . it doesn't matter. This is our home.

My name is Hassan Abdulla. I found these writings on the man I have been following for some time – Al-Qata, the desert poet. I think he died in the night of the cold, for he was an old man. I left him sitting in the rocks for the two Englishmen – the one with the blue eyes and his companion. They are close behind me and I wonder if they mean to kill me, since they have been following my trail for several weeks – since the time my son was separated from me by the sandstorm. Two nights ago we had the first rain for six years and the desert is blooming. Seeds carried on the wind from Africa, dormant for many years, have turned the desert into a sea of light green shoots. It will not last long, perhaps a few days. Then all will go brown and die. Its transient beauty cannot go unrecorded and I leave a few lines of verse on the rock, as Al-Qata would have done had he lived to see it. Perhaps my son will pass by this place and read them . . .

ON THE WATCHTOWER
AT PLATAEA

There was the chilling possibility, despite Miriam's assurance that she would dissuade the government from physical confrontation, that I might receive the order to go out and kill my adversary in the temple. They might use the argument that our future existence depended on an answer to be dredged up from the past. I wondered if I could do such a thing: and if so, how? Would I sneak from the watchtower in the night, like an assassin, and murder him in his bed? Or challenge him to single combat, like a true noble warrior is supposed to? The whole idea of such a confrontation made me feel ill and I prayed that if it should come to such a pass, they would send someone else to do the bloody job. I have no stomach for such things.

It was a shock to find that the expedition could go no further back than 429 B.C.: though for some of us, it was not an unwelcome one. Miriam was perhaps the only one amongst us who was annoyed that we couldn't get to Pericles. He had died earlier, in the part of the year we couldn't reach. So near – but we had hit a barrier, as solid as a rockface on the path of linear time, in the year that the Peloponnesian War was gaining momentum. It was the night that Sparta and its allies were to take positive action against the Athenians by attacking a little walled city-state called Plataea. Plataea, with its present garrison of 400 local hoplites and some eighty seconded Athenians, was virtually the only mainland supporter of Athens

in the war amongst the Greeks. It was a tiny city-state, even
by ancient world standards – perhaps a mile in circumference
– and it was heavily outnumbered by the besieging troops led
by the Spartan king, Archidamus. It didn't stand a chance, but
by God it put up resistance which rivalled The Alamo for
stubbornness, and surpassed it for inventiveness.

Miriam suggested we set up the recording equipment in an
old abandoned watchtower on a hill outside the city. From there
we could see the main gates, and could record both the Spartan
attempts at breaching the walls and the defenders as they battled
to keep the invaders at bay. The stonework of the watchtower
was unstable, the timber rotting, and it was probably only used
to shelter goats. We did not, therefore, expect to be interrupted
while we settled in. In any case, while we were 'travelling', we
appeared as insubstantial beings and were seldom confronted.
The tower was ideal. It gave us the height we needed to
command a good view, and had aged enough to be a respectable
establishment for spectral forms.

There were three of us in the team. Miriam was the expedition's leader; John was responsible for the recording equipment;
and I was the official communicator, in contact with base camp,
A.D. 2017. By 429, we were not at our harmonious best, having
been away from home for a very long time: long enough for all
our habits and individual ways to get on each other's nerves to
the point of screaming. I suppose we were all missing home to
a certain extent, though why we should want to go back to a
world where four-fifths of the population was on the streets,
starving, and kept precariously at bay by the private military
armies of privileged groups, was never raised. We ourselves, of
course, belonged to one of those groups, but we were aware of
the instability of the situation and the depressingly obvious fact
that we could do nothing to influence it. The *haves* were no
longer in a position to help the *have nots*, even given the desire
to do such. One of the reasons for coming on the expedition
was to escape my guilt – and the constant wars between the
groups. It was, as always, a mess.

'What do base say?' asked Miriam.

I could see the watch fires on the nearby city walls through her ghostly form, as she moved restlessly around the walkway of the tower. John was doing something below.

'They believe the vortex must have an outer limit,' I said. 'It would appear that we've reached it.'

This didn't satisfy her, and I didn't expect it to. Miriam did not operate on beliefs. She liked people to *know*.

'But why here? Why now? What's so special about the year 429? It doesn't make any sense.'

'You expect it to make sense?'

'I had hoped . . . oh, I don't know. An answer which wasn't still a question I suppose. Doesn't it worry you? That suddenly we come up against a wall, without any apparent reason?'

I shrugged. 'Surely natural limitations are a good enough reason. Human endeavour has often come up against such things – the sound barrier, for example. They believed that was impassable at the time, but they got through it in the end. Maybe this is a comparable problem?'

'It's a bitch, I know that much,' she replied in a bitter tone. 'I really wanted Pericles – and the earlier battles. Marathon. Thermopylae. Damn it, there's so much we'll have to leave. Mycenae and Agamemnon. We could have confirmed all that. If we can't go back any further, Troy will remain covered in mist . . .'

Which was not altogether a bad thing as far as I was concerned. Already too many illusions had been wiped away. Why destroy all myth and legend, simply for the sake of facts? It's a pretty boring world, once the magic has been stripped off.

'Well, perhaps we shouldn't do it all at once,' I suggested. 'I feel as if I'm drowning as it is . . . let someone else destroy Homer.'

She said, 'We're not *destroying* anything. We're merely recording . . .'

'The *truth*,' I said, unable to keep the sarcasm out of my tone.

She glared at me, a silvery frown marring her handsome

features. We had clashed in the same way several times recently and I think she was getting tired of my outbursts.

'You have an attitude problem, Stan – don't make it my problem, too.'

'I won't,' I said, turning away.

In the distance, I could hear the jingle of brass: the Spartan army tramping through the night, their torches clearly visible. These sounds and sights were the cause of some consternation and excitement amongst the Plataeans on the walls of the city. The enemy had arrived. Little figures ran to and fro, between the watch fires. They had known for a few hours that Archidamus was coming: Theban traitors, spies and double agents had been busy during the day, earning a crust. The warnings had come too late for flight, however, and it was now a case of defying the vastly superior force or surrendering the city. Some of the defenders were relying on the fact that Plataea was sacred ground – it had been consecrated after a successful battle with the Persians earlier in the century – but Archidamus was not a man to take much notice of that. There were ways of appealing to the gods for a suspension of holy rights, if the need was there.

I wondered how the Spartans would react if they knew they were being recorded, visually. They were already pretty good at strutting around in grand macho style, cuffing slaves and flaunting their long hair. We had been told that historical recordings such as this would be studied for possible answers to the problems of our own time. I couldn't help but feel cynical about this idea, though I did not have the whole picture. The future, beyond my own time, had been investigated by another team and the result was a secret known only to that expedition and our illustrious government, but I couldn't help feeling it was a very bleak picture.

Besides Spartans, the invading army consisted of slave auxiliaries, a few mercenaries and volunteer forces from the cities allied with Sparta: Corinth, Megara, Elis, Thebes and many others. These cities looked to their big cousin to lead them against the upstart Athens, a city-state of little significance until the early part of the century, when it had thrashed a hugely superior force of Persians at the Battle of Marathon, and had since become too big for its sandals. If there was one thing the ancient Greeks could not stand, it was someone thinking they were better than everyone else.

Except for Plataea. Athens stood virtually alone in mainland Greece, though its maritime empire encompassed almost all the Aegean islands and the coast of Asia Minor. One of the reasons why the war would last so long was because a stalemate was inevitable. Athens was a strongly walled city, which included its harbour, and could not be penetrated by a land force. Its formidable bronze-toothed fleet of ramming triremes discouraged any idea of a naval blockade. On the other hand, Sparta had no ships to speak of, was an inland unwalled city, but positively encouraged an invasion of their territory since they relished battles and their hoplites were considered almost invincible. Certainly no Spartan would leave a field alive unless victory had been assured. Direct confrontations with such warriors, cool and unafraid of death, were not courted at all keenly, even by brave Athenians.

So, a military might and a naval power, and rarely the twain met. Stalemate. Little Plataea was in fact nothing more than a whipping boy on which Sparta could vent some of its frustration and spleen.

Miriam was looking through night viewers, at the advancing hordes. She said, 'This may be the last historical battle we're able to record.'

I was glad of that. Expeditions like ours tend to start out fortified by enthusiasms and good nature, only to end in disillusionment and bitter emotions, as any geographical explorer will tell you. Discoveries exact a high price from the finders, who have to pay for them with pieces of their souls.

There was a terrible scream from down below, sending lizards racing up my back. I stared at Miriam. A few moments later, John came up the makeshift ladder, looking disgusted.

'Goatboy,' he explained. 'Wandered in looking for a place to hide from the troops, I suppose, now that they've closed the city gates. He saw me and ran. That earth floor already stinks to high heaven with goat droppings. They must have been using it for decades.'

Miriam said, 'Pull up the ladder, John. We may as well settle for the night. Nothing's going to happen until morning.'

Below us, the weary Allies began to arrive and put up tents, out of range of any archers who might be on the walls of the city. Trumpets were sounded, informing the Plataeans that a bloody business was about to begin, as if they didn't know that already. They were pretty noisy in unloading their gear, clattering pots and clanking bits of armour; bawling to one another as new groups arrived, in the hearty fashion of the soldier before the killing starts. We required rest, though we did not sleep while we were travelling, any more than we needed to eat or drink.

'Noisy bastards,' I grumbled. 'I wish they'd shut up.'

John, saying his prayers as he always did at that time of night, looked up sharply from his kneeling position and frowned. He did not like interruptions during such a time, and I found myself apologizing.

Here we were, making sure these squabbles amongst mankind reached a pitch of historical accuracy nobody needed. What the hell was it all about? And were our recordings doing even that useless job? I doubted it. Going back into history, you tend to get caught in the confusion of one small corner of an issue, just as if you lived in the times. One needs God's eyes to see the whole, and weigh the reasons.

It might be that God dwells beyond some far ripple of the time vortex. If you think of the vortex as an old-fashioned, long-playing record and the groove as linear time, you will have some idea how travellers are able to skip through the ages, as a too light arm of a record deck skates over a disc. It is a mental process, requiring no vehicle. Somewhere beyond those grooves, dwells the Almighty. Who wants to meet God and see *absolute truth* in all its blinding whiteness? Not me. Not me, my friend. *Eyes I dare not meet in dreams*, as the poet Eliot said.

By the next morning the Spartans had surrounded Plataea and were intent on encircling it with a palisade of sharpened stakes, leaning inwards. Archidamus wanted to be sure that no one could escape from the city. He wanted to teach the inhabitants a lesson: that siding with those nasty imperialists and free-thinkers, the Athenians, was a dangerous thing to do.

It was true that Athens had created a confederacy, mostly consisting of island states, which she subsequently milked of funds, using the money to build the Parthenon, generally beautify the city, and increase the number of ships in her fleet. It was true that anyone who requested to leave the confederacy found the equivalent of several British gunboats in their harbour within a few days. But it was equally true that the Spartans, with their two kings (one to stay at home, while the other was at war), really could not give a damn about anyone but themselves. Athens was full of woolly-minded intellectuals who not only indulged in progressive thinking and innovations, but were carefree and undisciplined with it. Sparta had long since fossilized. They had put a stop to progress some time ago. In Sparta it was forbidden to write new songs, poetry or plays, or introduce anything into society with a flavour of change about it, let alone the *avant-garde* stuff allowed in Athens. Why, the northern city was positively licentious in its attitudes towards art and science. Nothing which would disturb the perfection of the life-style Spartans had achieved at an earlier time was permitted in Lacedaemonia. Asceticism, the nobility of war, plain food and state-raised children destined for the army: these were the ideals to be upheld. Give a Spartan a coarse hair shirt, a plate of salty porridge, a lusty 300-year-old song to sing and send him out on to the battlefield, and he'll die thanking you. To the Athenians, who loved good food, new mathematics, eccentric old men asking interminable questions, incompre-hensible philosophies, weird inventions, plays making fun of the gods, love, life and the pursuit of happiness – to these people the Spartans were homicidal lunatics.

I suppose it was little wonder that these two Hellenic city-states disliked each other so much.

While the thousands of figures, the keen ones still sweating in their armour, scurried about below us, busy with siege engines, we got on with our regular tasks. John had set up a hologram at the entrance to the tower. It was supposed to represent Apollo and appeared instantly on any human approach, to warn away hoplites who would have otherwise used the tower as a toilet. The hologram uttered its threats in what was probably an appalling accent, but it was the best we could do with the devices to hand. It seemed to do its job, because by noon on the first day gifts had been placed at a respectable distance from the entrance to the watchtower. They could see us, of course, drifting around the top of the tower, but I suppose we were gods, too, witnessing the heroic struggles of mortals. I did my best to assume a Zeus-like posture. We had some 'thunder and lightning' for emergencies, but hadn't needed them up to that point.

The heat of the day made us generally testy and irritable, for although many of our bodily functions were suspended, we still had our senses. I found some shade under the parapet and proceeded to contact base. This time they had a little news for us which was still very vague. Something – they were not sure quite what, but told us to watch for the unusual – something was preventing a further spread of the vortex.

Watch for something unusual? Only those bloody deskriders back at base would say something like that, to travellers in an antique world, where the unusual was all around, in almost every facet of daily life. Personally, I hoped they didn't solve the problem. I was weary and homesick and a solution would mean continuing the journey. I didn't say that, of course.

I told Miriam what base had said, and she nodded.

'Thanks. We'll have to wait and see.'

Boredom, that's what time travel is mostly about. Like war,

it's 5 per cent feverish action, and 95 per cent sitting around with nothing to do. I settled down wearily for a game of chess with John.

'You're the Athenians and I'm the Spartans, so I get to have two kings,' he joked.

I thought John uncomplicated and open, and we seemed to get on well together, though he was a good deal younger than me. I was reticent, but he didn't seem to mind that. He had not lost the bubbling enthusiasm of youth, took religion seriously (both of which got on my nerves sometimes, when I was feeling bloody), and had a love for his fellows which was difficult to resist.

Miriam was of a similar disposition to myself. Sometimes to while away the hours, I imagined a romantic connection between us, which was actually as far-fetched as any fairytale romance. Although she is a fine-looking woman, with a strong will and good mind, I was not in the least attracted to her. Interested in her, but not attracted. One of those chemical negatives I suppose. I'm sure the feeling was mutual, if she thought about it at all. She had a husband back home, and two kids, not that she ever talked about them. I expect they were none of our damn business.

'Your move.'

John shifted his head, to interfere with my line of vision.

'Oh, yes – sorry. Daydreaming.'

'Occupational hazard,' he said, with more seriousness than was warranted, but I didn't have time to question his tone. At that moment a bird, a bee-eater I think, flew into the parapet with a *smack*. I picked the beautiful creature up, whereupon it pecked me, struggled from my grasp and took groggily to the air. It seemed to be all right.

John gave me a significant stare. It is one of his theories that the vortex interferes with the orientation of natural creatures (time travellers being *unnatural*, I expect) and he intended to write something of the sort when we returned to civilization. He could be right, but if he believed that anyone would care about such things, he was in for a disappointment. It is one of *my* theories that, back at base camp, they don't even care about the orientation of humans, let alone bee-eaters.

Over the next few weeks we watched the activity below with a little more interest. It became a battle of wits, not swords, the main combatants being the engineering corps of both sides. The Spartan army laboured long and hard to build an earth ramp against the city wall, up which they intended to march and take the city, at the same time catapulting fireballs through the air and making futile attempts at scaling the walls with ladders. Before the ramp was completed the wily Plataeans had raised the height of the wall at that point, cannibalizing their houses for stone blocks. It became a race. The taller grew the ramp, the higher went the wall. In the end, Archidamus put every available man on earth-carrying duty and by this means he managed to gain on the Plataeans, threatening to reach the top of the wall.

Undaunted, the defenders then tunnelled underneath their own wall and through the earth ramp, removing the loose soil until the ramp collapsed. On seeing his beautiful mound fall in on itself, Archidamus stamped around threatening death and destruction. He sacrificed a dozen goats to us, and to another shrine – a small temple about half a mile from our position – hoping we would intervene divinely on his behalf in subduing these irksome Plataeans. He came to us in full armour, wearing the classic Corinthian helmet, with its decorated, elongated cheek-pieces and transverse crest of horsehair, his brass-faced shield and muscled greaves, and a heavy bell cuirass. For a Spartan he was pretty flashy, but then he was a king. It was obvious that he was hot and testy, and I think it took all his reserve to remain polite to the gods who were giving his troops such a hard time. The goats' entrails stank like hell when thrown into the copper bowl of flames and we retreated below for a while, leaving a hologram of Athena to receive promises of temples to be erected, and pilgrimages to be undertaken, once victory was within Spartan grasp. On reflection it was not the most tactful thing to have done, since Athena was the goddess protector of Athens, but we didn't think about that at the time. In any case, what was irritating Archidamus was the fact that the enemy would not come out and fight like men. Spartans do not make the best besieging troops in the world. They hate messing around with mud, sticks and stones, when they could be looking their best, charging across a windy plain with their long black hair streaming and their mouths uttering terrible war cries, ready to stick in or be stuck by some sharp instrument. There were lots of jokes about the Spartans, even amongst their own allies. The one about the shrew's brain in a lion's skin was a particular favourite.

After delivering his dubious gifts, Archidamus then went to the small temple, inside the palisade, and repeated the exercise. Miriam became very curious about this rival for our affections and managed to find a spot around the tower wall where she could see the building through her viewers. Finally, she asked John to take some footage, though it was not possible to see directly into the obliquely positioned temple and our line of sight was hampered by the points of some tall stakes on the palisade. We ran this through, afterwards, and managed to catch a glimpse of a figure between the marble columns. He had some kind of tri-legged device with him, the head of which seemed to incorporate revolving flaps of stiff material, that flashed like mirrors when it was operated. More significant than this, however, was the fact that the white-robed figure working this machine seemed to have semi-transparent flesh. Certainly, he was treated with distant, wary reverence by the Hellenes, in the same way that we were ourselves. There was very good reason to suppose that we and this elusive person, and possibly any companions hidden by the temple walls, had a great deal in common.

'Look at those beggars – you've got to hand it to them,' said John, with admiration in his voice. He was, of course, talking about the Plataeans. Archidamus's engineers had stopped the Plataeans' little game of removing earth from under the ramp by packing baskets with clay and placing them as foundation blocks for the ramp. These could not be drawn away like loose earth. The defenders met this device by digging a subterranean mine to beyond the ramp and allowing the whole effort to collapse again. By this time, the earth was having to be carried from some considerable distance by the besiegers and they were becoming dispirited and thoroughly disgruntled by the whole affair. Deserters began to drift by our watchtower at night, and one or two minor kings packed their tents and took their citizen-soldiers home. Archidamus executed some malefactors, possibly to create an interesting diversion to the gruelling manual labour, but was unable to stem the increasing tide of dissatisfaction amongst his troops. He had sent for some Scythian archers of his own, but the Plataeans erected animal-hide screens on top of the walls to protect themselves and the bowmen were less than effective. Added to this there was the smell of sickness in the air, which was part of the sordid business of a war in stalemate.

Some time after calling base regarding the possible presence of another group of travellers, we were asked to obtain further information. Miriam had already spent a great deal of time studying the mysterious occupants of the small temple through the viewer, but there were too many obstacles in the way to get anything concrete.

'We'll have to go over there,' she said, 'and get a closer look.'

John and I glanced at one another. Although the watchtower was far from secure against aggressive action, it provided protection for us in that it had become a sacred building to the Greeks and was unlikely to be violated. It ensured that we remained distant, aloof figures which could be avoided simply by giving the crumbling structure a wide berth. Once we started wandering amongst them, like ordinary mortals, we were in danger of becoming too familiar. It was not beyond the realms of possibility that some brave hoplite might decide to challenge the 'gods': after all, Odysseus had got away with it. It was a risky business. Of course, we could protect ourselves with our own weapons, but never having had to resort to such drastic action, we were unsure of the consequences.

'What do you suggest?' asked John.

Miriam said, 'I'll take the portable and go over there for some close-ups – Stan, you come with me.'

Not *too* close, I thought, but nodded in assent. I must admit, the anticipation of some excitement gave me a charge, despite my apprehension.

We set off just as the Hellenic dawn was coming up. Miriam carried the hand recorder, while I self-consciously cradled a weapon in my arms. I knew how to use it, but it was more a question of whether it knew how to use me. I have never had to hurt anyone in my life – physically, that is. We walked between tents and lean-to shacks that had been raised by the invaders, without hindrance, though one or two wide-eyed early risers moved quickly out of our way. When we got to the gate in the palisade of stakes we had a problem. It was closed.

'What do we do?' I said. 'We can't walk through the damn thing. And gods don't fiddle with gates, wondering how they open.'

Before Miriam could answer, one of the sentries rushed forward and pulled at a leather thong. The gate swung open. He had not, of course, understood the language of the gods, but our intentions were obvious and the mere fact that I had voiced some strange words must have spurred him to action.

We made our way towards the temple. I prayed that the archers on the walls of Plataea would be too overawed by the sight of a pair of semi-transparent beings to fire any arrows.

We stood off about a hundred yards from the temple, where we had a clear view into the interior, and Miriam began recording. Half-hidden in the heavy shadows thrown by the columns we could see a translucent form operating the instrument with the metallic flaps, which was possibly some sort of heliographic recording device, though it looked like something knocked-up in a Swiss toymaker's workshop for an Arabian prince. The stand was fashioned of polished wood covered in hieroglyphics and there were lead weights on plumblines which balanced wooden arms connected to cogged wheels. Behind the operator, hanging from the pillars, were two elongated scrolls of painted parchment, one with a picture of a dog's body with a monkey's head, the other depicting some sort of wading bird.

As we stood, both he and us, recording each other – a situation that struck me as rather ironical – another wraith-like figure appeared, wearing a long, flowing robe and decorated headcloth. He whispered to his companion, then went back into a side-room. I was sure that the directional mike would capture that whisper, which when amplified would reveal their language.

Miriam gestured to me without speaking and we stopped recording, making our way back.

The gate had been left open for us and we passed through without any problem, but on the other side of the palisade it was a different matter. Word had got around that the gods were abroad and a huge crowd had gathered, though there was a wide path through the middle of it leading to the tower. I could see John on the ramparts of the watchtower with a weapon in his hands.

'Okay,' said Miriam, 'let's go, Stan. Don't look back . . .'

I had no intention of doing anything of the sort. All I wanted to do was reach the tower, safely.

As we walked down the avenue a murmuring broke out amongst the troops, which grew in volume to uncoordinated chants. I hadn't any doubt we were being petitioned for various miracles, both collective and individual. Two-thirds of the way along there was a horrible incident. A young man broke from the crowd and threw himself at my feet, attempting to clutch my ankle. Before he could lay a hand on me, he was pinned to the mud by several spears, thrown by his comrades. I wanted to be sick on the spot as I watched him squirming in the dust like some wounded porcupine. We made the tower without any further problems and shortly afterwards the crowd broke up as

Spartan officers moved amongst them with whips. The young man's body was removed and as he was carried away I wondered what had made him so desperate as to brave touching a god. Maybe his mother or father was terminally ill? Or a close friend had been killed whom he wished us to raise from the dead? Or perhaps he was just a helot, a slave, who thought we could free him from the oppression of his Spartan masters with a wave of our hands? Poor bastard.

Later, I went to Miriam and asked her about our friends in the temple. We had already mentioned the word *Egyptian* to each other, though all we had as evidence for that were the hieroglyphics and the pictures. A group of future ancient Egyptian revivalists? Just because they wore the costume and carried the artifacts didn't make them residents from the banks of the Nile. Though there didn't seem any logical reason for a masquerade, cults are seldom founded on reason, or by rational thinkers.

'The bird picture was an ibis,' said Miriam, 'and the dog-monkey . . . well, the ancient Egyptian god Zehuti was represented by both those symbolic characters.'

'Zehuti?' I knew a little of the culture in question, but this was a new one to me.

'Sorry, you probably know him as Thoth – Zehuti is his older name. The Greeks identified him with Hermes, which makes sense. Hermes the messenger – a *traveller?*'

'Anything else?'

'Yes – Thoth was also the patron of science and inventions, the spokesman of the gods and their keeper of the records. Thoth invented all the arts and sciences, including surveying, geometry, astronomy, soothsaying, magic . . . do I need to go on?'

'No. I get the picture. If you wanted a god of time travel, Thoth fits the bill quite nicely. So what do we do now?'

She gave me a grim smile.

'Wait. What else? Once you've transmitted the recording back to base, we wait until they come up with definites.'

So we did what we were best, and worst, at: waiting.

One evening the three of us were sitting, more or less in a rough circle, engaged in frivolous tasks. I was actually doing nothing. The stars were out, above us, and I could hear the snuffling of livestock and the clank of pots from down below. The area around Plataea was becoming as unsavoury as the no man's land of World War Two, with cess pits filling the air with an appalling stink and churned mud giving the landscape an ugly, open-wound appearance. We had been discussing our situation. Something was preventing the outer ring of our vortex from going any further, and base believed that what was stopping it was another vortex, coming from the other direction, the distant past. The two whirlpools were touching each other, and neither could proceed before the other retreated. Our friends were indeed early Egyptians. It had taken a while for this idea to sink in, but when I thought deeply about it, it was not at all far-fetched.

On a simple level, time travel involved a psychological state induced by the use of darkness and light, resulting in the fusion of infinites, of space and time. The dark and light became unified into a substance which formed a shape. That shape was common enough in the night sky: a spiral on a flat plane, moving outwards from the centre of the group, some of whom remained behind to form an anchor point for the vortex. The base camp group. The room in which we had begun the vigil was no longer a room, but something else: a superphysical universe that possibly exists in all minds at some level of perception. There was no technological reason why an earlier civilization could not have made the same mental discovery. On the other hand, people of our rank were still not privy to the source of the discovery, and it could well be that the knowledge had *come* from the past. Egyptian documents perhaps, only recently decoded? I remembered something about mirrors being used to flood the dark interior passages of the pyramids with light from the sun.

A horrible thought occurred to me.

'We're not going to stay here, until they go back?'

Miriam shrugged.

'I don't know. I'm awaiting instructions from base.'

'Now look, we're the ones that are here. Not them.'

'You know how it is, as well as I do, Stan.'

I stared at her.

'I know how it is,' I said, bitterly.

Her phantom features produced a faint smile.

I lay awake that night, thinking about the stalemate I had got myself into. Egyptians? If they had had time travel for so long, why hadn't they visited future centuries? But then, of course, they probably had and we had run screaming from them, just as the goatboy had fled from us. They probably had a similar policy to ourselves: no interference, just record and return. So, on their umpteenth journey into the future, they had come to a halt, suddenly, and had no doubt come to the same conclusion as we had: someone was blocking the path.

It wasn't difficult either to see how such a discovery might be lost to future civilizations. Hadn't certain surgical techniques been lost too? Time travel would undoubtedly have been in the hands of an élite: probably a priesthood. Some pharaoh, his brain addled as the result of a long lineage of incestuous relationships, had destroyed the brotherhood in a fit of pique; or the priests had been put to death by invading barbarians, their secret locked in stone vaults.

On the current front, the Plataeans were still one jump ahead of the Spartans. They had abandoned their mining operations and instead had built another crescent-shaped wall inside their own, so that when the ramp was finally completed, the Spartans were faced with a second, higher obstacle. Peltasts tried lobbing spears over the higher wall, only to find the distance was too great. Archidamus had his men fill the gap between the two walls with faggots and set light to it, but a chance storm doused this attempt to burn down the city. We got a few indignant looks from the Spartans after that. As gods, we were responsible for the weather. The war trumpets of the invaders filled the air with bleating notes which we felt sure were a criticism of us and our seeming partiality towards the defenders.

Finally, battering rams were employed, over the gap between the walls, but the Plataeans had a device – a huge beam on chains – which they dropped on to the ram-headed war machines and snapped off the ends.

Archidamus gave up. He ordered yet another wall to be built, outside the palisade of stakes, and left part of his army to guard it. Winter was beginning to set in and the king had had enough of the inglorious mudbath in which he had been wallowing. He went home, to his family in the south.

The majority of the Egyptians also withdrew at this point. One of them remained behind.

We received our orders from base.

'One of us must stay,' said Miriam, 'until a relief can be sent. If we all go back, the vortex will recede with us and the Egyptians will move forward, gain on us.'

'A Mexican stand-off,' I said, disgustedly.

'Right. We can't allow them the opportunity to invade the territory we already hold . . .'

'Shit,' I said, ignoring a black look from John, 'now we've got a cold war on our hands. Even *time* isn't safe from ownership. First it was things, then it was countries . . . now it's time itself. Why don't we build a bloody great wall across this year, like Archidamus, and send an army of guards to defend it?'

Miriam said, 'Sarcasm won't help at this stage, Stan.'

'No, I don't suppose it will, but it makes me feel good. So what happens now? We draw straws?'

'I suggest we do it democratically.' She produced three shards of pottery that she had gathered from the ground below, and distributed one to each of us.

'We each write the name of the person we think most competent to remain behind,' she explained, 'and then toss them in the middle.'

'Most competent – I like the diplomatic language,' I muttered. John, I knew, would put down his own name. He was one of those selfless types, who volunteered for everything. His minor household gods were Duty and Honour. He would actually *want* to stay.

I picked up my piece of pot. It was an unglazed shard depicting two wrestlers locked in an eternal, motionless struggle, each seemingly of equal strength and skill, and each determined not to give ground. I turned it over and wrote JOHN in clear letters, before placing it, picture-side up, in the middle of the ring.

Two other pieces clattered against mine. Miriam sorted through them, turning them over.

My name was on two of them.

I turned to John.

'Thanks,' I said.

'It had to be somebody. You're the best man for the job.'

'Bullshit,' I said. I turned to Miriam. 'What if I refuse to stay? I'll resign, terminate my contract.'

Miriam shook her head. 'You won't do that. You'd never get another trip and while you get restless in the field, you get even worse at home. I know your type, Stan. Once you've been back a couple of weeks you'll be yelling to go again.'

She was right, damn her. While I got bored in the field, I was twice as bad back home.

'I'm not a type,' I said, and got up to go below. Shortly afterwards, Miriam followed me.

'I'm sorry, Stan.' She touched my arm. 'You see it for what it is – another political attempt at putting up fences by possessive, parochial old farts. Unless I go back and convince them otherwise, they'll be sending death squads down the line to wipe out the Egyptians. You do understand?'

'So it had to be me.'

'John's too young to leave here alone. I'll get them to replace you as soon as I can – until then . . .'

She held out her slim hand and I placed my own slowly and gently into her grip. The touch of her skin was like warm silk.

'Goodbye,' I said.

She went up the ladder and John came down next.

I said coldly, 'What is this? Visiting day?'

'I came to say goodbye,' he said, stiffly.

I stared hard at him, hoping I was making it difficult, hoping the bastard was uncomfortable and squirming.

'Why me, John? You had a reason.'

He suddenly looked very prim, his spectral features assuming a sharp quality.

'I thought about volunteering myself, but that would have meant you two going back alone – together, that is . . .' He became flustered. 'She's a married woman, Stan. She'll go back to her husband and forget you.'

I rocked on my heels.

'*What?* What the hell are you talking about?'

'Miriam. I've seen the way you two look at each other.'

I stared at him, finding it difficult to believe he could be so stupid.

'You're a fool, John. The worst kind of fool. It's people like you, with twisted minds, that start things like that war out there. Go on – get out of my sight.'

He started to climb the ladder, then he looked down and gave me a Parthian shot. 'You put *my* name on your shard. Why should I feel guilty about putting yours?'

And he was right, but that didn't stop me from wanting to jerk the ladder from under him and breaking his bloody neck.

They were gone within the hour, leaving me to haunt the Greeks all on my own, a solitary ghost moving restlessly around the parapet of the tower. I saw my Egyptian counterpart once, in the small hours, as a shimmering figure came out into the open to stare at my prison. I thought for a moment he or she was going to wave again, but nothing so interesting happened, and I was left to think about my predicament once more. I knew how slowly things moved back home. They had all the time in the world. I wondered whether Egyptians could learn to play chess. It was a pity Diogenes wasn't yet alive, or I might have been tempted to wander down to Corinth. He would certainly have enjoyed a game, providing I stayed out of his sun. Me and

Diogenes, sitting on top of his barrel, playing chess a thousand years before the game was invented – that would have been something. Plato was a newborn babe in arms. Socrates was around, in his early forties, but who would want to play with that cunning man. Once he got the hang of it, you'd never win a game.

Flurries of snow began to drift in, over the mountains. The little Plataeans were in for a hard winter. I knew the result of the siege, of course. Three hundred Plataeans and seconded Athenians would make a break for it in a year's time, killing the sentries left by Archidamus on the outer wall and getting away in the dark. All of them would make it, to Athens, fooling their pursuers into following a false trail, their inventive minds never flagging when it came to survival. Those Plataeans whose hearts failed them when it came to risking the escape, almost two hundred, would be put to death by the irate Spartans. The city itself would be razed. Perhaps the Spartans would learn something from the incident, but I doubted it. There was certainly a lot of patience around in the ancient world.

Patience. I wondered how much patience those people from the land of the pharaohs had, because it occurred to me that the natural movement of time was on their side. Provided we did nothing but maintain the *status quo*, standing nose to nose on the edges of our own vortices, they would gain, ever so gradually. Hour by hour, day by day, we were moving back to that place I call home.

We might replace our frontier guards, by one or by thousands, but the plain fact of the matter is we will eventually be pushed back to where we belong. Why, they've already gained several months as it is ... only another twenty-five centuries and I'll be back in my own back yard.

Then again, I might receive that terrible message I have been dreading, which would turn me from being the Athenian I believe I am, into a Spartan. Which would have me laying down my scroll and taking up the spear and shield. A ghost-warrior from the future, running forth to meet a god-soldier from the past. I can only hope that the possible historical havoc such action might cause will govern any decision made back home. I can't help thinking, however, that the wish for sense to prevail must have been in the lips of a million-million such as me, who killed or died in fields, in trenches, in deserts and jungles, on seas and in the air.

The odds are stacked against me.

THE WALL

In the year of Ninth Dragon, Emperor Teng Wu the Seventeenth, old enough to appreciate the sharp sting of snuff
but young enough for the act not to have developed into a habit,
ordered the building of a wall to encompass his garden states.

For thirteen centuries his ancestors had been cultivating the
land around the palace, building parks and establishing farms
on the tiered hillsides, until the whole territory was a flourishing
garden and the envy of neighbouring lands. In the lowlands
were orange groves, vineyards, fields of golden maize, melons
of honey hue and melons with flesh the colour of sunsets. Higher
up on the slopes were orchards dripping with angry plums, crisp
apples and blackcurrants with the complexion of summer
stormclouds. There were also lichee nuts with thin shells and
pale green translucent flesh, and rose-tinted gooseberries that
filled the baskets of his tenant farmers. Crisp ears of lettuce grew
in his kitchen garden in the seasons of warmth, and tightly
layered winter cabbage when the white frost covered the land.
The smell of herbs drifted amongst the chestnut, almond and
walnut trees and pomegranate blooms shed their petals over
the paths to form crimson carpets. Every manner of exotic fruit
tree and plant found a place in Wu's kingdom.

Naturally, we were jealous.

Over the hundreds of years, earlier emperors had robbed
neighbouring coastal areas of their rich alluvium, their peasant
armies carrying it by the thousand basket-load and depositing
the dark, fertile silt in Wu's valleys. The soil from the slopes of
volcanic hills, dense with nitrates, was lifted away in hods and

yoked boxes, to adorn the steppes and tiers of the Wu hills. Streams had been diverted and rivers dammed, until we poorer farmers, under weaker rulers, could barely scratch a living from the meagre dust bowls that remained.

Our dissatisfaction was brought to the notice of the might Wu by his network of spies and the building of the wall began. At first it was an earthwork of rubble and scree, patched with yellow river clay, and followed the line of Wu kingdoms from east to west, in a semi-circle, the north being protected by a ring of ironstone mountains that rose like a forest of giant spearpoints tipped with white. The mortar was allowed to harden in the sun to the consistency of amber.

This wall was more than seventy feet high.

But we were able, like our goats, to scramble up this rampart and look down upon the kingdoms below, glistening with their succulant jewels, and the emperor ordered a higher wall to be built, this time of granite, obsidian and flint, sheathed in slippery glass.

For twenty years we heard the clinking of chisels on stone, night and day, and watched the huge blocks being drawn and pushed into place. The wall grew higher and higher, so that even the bravest of us was afraid to attempt the climb and we looked down on the hated kingdoms of Wu no more.

Then, one day as the wan moon slipped away below the dark sea, we awoke and turning to one another, said 'Listen! What do you hear?'

And we answered each other, saying, 'Only the birds in the thorn bushes and the rustle of papery leaves on dry bark,' for the ring of metal on stone had ceased and all activity had stopped behind the wall.

The one of us had the idea of building huge man-carrying kites, so that we could hover above the wall and see what we were missing in the green kingdoms of Emperor Wu.

This activity so incensed the ruler that he ordered all the drystone walls to be stripped of bricks and stones, and the houses of his peasants to be torn down, to add to the height of the great wall. Marble gravestones were ripped from the resting places of the dead; fine monuments and beautiful statues to past heroines and heroes were knocked from their pedestals; alabaster ceilings and roofslates from pagodas were broken up; onyx paths were robbed from the parks and jade panels taken from temple doors: all going to form yet more layers to the wall. Soon, the kites would not fly high enough and were in danger of crashing because of the fierce updraughts created by the wall. We had to abandon them, relinquishing all hope of ever seeing the garden kingdoms again.

Instead, we found what soil we could, scraping it from the shallow basins of rock and packing it into the cracks and crevices of the wall. There we planted strawberries, and in the deeper crannies, edible fungi. The strawberries flourished in the southern aspect – the mushrooms in their dark damper holes proliferated, tender and succulent. We pressed the sweet red fruits to our lips as we gathered in the harvests and inhaled the smell of the silk-vented mushrooms as the crops were collected. Over the course of the years we established our territories as fine regions for such produce.

Yet still we were angry and full of hatred for those behind the wall, who lived a better life than we did, their yield much higher and the variety of their produce far exceeding our own. We burned effigies of Emperor Wu during the fertility rites and beat the wall with sticks to symbolize our hatred. At the annual Festival of Noise, trumpeters marched up and down the wall blaring out our anger; horns bellowed, cymbals clashed and a mighty furore was created out of drums, gongs and scream-whistles. Priests would curse those behind the stone barrier and spit upon the blocks and pyrotechnical dislays of bloodlust filled the skies at harvest time.

As we grew richer from our harvests we bought new tools and with these shiny implements we burrowed away at the foot of the wall, hoping to get at the rich, dark soil on the other side and drain it away.

Then, when the seasonal monsoons came, the water rushed

along the tunnels we had scooped out, eroding what was left of the earth foundations.

Finally, there came a day when a thunder shook our lands from coast to coast. The wall collapsed like a range of mountains toppling into a chasm. Such tremendous din. Such a mighty thump. Every man, woman and child was thrown high into the air with the impact and the very surface of the world rippled like a shaken reedmat. Villages were razed and trees were felled.

When the rain ceased, we scrambled over the rubble to find an arid land on the far side. The precious soil had all been banked high against the foot of the wall, covered in thick moss, and now lay buried under tons of boulder rock. The cracked and desolate hinterland beyond was windswept desert. The only dwelling visible was the palace of Emperor Wu the Seventeenth, which stood on a high knoll surrounded by wasteland.

We realized from the evidence what had happened. The mistrals from the north had swept down from the mountains, across the land stripped of its drystone windbreaks, and had carried the surface soil towards the great wall, there to be cast in the shade from the giant barrier. The orchards and gardens had died in the hinterlands and little would grow but thick moss in the cold shadow of the wall.

In his selfishness to retain all he had, Emperor Wu had destroyed his garden and had established ours. In our eagerness and greed to get at greener fields, we had erased what new riches we had gained from his foolishness. The only benefactor is the storyteller, who makes gain from the mistakes of others, for who listens to stories of good emperors and satisfied people? Certainly not emperors, who all hate each other and delight in the fall of their contemporaries. Nor those who toil in the fields for a few grains of rice, who listen with distaste to tales of those more fortunate than themselves. The storyteller knows that both emperors and subjects are pleased to hear of the destruction of a ruler, for different reasons. The storyteller knows that subjects and emperors are pleased to hear of the misery of other people, for the same reasons.

MEMORIES OF THE FLYING BALL BIKE SHOP

The old Chinese gentleman was sitting cross-legged in the shadow of an alley. He was smoking a long bamboo pipe, which he cradled in the crook of his elbow. I had noticed him as we climbed the temple steps, and the image stayed with me as we wandered through the buddhist-tao shrine dedicated to Wong Tai Sin, a shepherd boy who had seen visions.

It was so hot the flagstones pulsed beneath our feet, but despite that David was impressed with the temple. We waded through the red-and-gold litter which covered the forecourt, the dead joss sticks cracking underfoot. Cantonese worshippers were present in their hundreds, murmuring orisons, rattling their cans of fortune sticks. Wong Tai Sin is no showcase for tourists, but a working temple in the middle of a high rise public housing estate. Bamboo poles covered in freshly washed clothes over-hung the ornate roof, and dripped upon its emerald tiles.

The air was heavy with incense dense enough to drug the crickets into silence. We ambled up and down stone staircases, admiring carvings the significance of which was lost in genera-tions of Western nescience, and gazed self-consciously at the worshippers on their knees as they shook their fortune sticks and prayed for lucky numbers to fall to the flagstones.

We left the temple with our ignorance almost intact.

The old man was still there, incongruous amongst the other clean-shaven Hong Kong men, with their carefully-acquired sophistication, hurrying by his squatting form.

He had a wispy Manchu beard, long grey locks, and dark eyes

set in a pomelo-skin face. A sleeveless vest hung from bony shoulders, and canvas trousers covered legs that terminated in an enormous pair of bare feet. The bamboo pipe he was smoking was about fifty centimetres long, three centimetres in diameter, with a large watercooled bowl at one end, and a stem the size of a drinking straw at the other. He had the stem in his lipless mouth, inhaling the smoke.

There was a fruit stall owner, a man I had spoken to on occasion, on the pavement nearby. I told David to wait by the taxi stand and went to the vendor. We usually spoke to each other in a mixture of Cantonese and English, neither of us being fluent in the foreign language. He was fascinated by my red hair, inherited from my Scottish highland ancestors.

'*Jo san*,' I said, greeting him, '*leung goh ping gwoh, m'goi.*'

I had to shout to make myself heard above the incredibly loud clattering coming from behind him, where sat three thin men and a stout lady, slamming down mah-jong tiles as if trying to drive them through the formica table top.

He nodded, wrapped two apples in a piece of newspaper, and asked me for two dollars.

Paying him, I said, 'That man, smoking. Opium?'

He looked where I was pointing, smiled, and shook his head vigorously.

'Not smoke opium. No, no. *Sik yin* enemy.'

I stared at the old gentleman, puffing earnestly away, seeming to suck down the shadows of the alley along with the smoke.

'*Sik yin dik yan-aa?*' I said, wanting to make sure I had heard him properly. 'Smoke *enemy?*'

'*Hai.* Magic smoke-pipe,' he grinned. '*Magic*, you know? Very old *sik yin*-pipe.'

Gradually I learned that the aged smoker had written down the name of a man he hated, on 'dragon' paper, had torn it to shreds, and was inhaling it with his tobacco. Once he had smoked the name of his enemy, had the hated foe inside him, he would come to *know* the man.

The idea was of course, that when you knew the hated enemy

– and by *know* the Chinese mean to understand completely –
you could predict any moves he might make against you. You
would have a psychological advantage over him, be able to
forestall his attacks, form countermoves against him. His
strategy, his tactics, would be yours to thwart. He would be
able to do nothing which you would not foresee.

'I think . . .' I began saying, but David interrupted me with
a shout of, 'I've got a taxi, *come* on!', so I bid the stall owner a
hasty goodbye, and ran for the waiting vehicle. We leapt out
into the fierce flow of Hong Kong traffic, and I put the incident
aside until I had more time to think about it.

That evening, over dinner at the Great Shanghai Restaurant in
Tsimshatsui, I complained bitterly to David about John Chang.

'He's making my life here a misery,' I said. 'I find myself
battling with a man who seems to despise me.'

David was a photographer who had worked with me on my
old Birmingham paper. He had since moved into the big time,
with one of the nationals in London, while I had run away to
a Hong Kong English-language newspaper, after an *affaire* had
suffered a greenstick fracture which was obviously never going
to heal.

David fiddled with his chopsticks, holding them too low down
the shafts to get any sort of control over them. He chased an
elusive peppered prawn around the dish. It could have still been
alive, the way it evaded the pincers.

'You always get people like that, on any paper, Sean – you
know that. Politicians, roughriders, ambitious bastards, you
can't escape them just by coming east. Some people get their
kicks out of stomping on their subordinates. What is he,
anyway? Senior Editor?'

David finally speared the prawn with a single chopstick and
looked around him defiantly at the Cantonese diners before
popping it into his mouth.

'He's got a lot of power. He could get me thrown out, just
like that.'

'Well, suck up to the bastard. They like that sort of thing, don't they? The Chinese? Especially from European *gwailos* like you. Take him out to lunch, tell him he's a great guy and you're proud to be working with him – no, *for* him. Tell him the Far East is wonderful, you love Hong Kong, you want to make good here, make your home here. Tell the bastard anything, if it gets him off your back. Forget all that shit about crawling. That's for school kids who think that there's some kind of virtue in swimming against the tide. You've got to make a go of it, and this bloke, what's his name? Chang? If he's making your life hell, then neutralize the sod. Not many people can resist flattery, even when they recognize what it is – hookers use it all the time – "you big strong man, you make fantastic lovey, I never have man like you before". Codswallop. You know it, they know it, but it still makes you feel good, doesn't it? Speaking of hookers, when are you going to take me down the Wanch . . . ?'

He was talking about Wan Chai, the red-light district, which I knew I would have to point him towards one evening of his holiday. David liked his sex casual and stringless, despite all the evil drums in such a life-style these days. I needed emotion with my love-making, not cheap scent and garlic breath.

I lay in bed that night, thinking about what David had said. Maybe the fault did lie with me? Maybe I was putting out the wrong signals and John Chang thought I did not like him, had not liked him from our first meeting? Some men had sensitive antennae, picked up these vibrations before the signaller knew himself what messages he intended to transmit.

No, I was sure that wasn't it. I had gone out of my way to be friendly with John Chang. I had arrived in Hong Kong eager to get to know the local people, and had seen John Chang as a person to whom I would have liked to get close. But from the beginning he had come down hard on me, on my work, on everything I did. I had been singled out for victimization and he piled adverse criticism on my head whenever he got the chance.

However, I was willing to admit that I was not the easiest of employees to get along with, from a social point of view.

John Chang had a happy marriage. I had never met his wife, but she phoned him at the office quite often, and the tone and manner of the conversation indicated a strong loving relationship. This caused me to be envious of him. I once dreamed of having such a relationship with Nickie, and had failed to make it work. I still loved her, of course, and on days I missed her most I was testy and irritable with everyone, including John Chang.

I fell asleep thinking that perhaps I was more than partly to blame for John Chang's attitude towards me. I vowed to try to improve things, once my vacation was over and I was back at work.

There was a cricket making insistent noises, somewhere in the bedroom. It took several sleep-drugged minutes for me to realize that it was the phone chirruping. David? Had he gone down the Wanch and got himself into trouble?

'Hello, Sean Fraser . . .'

'Fraser?' John Chang's clipped accent. 'Get down to the office. We need you on a story.'

I sat up in bed.

'I'm on vacation. I've got a guest here, dammit!'

'Sorry, can't help that. Tim Lee's gone sick. He was covering the Governor's annual speech. You'll have to do it.'

The line went dead. He had replaced the receiver.

I slammed the phone down and seethed for a few minutes, before getting out of bed to have a shower and get dressed. David was still asleep on the living-room couch when I went through to the kitchen. I woke him and told him what had happened, apologized, and said I would see him that evening.

'Don't worry about me, mate. I can sort myself out. It's that bastard of a boss *you* want to sort out.'

Once I had covered the usual bland yearly speech presented by the British Governor of Hong Kong – written by a committee

into a meaningless string of words – John Chang wanted me to
visit a fireman who lived in the Lok Fu district. The man had
been partially blinded six weeks previously while fighting a fire
in Chung King Mansions, a notorious giant slum where holiday-
ing backpackers found relatively cheap accommodation in an
impossibly expensive city.

'It's five o'clock,' I protested to Chang, 'and I have a guest to
look after.'

He regarded me stone faced.

'You're a reporter. You don't work office hours.'

'I'm on bloody holiday.'

'That's tough. You cover this, *then* you're on vacation –
unless I need you again. If you want to work for someone else,
that's fine too. Understand me?' He stared hard at me, probably
hoping I would throw his job in his face. I was not about to do
that.

I said coldly, 'I understand.'

I rang David and said I would be home about nine o'clock. I
advised him to go out and eat, because I was going to grab some
fast food on my way to Lok Fu. He seemed happy enough, and
told me not to worry, but that wasn't the point. The point was
that I was close to strangling John Chang with my bare hands.

I saw the young fireman. He seemed philosophical about his
accident, though to me his disability pension seemed incredibly
small. His wife was working as a bank clerk and now he could
look after their two infants, instead of sending them to the
grandparents for the weekdays. He could still see a little, and
as he pointed out, government apartments, like most private
apartments in Hong Kong, were so small it had only taken him
a short while to get a mental picture of his home.

During the interview the fireman pressed brandies upon me,
as is the custom amongst the Hong Kong Chinese. By the time
I left him, I was quietly drunk. I caught a taxi. The driver took
me through Wong Tai Sin, and I passed the temple David and
I had visited the previous evening. On impulse I told the driver
to stop and paid him off.

The old man was still there, at the opening to the alley. He was sitting on a small stool, staring dispassionately at passers-by with his rheumy eyes. The pipe was lying on a piece of dirty newspaper, just behind him. I stumbled over to him, trying to hide my state of inebriation.

I pointed to the pipe.

'Ngoh, sik yin-aa?' I said, asking to smoke it.

Cantonese is a tonal language, the same words meaning many different things, and by the way he looked at me I knew I had got my tones wrong. I had probably said something like 'Me fat brickhead' or something even more incomprehensible.

'M'maai,' he said emphatically in Cantonese, thinking I wanted to buy the pipe and informing that it was not for sale.

I persisted, and by degrees got him to understand that I only wanted to smoke it. I told him I had an enemy, a man I hated. I said I wished to know this man, and would pay him for the use of his magic pipe. He smiled at me, his face a tight mass of contour lines.

'Yi sap man,' he agreed, asking me for twenty dollars. It was a very small sum for gaining power over the man that was making my life a misery.

I tore off a margin piece of newspaper and wrote JOHN CHANG on it, but the old man brushed this aside. He produced a thin strip of red-and-gold paper covered on one side with Chinese characters and indicated that I should write the name on the back of it. When I had done so, he tore it into tiny pieces. I could see the muscles working in wrists as thin as broom handles, as his long-nailed fingers worked first at this, then at tamping down the paper shreds and tobacco in the pipe bowl.

He handed the musty-smelling instrument to me and I hesitated. It looked filthy. Did I really want that thing in my mouth? I had visions of the stem crawling with tuberculosis bacilli from the spittle of a thousand previous smokers. But then there was a flame at the bowl, and I was sucking away, finding the tobacco surprisingly smooth.

I could see the dark smoke rising from the rubbish-burning

cauldrons of Wong Tai Sin Temple, and as I puffed away on the ancient bamboo pipe, an intense feeling of well-being crept over me. I began to suspect the tobacco. Was it indeed free of opium? Had I been conned, by the fruit seller and the old man both? Maybe the old man was the fruit stall owner's father? It didn't seem to matter. I liked the pair of them. They were wonderful people. Even John Chang seemed a nice man, at that moment in time.

When the holiday was over, David left Hong Kong, and I returned to work. John Chang was in a foul mood the morning I arrived, and was screaming at a young girl for spilling a few drops of coffee on the floor. A female reporter caught my eyes and made a face which said, 'Stay out of his way if you can.'

The warning came too late.

'You,' snapped John Chang, as I passed him. 'That fireman story was bloody useless. You didn't capture the personal side *at all*.'

'I thought I did,' I said, stiffly.

'What you think is of no interest to me. I asked you to concentrate on the man and his family, and you bring in all that rubbish about government pensions.'

'I thought it needed saying.'

He gave me a look of disgust and waved me away as if I were some coolie that was irritating, but not worth chastising further. I felt my blood rise and I took a step towards him, but Sally, the female reporter, grabbed my arm. She held me there until John Chang had left the room.

I turned, the fury dissipating, and said, 'Thanks.'

She gave me a little smile.

'You would only be giving him the excuse he needs,' she said in her soft Asiatic accent. Peter Smith, another reporter, said, 'Too bloody right, mate. Don't give him the satisfaction.'

'He looked as if he could have killed that girl,' I said to Sally, a little later. 'All over a few spots of coffee.'

'It was her perfume. For some reason that brand drives him crazy. I used to wear it myself, but not any more. Not since I realized what it does to his temper . . .'

Understand the one you hate.

I had to admit my temporary drunken hopes for a magical insight into John Chang had failed. There was no magic on the modern streets of Hong Kong. An antique pipe, nicotined a dirty yellow, stained black with tobacco juice, dottle clinging to the bowl, was nothing more than what it was – a lump of wood. Had I really believed it would help me?

I guess a desperate man will believe anything, even that he will some day manage to forget a woman he loves: will wake up one morning free of her image, the sound of her voice in his head gone, her smell removed from his olefactory memory. Memory sometimes works to its own secret rules and is not always subject to the will of its owner.

Memories can be cruel servants.

I began to have strange dreams, even while awake, of a woman I did not know. She was small, slim and dark, with a familiar voice. We were very intimate with one another. I pictured her in a kitchen, her hands flying around a wok, producing aromas that drove my gastric juices crazy. I saw her brown eyes, peering into mine from behind candles like white bars, over a dining-room table made of Chinese rosewood. There was love in those eyes. We drank a wine which was familiar to my brain but not to my tongue. She chattered to me, pleasantly, in Cantonese. I understood every word she said.

These pictures, images, dreams, began to frighten me a little, not because they were unpleasant, but because they felt comfortable. They worried me with their cosiness. I wondered whether they were some kind of replacement for the memories that I was attempting to unload: the result of a compensatory mental illness. Perhaps I was trying to fill emotional gaps with strange fantasies of a Chinese woman.

I began to look for her in the street.

There were other, more disconcerting thoughts, which meant very little to me. Scenes, cameos, flashes of familiar happenings that meant nothing to me emotionally. I pictured myself going into stores and shops I did not recognize, for articles I had never even considered buying. There was an ambivalence to my feelings during these scenes. I saw myself buying an antique porcelain bowl, the design of which I instinctively and intensely disliked. Yet I purchased it with loving care and a knowledge of ceramics I had not previously been aware of possessing. In another scene, I went into a bakery and bought some Chinese moon cakes, a highly-sweetened, dense foodstuff which most *gwailos* avoid, and I was no exception.

I was sure I was going quite mad.

John Chang kept me busy, hating him. He did not let up on me for one moment during the sweltering summer months, when the wealthy fled to cooler climes and school teachers blessed the long vacations they got during the season when Hell relocated to the Hong Kong streets.

During this humid period the Chinese lady with the loving eyes continued to haunt me. I would languish at my desk after work, reluctant to leave the air-conditioned building, picturing myself making love with this woman in a bed with satin sheets, surrounded by unfamiliar furniture. It seemed right. Everything about it seemed right, except when I questioned it with some other part of my mind, the part firmly based in the logic that said, *you do not know this woman*. It was true. I had never met anyone like her, yet she looked at me as if I were hers, and some unquestioning area of my mind, less concerned with what I *knew* and content to be satisfied with what I *felt*, told me yes, this had happened, this was a proper interpretation of my experiences.

I began to read about schizophrenia, wondering whether I was one of those people who have more than one personality, but the books that I read did not seem to match what was happening to me. I baulked when it came to seeing a therapist.

I was afraid there was something quite seriously wrong with me.

In October, some people organized a junk trip to Lamma Island, the waterfront of which is lined with excellent fish restaurants. Sally asked me if I was going and I said I might as well. Most of the newspaper's employees would be there, and a few of the employers as well. The weather had turned pleasantly hot, had left the dehumanizing summer humidity behind in September. It promised to be a good evening.

There were rumours that John Chang would be going, but that did not deter me. I wondered if I could get drunk enough to tell him what I thought of him.

I was one of the last to jump aboard the junk, which then pulled out into the busy harbour. I stared at the millions of lights off to port: Causeway Bay, Wan Chai and Central, resplendent during the dark hours. A beer was thrust into my hand. I drank it from the can and looked around me. Sally was there. She waved. Peter Smith stood in animated conversation with another of our colleagues, his legs astride to combat the rolling motion of the craft in the choppy harbour waters. Then I noticed John Chang, sour faced, standing by the rail.

Beside him was a lady I had never seen before, not in the flesh, but a woman with whom I had made love, in my head, a thousand times. My heart began to race and I felt myself going hot and cold, alternately, wondering whether I should try to hide somewhere until the evening was over. If she sees me, I thought, she's bound to recognize me as the one . . .

Then I pulled myself up short. One *what?* What had I done to her? Nothing. Not a blessed thing. So where did these pictures come from, that had invaded my head? The best way to find out, was to talk to her. I tried to catch her eyes, hoping she would come over to me without bringing John Chang.

Eventually I captured her attention and she looked startled. Did she know me after all? Was I indeed living some kind of Jekyll and Hyde existence? It was only after a few minutes that I understood she was not staring into my face at all: it was my red hair that had her attention. Then she realized she was being rude and averted her gaze, but Chang had caught us looking at each other and motioned for her to cross the deck with him. Before I could turn away, he was standing in front of me, gesturing towards the woman at his side.

'I don't believe you've met my wife, have you, Fraser?'

She spoke in gentle tones, admonishing him.

'John, Mr Fraser must have a first name?'

He looked a little disconcerted.

'Yes, of course,' he said stiffly. 'Sean. Sean Fraser. Scottish I think.'

'My ancestors were,' I blurted, 'but we've lived south of the border for two generations. The red hair, you know, is proof of my Celtic origins. I'm still a Scot, in spirit.'

I shook her hand, acutely embarrassed by the fact that I knew what she looked like naked, lying on the bed, waiting for me to press myself against her. *John Chang's wife.* There were two small brown moles under her left breast. There were stretch marks around her abdomen.

I felt the silkiness of her palm, knowing that soft touch. I remembered the time she had whispered urgent nonsense into my ear, the first time our orgasms had coincided exactly, a miracle of biology which had left us breathless for several minutes afterwards, when we had both laughed with the utter joy of the occasion.

Staring into her eyes, I knew that if there was a memory of such happenings, they did not include *me*. What I saw there was a terrible sadness, held in check by a great strength. Alice Chang was one of those splendid people who find a natural balance within themselves. When a negative aspect of life causes them to lose equilibrium, a positive one rises from within their spirit, to meet it, cancel it out.

'I'm very pleased to meet you, Alice,' I said.

'Oh, you know my name.' She laughed. 'I thought John tried to keep me a secret. Do you know this is the first time he has allowed me to meet his colleagues?'

I looked quickly at John Chang, and then said, 'I'm afraid I've heard him speaking to you on the phone. The office has good acoustics. I don't eavesdrop intentionally.'

'I'm sure you don't,' she said, and then he steered her away, towards one of the directors, leaving me sweating, holding on to the rail for support. Not because of the rocking motion of the boat, but because my legs felt weak.

The following weekend I took a boat trip to Lantau Island and sat at a beach restaurant, staring at the sea and sand. I needed a peaceful place to think. Hong Kong's national anthem, the music of road drills, pile drivers, traffic, buzz saws, metal grinders *et al.* was not conducive to reflective thought.

There were evergreens along the shoreline of Silvermine Bay, decorated with hundreds of tattered kites. The children used the beach to fly their toys, which eventually got caught in the branches of the large conifers, and remained there. The brightly-coloured paper diamonds gave the firs the appearance of Christmas trees. Around the trunks of the kite-snatchers were dozens of bicycles, chained to each other for security, left there by adolescents now sprawled on the sands.

I had managed to engineer one more chat with Alice Chang, before the end of that evening on Lamma, and spoke about the antique porcelain bowl, describing it. I had to lie to her, telling her that John had spoken to me about it, seemed proud to be its owner.

'Oh, yes. He loves ceramics you know. It's his one expensive hobby.'

I knew now I was experiencing John Chang's memories.

It was nothing to do with me. I had not made love to Alice Chang, but I carried John Chang's memories of such occasions, those that he wished to recall, and some he did not. It was a disturbing ordeal. There was a grim recollection of being hit a glancing blow by a truck, when he was small, and another when he was falsely accused of stealing from his school friends. I was gradually getting to *know* my Chinese boss and there were some dark areas in there which terrified me. I woke up at night, sweating, wondering where the fear was coming from, what was causing the desire to scream.

The night after the junk trip, I had spoken to Sally.

'How many kids has John Chang got?' I asked her casually.

She shook her head.

'None, so far as I know. Why do you ask?'

'Oh, no reason. I met his wife, last night. I thought she mentioned something about a child, but I couldn't be sure. I suppose I must have been mistaken.'

Sally said, 'I'm positive you are.'

I drank steadily, as I tried to puzzle through my jumbled memories of his early marriage, and my eyes kept being drawn towards the bicycles, chained to the tree trunks. I struggled with a black beast of a memory, which was utterly reluctant to emerge from a hole it had dug itself.

A bicycle.

This was the key, but something prevented me from opening the lock. There was the idea that a bicycle was a detested thing, a deadly, ugly machine that should be outlawed, banned from use. *People who sell bicycles should be prosecuted, imprisoned, hung by the neck . . .*

That was very strong, *very* strong.

One of the kids from the beach came and unlocked her bike, climbed into the saddle, and rode away along the path. I experienced a forceful desire to scream at her, tell her to get off, return the machine to the salesman.

Where?

A shop sign popped into my head, which read: THE FLYING BALL CYCLE CO.

Then that dark cloud extended itself from the back of my brain, blacking out anything that might have followed.

Back at the flat I received a surprise telephone call from England. From Nickie. She asked me how I was. Did I like the Far East? Yes, she was fine. She was seeing one or two people (she didn't call them men) and things were absolutely fine.

Her voice was recognizably thin and tight, even over the phone. There was great anger there, pressing against her desire to sound casual. I noticed that it was three o'clock in the morning, her time, and I guessed she had been unable to sleep, obsessed with relentlessly reviewing the bitter times, furious with herself for failing to retaliate strongly, when something hurtful had been said, wishing she could raise the subject again, but this time be the one to wield the knife, cut the deepest.

I knew how she felt, having gone through the same cycle, many nights. We had both fired words, intended to wound, but we both remembered only being hit.

I told her I was having some trouble with one of my bosses. She sympathized coldly, but what she had really called about was the fact that I still had two of her favourite poetry books. She would like them back again, please, the Hughes and the Rilke.

Oh, those, yes, but three o'clock in the morning? – she really must want them badly, I said. I told her I remembered seeing them just before leaving England for Hong Kong, but could not put my hand on them at this time. Could she call again later, when I had done some more unpacking?

No, she couldn't. I had been in Hong Kong for nearly a year. Hadn't I unpacked my things *yet*?

Her words became more shrill as the anger seeped through like a gas, altering the pitch of her voice.

When I did manage to unpack, could I please post them back to her? Yes, she was aware they were only paperbacks and could be replaced, but she didn't see why she should buy new copies when she already owned some – goodbye.

The emptiness that filled the room, after she had put down the phone, would have held galaxies.

I tried not to hate her, but I couldn't help it. She was there, I was here. Thousands of miles apart.

I picked up the Rilke, from the bedside table, open at *Orpheus, Eurydice, Hermes*. It was pencil-marked in the margins, with her comments on the text. It was her handwriting I had been reading, not Rilke's poem. The flourishes were part of her, of the woman I had loved, and I had been sentimentalizing, as well as studying them for some small insight into her soul. I wanted to understand her, the secret of her self, in order to discover *why*. Why had it gone wrong?

The terrible ache in me could not be filled by love, so I filled it with hate instead. I wanted to kill her, for leaving me, for causing me so much emotional agony. I wanted to love her. I wanted her to love me. I hated her.

On Monday afternoon, I cornered Peter Smith. I recalled that he used to cover cycling stories for the paper. At one time his speech had been full of jargon – *accushift drivetrains, Dia-Compe XCU brakes, oversized headsets, Shimano derailleurs*. The language of the initiated, for the enthusiasts.

'You're a bike fanatic,' I said. 'You cycle in New Territories, don't you?'

'Not so much now,' he patted a growing paunch, 'but I used to. Why, you looking for a sport to keep you fit?'

'No, I came across this guy who kept raving about the Flying Ball Bike Shop. Know it?'

Smith laughed.

'My boy, that shop is a legend amongst cyclists. You can write to the owner of the Flying Ball from any corner of the earth, and he'll airmail the part you need and tell you to pay him when you eventually pass through Hong Kong.'

'Why *Flying Ball*? Is that some kind of cog or wheel-bearing invented specifically for push bikes?'

Smith shook his head.

'I asked the owner once. He told me the shop had been named by his grandfather, and he forgot to ask the old man what it meant. The secret's gone with grandpa's polished bones to a hillside grave overlooking water. Part of the legend now.'

'Where is it? The shop, I mean.'

'Tung Choi Street, in the heart of Mong Kok,' he said, 'now buzz off. I've got a column to write.'

I went back to my desk. A few moments later I experienced a sharp memory pang and looked up to see the office girl placing a polystyrene cup of steaming brown liquid on my desk top. She smiled and nodded, moving on to Sally's desk. I could smell her perfume. It was the same one she had been wearing the day John Chang had bawled at her.

It was twilight when I reached Tung Choi Street. Mong Kok is in the *Guinness Book of Records* as the most densely populated area on the face of the earth. It is teeming with life, overspilling, like an ants' nest in a time of danger. It is run down, sleazy, but energetic, effervescent. Decaying tenements with weed-ridden walls overhang garage-sized factory-shops where men in dirty vests hammer out metal parts for everything and anything: stove pipes, watering cans, kitchen utensils, car exhausts, rat cages, butter pats, fish tanks, containers, and so on. What you can't buy ready-made to fit, you can have knocked up within minutes.

Over the course of the day the factory-shops vomit their wares slowly, out, across the greasy pavement, into the road. The vendors of fruit and iced drinks fill in the spaces between. Through this jungle of metal, wood and plastic plough the taxis and trucks, while the pedestrians manage as best they can, to hop over, climb, circumnavigate. Business is conducted to a cacophony caused by hammers, drills, saws, car horns. It can have a rhythm if you have a broad musical tolerance and allow it flexibility.

THE FLYING BALL CYCLE CO.

I found the shop after two minutes walking.

I stood on the opposite side of the road, the two-way flow of life between me and this unimposing little bike shop, and I remembered. It hit me with a force that almost had me reeling backwards into the arms of the shopkeeper amongst whose goods I was standing. The dark area lifted from my brain and the tragedy was like an awful light, shining through to my consciousness. The emotional pain revealed by this brightness, so long covered and now unveiled, was appalling.

And this was not my agony, but *his*.

I turned and stumbled away from the scene, making for the nearest telephone. When I found one I dialled John Chang's home number. It had all come together the moment I laid eyes on the Flying Ball: the hate John Chang bore towards me; the unexplained stretch marks on Alice Chang's abdomen; the blankness in his eyes, the sadness in hers.

'Mrs Chang? This is Sean Fraser. We met on the junk – yes, the other night. I wonder if you could ask John to meet me, in the coffee shop by Star Ferry? Yes, that's the one. Can you say it's very important. It's about your son. Michael . . . Yes, I know. I know, but I have to talk to him just the same. Thanks.'

I put down the receiver and hailed a taxi.

I was on my second cup of coffee when he arrived. He looked ashen and for once his façade of grim self-assurance was missing. I ordered him a cup of coffee and when it arrived, put some brandy in it from a half-bottle I had bought on the way. He stared at the drink, his lean face grey, his lips colourless.

'What's all this about?' he said. The words were delivered belligerently, but there was an underlying anxiousness to the tone. 'Why did you ask me to come here, Fraser?'

He hadn't touched his coffee, and I pushed it towards him.

'I know about Michael,' I said.

His eyes registered some pain.

'I know how he died.'

'What business is it of yours?' he said in a low voice. 'How dare you? You're interfering in my family affairs. You leave my family alone.'

'I'm not interested in your family. I'm interested in the way you treat *me*. Since I've been in Hong Kong you've made my life hell. I didn't bring your family into the office, *you* did. You're punishing me for something you won't even allow yourself to think about. You've blocked it out and the guilt you feel is causing you to hurt other people, especially red-headed *gwailos*.

'I've been the target for your suppressed anger, your bottled grief, for as long as I can stand. It's got to stop, John. I'm not responsible for Michael's death, and you know it, really. I just happen to be a European with red hair. I wasn't even in Hong Kong when that driver took your son's life . . .'

'Shut up!' he shouted, causing heads to turn and look, then turn back again quickly. His face was blotched now, with fury, and he was gripping the cup of coffee as if he intended to hurl it into my face.

'This is what happened, John,' I said quietly, ignoring his outburst. 'It was Christmas, and being a Christian, you cele- brated the birth of Christ in the way that *gwailo* Christians do. You bought presents for your wife and twelve-year-old son. You gave your wife some perfume, a brand you won't allow her to use now because it reminds you of that terrible time, and you asked your son what he would like most in the world . . .'

There were tears coming down John Chang's face now, and he stumbled to his feet and went through the door. I left ten dollars on the table and followed him. He was standing against the harbour wall, looking down into the water still crying. I moved up next to him.

'He said he wanted a bicycle, didn't he, John? One of those new mountain bikes, with eighteen, twenty gears. You took Michael down to Mong Kok, to the Flying Ball Bike Shop, and you bought him what he wanted because you were a loving father, and you wanted to please him. He then begged to be allowed to ride it home, but you were concerned, you said no, repeatedly, until he burst into tears and finally, you relented.

'You said he could ride it home, if he was very, very careful, and you followed behind him in the car.'

I paused for a moment and put my arm around his shoulders.

'The car that overtook you, halfway home, was driven by a red-headed foreigner, a *gwailo*, and he hit Michael as he swerved in front of you to avoid an oncoming truck. The bike itself was run over. It crumpled, like paper, and lay obscenely twisted beside your son's body. You stopped, but the other driver didn't.

He sped away while you cradled Michael's limp body in your arms, screaming for an ambulance, a doctor.

'They never caught the hit-and-run driver, and you've never forgiven yourself. You still want him, don't you, that murdering red-headed *gwailo*, the man that killed your son? You want to punish him, desperately, and maybe some of that terrible guilt you feel might go away.'

He turned his tear-streaked face towards me, looked into my eyes, seeking a comfort I couldn't really give him.

I said gently, 'That wasn't me, John. You know it wasn't me.'

'I know,' he said. 'I know, I know. I'm so sorry.'

He fell forward, into my arms, and we hugged each other, for a brief while. Then we became embarrassed simultaneously, and let go. He went back to leaning on the wall, but though the pain was still evident, his sobbing had ceased.

Finally he turned and asked the obvious question: how did I know so much detail, about Michael's death? It had happened many years ago.

Rather than go into the business with the pipe, I told him I had been to Wong Tai Sin, to a clairvoyant, and the man had looked into John's past for me.

'It cost me a lot of money,' I said, to make it sound more authentic. If there's one thing that Hongkongers believe in, it's the authority money has to make the impossible possible. John Chang did not laugh at this explanation or call me a liar. A little brush with the West does not wipe out five thousand years of Chinese belief in the supernatural.

Then he went home, to his wife, leaving me to stare at the waters of the fragrant harbour and think about my own feelings of love and hate. *Understand the man you hate.* How can you hate a man you understand? I began to realize what the old man with his magic pipe was selling. Not power over one's enemy. Love. That's what he had for sale. His was a place where you could look at hate, understand it enough to be able to turn it into love.

I knew something else. Now that I had confronted John, now

that we understood one another, the memories of his past would cease to bother me. The pipe had done its work.

The following week, one evening when a rain as fine as Irish drizzle had come and gone, leaving a fresh scent to the air, I took a taxi to Wong Tai Sin Temple. The old man was still there, sitting at the entrance to the alley, his pipe by his side.

I went up to him and gave him twenty dollars, and he smiled and silently handed me the pipe and a piece of red-and-gold paper decorated with Chinese characters.

On the back of the paper I wrote the name of a person I loved and hated – NICHOLA BLACKWOOD – and tore it into tiny pieces hoping that distance was no barrier to magic.

X-CALIBRE

The Dark Age

A dark age has fallen upon the ancient halls of Whorestraete. Men gather in groups, heavy-eyed, hollow-eyed, whispering from gaunt faces. Others stand alone, in the washrooms, staring into mirrors which appear to have no finite depth. There are those who have plunged from high places, some figuratively, some even physically.

Whorestraete was once a flourishing stronghold, its floors sounding with the soles of expensive shoes, its walls ringing with the shouts of dealers. Its noble houses seemed indestructible, its stockbroker lords immortal. Now and then one might fall prey to the temptation of insider dealing and be struck off the lists of the mighty families, or destroy itself from within, but these had hitherto been isolated misfortunes. The oligarchies whose assets had once seemed invincible had now been shown the index finger. Since the crash fortunes have been lost overnight. Out of this darkness has come widespread corruption as men try to save themselves from the pit. The red figure of bankruptcy stalks the kingdom: he prowls through halls, offices and corridors, and gathers men to him in a harvest of broken dreams. Ruin is upon the land.

In the house of Utha, prayers are muttered before VDUs, murmured into telephones: prayers for a saviour, who might deliver them from chaos and restore confidence in the market once again.

The Legend

Amongst the rubble of fallen firms, in the basements of

crumbling companies, it has long been whispered that a Hero strong enough to restore order and sanity to the kingdom will arise. It is said that this man will come from the family of an aristocratic firm of stockbrokers, will be of inherited wealth, but by necessity will have been raised in ignorance of the vagaries and vicissitudes of the market. Thus he will be pure of spirit, untarnished by the sordid dealings of the Dark Ages and able to operate with a clear conscience.

He was expected to be, like all great stock market heroes, a man of great wisdom, without fear; ruthless but with an impeccable integrity. He would no doubt continue the practice of worshipping Chance, the god of Whorestraete, but with a clean mind capable of restoring the treasure house to its former respectability and glory. Security would be his watchword and all would yield to his advice.

The New King

And a Hero does emerge from the mists, fresh from the College of Business Administration. Her name is Gwenyth and, being a woman, the remnants of the Old Families of Bankers and Stockbrokers refuse to accept her. Never before has a female warrior stood at the head of their armies, led them into battle against their foes.

There is a split amongst the nobles and some leave with her half-brother Morton, a man dedicated to corruption, and some remain with Gwenyth who forms a new company. Gwenyth is elected President of the new company which she calls The Avalon Group. She insists that all the board members have an equal vote, and that there shall be no lobbying and no yes-men, and the board table shall be *round* to emphasize the fact that it is a *group* effort and no single member is more important than another. Gwenyth is aware that internal petty jealousies can be more devastating than any damage an outsider may inflict.

The Magic Weapon

Gwenyth knows she needs a symbol of authority to give her the strength to rid Whorestraete of the damned Morton, who has already covered his ass with gold and silver. Gwenyth has a childhood sweetheart by the name of Merle, who is an electronics wizard. Merle invents for her a computer the like of which has never been seen before. The magic of Merle is not only in the system, which is able to accommodate any software program in the known world, but in the flexibility of its disc drive slot, which will expand and contract to accept any kind of disc that was ever forged on the anvils of computersmiths. Thus a disc from any region of the known world can be inserted and its information accessed immediately. In Whorestraete, fractions of seconds count, and fortunes are made by the quick, leaving competitors dead. In Merle's computer, Gwenyth has her taliswoman.

$x = $ Slot vol, where x is lxbxh of disc

The wizard Merle explains that x equals the calibre of the disc drive slot when x is the size of any given disc. Gwenyth bestows upon her magic weapon the access code 'x-calibre'.

Right-hand Man

Once she has her magic weapon, Gwenyth discovers that great heroes also require a special friend and adviser, a trouble-shooter who will go through fire. Although she trusts those around the board table, she needs a consultant with unshakable loyalty. This person must have impeccable credentials, be afraid of nothing, be pure of spirit. She asks her secretary to search the lists for one who is not afraid to joust with dark market forces.

The Stranger

Such a person sweeps into her office one day. She has travelled from a distant land called Lundun, and has knowledge of Hung Gung and Toakio stock markets. She is the ex-vice-president of French and French Inc., a family business famous for its integrity and morals. The woman's name is Lily. She states that private domestic misfortunes caused her departure from F&F Inc., that she has heard of Gwenyth and now wishes to serve The Avalon Group in any capacity.

Gwenyth is overjoyed. With Merle's x-calibre computer in her hands and an ex-inc vip for an ally, she is convinced that Morton will soon need more than heavy metals to protect his arrears. Her half-brother is casting a dark shadow over Whorestraete, and brokers go in fear of him, for he has destroyed many of their options in his greed for power. His self-interest is boundless. Now Gwenyth has the means to meet him on the battlefield in a final confrontation. She begins to make her plans.

There is some jealousy in the Avalon camp because Gwenyth shows a marked preference for the views of Lily and favours her new companion with more time than she gives others. The Company President is aware of this dissatisfaction, but considers there are more important things with which to concern herself.

The Unknown Factor

Illicit love will penetrate the strongest armour with its barbed and wicked arrows. Until Lily arrived at Whorestraete, Merle and Gwenyth had an understanding, a close relationship of the shared kind. Gwenyth possessed a high retreat to which they escaped from time to time, but when they could not they played bondage games behind the gates of their office citadel, finding great excitement in locking each other in Gwenyth's personal stocks.

Now that the great battle is almost upon her, however, Gwenyth has to work late. She cannot meet with Merle in her high tower, nor does she have time for manacled love in the shadowed recesses of her office fortress. She tells Lily she would appreciate it if her right-hand man would keep Merle company of an evening, warning her that though Merle is magic with electronic equipment he bores the socks off most people with his interest in computers.

Suspicion and Envy

There is talk behind closed doors in The House of Avalon, of how Lily is having an *affaire* with Gwenyth's lover. Noble lords and ladies mutter through gritted teeth that 'the woman must go' for she has committed the cardinal sin of monopolizing all sexual intrigue, and is driving everyone mad with envy and suspicion.

They all add their own dark misgivings, at the same time craving similar liaisons with Lily, Merle and each other, but not daring to make the first move for fear of rejection. Lust is in every noble's mind. It eats away at the very mortar of their foundations, it gnaws at the bastions and keeps and the company begins to crumble.

Gwenyth will hear nothing against her friend, nor against her lover, both of whom she would trust with her bank balance. When Merle and Lily run away together to Akapulko, Gwenyth falls into deep despair and neglects the management of the kingdom.

Regrets and Betrayal

Lily dispatches a message to Gwenyth from Akapulko, repenting of her deeds and stating that before she left Whorestraete she had uncovered treachery. Lily's note tells Gwenyth that the user manuals Merle wrote for the x-calibre system have been stolen, lock, stock and barrel, by Gwenyth's secretary, who is an agent for the Morton Group.

The Holy Grail

Without Merle to advise her on the system, the user instructions for x-calibre are essential, and Gwenyth sends her knights out, to seek the traitorous secretary. They are in the field for many weeks, some of them never return from their quest. They are lost out in the wildernesses of concrete and brick. Some fall prey to higher offers from other giants and dragons of the business world. Others do battle with terrible bulls and savage bears, occasionally making a killing, but more often than not going under. Those that do return are empty-handed, dispirited and unable to assist her in the final fight for the controlling shares of key companies.

At the fateful hour of the battle with Morton, x-calibre goes down. Merle, her electronics wizard, is somewhere else humping her right-hand man.

Gwenyth stands in the fray with the remnants of her army, teeth gritted and with blood in her eyes, but without her magic weapon. She is still determined to destroy Morton for good and all. She has right on her side, and she prays that her god will see her triumph over her half-brother.

The carnage that follows is awful to witness. Holdings are lost, trusts destroyed, bondsmen are driven back and forth, stockades fall, shares are forged into weapons on the fires of wrath. Votes are cast and the air is thick with oaths. Finally, just before the market closes only Morton and Gwenyth stand head to head trading blows. At the height of single combat, the swaying Whorestraete god finally settles his support on the corrupt Morton. Chance is amoral and distributes his favours by whim. Gwenyth is forced to yield and crawls away at the end of the day, hollow and defeated.

The Aftermath

Gwenyth never recovers from this last betrayal. She is found sitting before a blank screen, punching at random keys in a daze, and is finally prised from x-calibre. To her credit, her last quotation is spirited and full of venom.

'Throw the fucking thing in the lake!'

Gwenyth has not failed because she is pure, nor because she put her faith in the wrong kind of people, nor because x-calibre went down at a crucial time. She has not fallen from grace because love has no place in a board room nor even because her secretary was a spy for the Morton Group.

She failed because she chose a fickle god.

BRONZE CASKET FOR A MUMMIFIED SHREW-MOUSE

I expect you're wondering what the hell has gone wrong with the world in the last few months. I expect you're asking yourself why all the earthquakes, floods, pestilence, famine, accidents, incidents, tragedies, disasters. Why, you are saying to your neighbour, are the stars going out (one by one); why have the laws of science and nature gone berserk; where have lost bits of the Earth gone to? You needn't ask, because I'm going to tell you anyway. Look on this as something of a confession. I don't think it *really* matters whether I confess or not: Old Nick is warming up a floppy disc for me right now, if I'm not mistaken. You can't do what I did and expect to be forgiven, no matter how many confessions you indulge in. And this is in the nature of an indulgence. I've just got to get it off my chest. It all began when I was under the surgeon's knife and my heart stopped beating. In the middle of an operation . . . No, perhaps it's not *all* my fault. He's got to take a bit of the blame.

You see, God has just discovered he likes to use a word processor.

I'm not kidding. Up until now God has been writing it all up by hand, first the old pen and ink, then (a reluctant change) a ballpoint, occasionally using the typewriter when he wanted things clearer in his mind. Writing the story of the world, making it up as he goes along, like any creative author.

Now he's written computers into the scheme of things. It took him a while to get around to trying one himself. Comes of inventing things second hand, I suppose. I mean, what he does is write down something like '... on the third of October, dah-dah-dah-dah (note: enter year later), Alexander Graham Bell invents the telephone.' Big J doesn't actually invent the thing himself, you understand. I doubt the Old Man even understands how the telephone system works. (Does *anyone* understand how the telephone systems works?) He gets one of us to do it and then, later, when he's overcome his prejudices of the thing, tries it out himself. Sometimes he's delighted, sometimes he's not. It's not a generally well known fact but God can be a bit of a materialist at times. I mean, he likes gadgets and appliances, especially things that revolve at high speed, like kitchen mixers and whisks. He's still a kid at heart, though the rest of him is older than time. Automatic toasters are also a great hit with the Ancient of Days, even though he never eats toast. He likes to see it jump, he says.

What?

Who am I?

Actually there's no reason why you should know me, even if I gave you my name. I'm one of those guys that 'died' on the operating table, only to be brought back to life a few minutes later – and if you think a few minutes is not enough to get an insight into what happens up there, you don't know anything about time my friend. Three minutes of eternity is long enough to get to know the whole shebang inside out.

So, as I was saying, God's into computers. He's also making a mess of what was once a pretty good system. Okay, it wasn't *perfect*: things didn't dovetail all the time. But now? Now the whole PLAN is going awry.

How do I know? I'll tell you how I know. Remember the last but one President of the United States, Tom Mishnler? President for exactly four months? No, of course you don't. Know why you don't know? Because God used the erase key on him, that's why. He hasn't had the word processor long and he's been practising with things like that lately. Why do I remember Tom Mishnler, and nobody else? Well, the fact is, be it coincidence or what, I 'died' on the operating table just as the Old Man was preparing to wipe out the President, so I was up there when it happened, looking over his shoulder with the rest of the angels, saints and souls. When he had effectively zapped Mishnler, much earlier than planned, he spun round on his typist's stool (which he *loves* by the way) and asked, 'Who was last up?'

'Me,' says I. 'Couple of minutes ago.'

'Okay,' says the Old Man, 'we've got to replace that latent Fascist Mishnler, to keep the numbers straight, so you get a second shot. I should erase your memory, but,' he looked at his Longines, 'I've got to cause a tsunami in the Pacific – fact I should have done it three nano-seconds ago. Don't tell anyone about this place or I'll zap you quick as look at you. Understand?'

'Understood,' I gulped (he's a fearsome-looking fella, is God).

Thus the doctors down below, who had been busy with my body, pumping it full of injections to get the old heart going again, looked up to see a blip on the heart monitor. *Blip, blip, blip*, regular as twenty-one jewel movement clockwork.

'We did it!' they cried, and the intern who had given me the wrong anaesthetic fainted in relief.

Swop one fiction writer for a President.

But did God do right? Ah, there's the rub. God is omniscient, he *knows* all things – but can he remember to actually *do* all things? There's a great difference. He's like the professor who can remember whole chunks of math theory, quote it verbatim, but ask him where his car keys are and he looks at you as if you'd just discovered a cure for cancer.

Like I said, Big J was just playing with the keys, trying out things, that's how you get to know your word processor. Now, an erase key in the wrong hands can be a very dangerous tool. I wouldn't go so far as to say God's hands are 'wrong', but as everyone knows, you got to start young if you want to be an expert. Get any eight-year-old kid and his dad together, on a home computer, and see which one's the whizz at video games.

God is no eight-year-old. Eight years is a finger-snap to 'I AM'. God's got socks that are older than my grandfather.

What I'm trying to say is, he's not your flashbrained whizzkid.

Okay, the answer to the question. *I* think, and this is purely a personal observation you understand, I think God erased Mishnler because the President was showing neo-Nazi tendencies from the moment he entered office. The guy was beginning to reveal strong Fascist policies and we had already been through all that once. Hitler, Franco, Mussolini, Papa Doc – God is bored with Fascists. I can see him, chin in hand, when, having just written Mishnler into office and seeing what he's doing once he's there, groaning and saying, 'Not *again*! Where's my fershlugner erase key.'

Now, this is where the problem lies. Let's go back to when the Old Fella used pen and ink. If he didn't like Tom Mishnler then he would write in his big book, 'Mishnler snuffs it after four months in office. Heart attack on the steps of the White House while he's inspecting a regiment of Mishnler Youth. Streatham, the Vice-President, sworn in. First black President of the United States. etc, etc'. So, everyone would remember Mishnler, many would have seen what they were in for and heaved a sigh of relief. 'Squeaked through that one,' they would say. 'Better watch for it in future. We're getting too damn complacent.'

Okay, that's the pen and ink job. But what about erase keys? Ah, that's where the system starts to break down. It may seem clean and efficient and all that, but what you haven't got is a continuing script, with all the historical bits still there, if you care to go back a few pages. The History of the World is no longer a diary or a journal, so to speak, but a single chunk of writing, constantly being revised and rewritten. There's not even a first draft lying around somewhere. It's all pristine copy. So once God gets used to his erase key, and he decides it's easier than writing a continuing saga, bang goes the History of the World. We just sort of do a mark time. With the erase key comes memory wipe, because once God has done the biz with the magic key, that piece of history no longer exists. It ain't in the big book. It's nowhere.

Or is it?

This is where the second part of the problem comes in.

As I said before, the Almighty, bless his ancient cotton socks, hadn't thought it through enough. What he hadn't realized was that the word processing software on his PCW contained failsafes for at least the first six files erased from any block. What happens is simple: you erase a file and it goes into a *limbo file*. The device is so new to the Lord of Hosts that he hasn't found out about limbo files yet. Mishnler was still somewhere in his machine, just waiting to get out again, like all the souls in the real Limbo. All God had to do was press a few wrong keys in sequence one day – granted, *unlikely*, but as that great humorist P. G. Wodehouse once wrote, never confuse the unusual with the impossible – and Mishnler was back in the totalitarian governing business, somewhere on the globe. Don't forget, Mishnler didn't die, as such. He was just erased. And since he wasn't erased completely, he's still there, behind a couple of locked doors.

When I was up top I noticed that God was having a few more terminals put in and my guess was that he was going to train the Archs, Gabriel and his buddies, as computer operators, so that they could transpose the History of the World from book form to computer program. I'm sure some bright recently- dead soul has done the salesman pitch with the Old Man and convinced him that his archives would take up far less room if everything was on disc. Heaven may be infinite but you've still got to walk around or climb over the racks of paper files. I can see the guy now:

'You see, Sir, the *paperless* office is the thing of the future. Get everything on microfiche or disc is my advice. You won't regret it, I can assure you . . .'

Well I can assure both of them that they *will* regret it.

You see, I've done a very foolish, not to say, evil thing.

Fact is, at first I didn't really care whether or not Mishnler got out and began his reign of terror somewhere in the world. Chances are it would be some small republic on an island off South America and the people would end up burning him on a bonfire with chickens tied to his legs, or something of that nature. But I have a personal problem at stake here. I mean, if Mishnler got out and came back, what would happen to me? I *like* being alive. I enjoy the pleasures of the flesh. I'm not saying I'm debauched or depraved or anything. I'm no de Sade or mad Russian monk. I'm no Louis XIV. I'm just your average guy who likes his pint, enjoys a take-away on a Friday, and has a regular girlfriend who is willing to participate, if you know what I mean. Nothing kinky, nothing illegal. You see, I *know* what's up there, and I don't want to go *down*. I'm not ambitious. I'm happy to be a ranker when I go back. Let the keen ones go for Sainthood, whatever. I just want to do my job, live my life best as I can, and still enjoy it a little.

Now God did indicate something to the effect that there was a balance of some kind. I don't think he would claim to be neat and tidy, but it seems everything has got its place. If Mishnler were to escape from his hidden file, I might find myself in a nasty traffic accident, in order to make up the number of dead souls.

One day I was wandering around the British Museum, worrying the hell out of this problem, when I found myself in the Egyptian section. I walked amongst the glass cases, in between the sarcophagi, staring moodily at the contents. I was trying to think of some way of screwing up the system in Heaven to take God's attention away from his new toy. You see, nothing ever goes wrong up there, and if I could throw a glitch into the system God might hand over the keyboard to a soul expert in such matters (some new guy who worked for IBM in his mortal years?) and turn his omnipotence to putting his own house in order. No one who knows what they're doing would call a *limbo file* forward except on purpose, and I was sure I'd be safe for at least my own lifetime.

Suddenly, I stopped, and an idea came to me.

The object that had caught my attention was a tiny metal oblong box labelled BRONZE CASKET FOR A MUMMIFIED SHREW-MOUSE. You see, the ancient Egyptians had it right:

animals do have souls. They actually deserve the same rites as humans get, whatever the religion. (By the way, there *is* only one bloke up there, whether you call him Jehovah, God, Sun, Moon, Tree or John Frum.) During my eternal three minutes I saw every kind of animal-soul wandering around. Wild animals always go to Heaven, though there are one or two of the domestic beasts that go to the other place. This is because they have been warped by contact with some evil human during their lives and animals have a choice too. They can be bad or good. But God doesn't even bother to personally vet (ha, ha,) wild animals, because they operate by instinct and therefore you're extremely unlikely to get a bad one. Yes, they kill, and fight, and bonk each other randomly, but these are all instincts, built in, and uncontrollable. When humans do it, we do it *knowingly*. Apparently there hasn't been a bad wild animal since Noah's ark, and the crocodile in question was forgiven because the circumstances were considered to be mitigating. The croc had, after all, been cooped up for weeks with a lot of other beasts, birds and insects. No, I'm not going to tell you what it did, that wouldn't be fair on the creature now that God's given it a clean slate. Suffice to say that it would have gone up in smoke in one of two biblical cities had it been around at that time and there was no blame attached to the other party because *that* unwitting correspondent, a wallaby, was already dead at the time the act took place.

However, the scheme that unravelled in my mind required that P. G. Wodehouse adage to work. It is extremely unusual for a wild animal to go bad, *but not impossible*. The archangel responsible for doing the checks had become remarkably complacent about the beasts of the field, and gave them but a cursory once-over, if that. What I had to do was first get myself an evil beast of the field, and secondly, get him into Heaven.

My plan was to get a 'bad' soul up there and screw up the system, so that God and his archminions would have more to worry about than playing with word processors. The Lord and his Band of Angels would know that something was rotten in the state of Paradise, but they would have one hell of a time finding what and where it was, especially if it was *very very small*. Imagine the fuss it would take looking for a tiny bad soul in infinite space and eternal time!

For my purpose, what better trainee than one of those nasty-tempered little mammals, the shrew?

It took me a week to catch the little devil and training began in earnest, straight away. At the end of a certain period of time I had corrupted the shrew completely. Its soul was as black as sin. It would kill at the drop of a hat, that is to say, for gain. It attacked and raped lady shrews out of season, just for the hell of it, and had lust coming out of every orifice. It envied all other creatures, for one thing or another. It collected and hoarded food it would never eat, and would rather the stuff rotted than give it away to some starving brother shrew. It ate all kinds of delicacies, from honeyed humming-bird's wings to pickled bees-livers, always to excess. It drank any kind of alcohol I put in its dish, to the point of vomiting. It was fat, lazy and cruel. It tortured and maimed, sending other shrews into nests far afield, in order to get the edge on its enemies. It would tear the eyes out of a jenny wren as soon as look at it.

I assisted it in forming an empire in the wood outside my home, where it gathered slaves to itself, took concubines, encouraged prostitution and graft, made other shrews fight to the death for its own entertainment. It massacred babies and pillaged the nests of birds and voles and wood mice, robbing the rich and poor alike, storing all for itself in huge empty molehills. It was paranoid and was not slow in indicating which other creatures I was to execute when it felt a plot might be forming against its despotic rule. It set up an opium route to feed its own habit, getting shipboard rats to smuggle the stuff in from Thailand. It chased dragons and mainlined until its eyes were popping and its tail as stiff as a needle.

It dabbled in black magic, calling forth Mephistopheles with more frequency than did Dr Faustus, selling instead of its *own* soul to the devil, those of yet unborn generations of amphibians, damned by a shrew even before the metamorphosis from tadpole to frog. It scrawled letters in blood on the trunks of trees and hanged infant squirrels for the theft of a single seed. The skulls of innocents were piled high in the woods and the bones of unwary animal travellers were scattered amongst the grasses of my lawn.

It invented tortures unknown to Orientals: tortures de Sade would have given his mistress's eyes to have at his fingertips. There were nights when the screams of the dying penetrated every corner of my garden and days when the vegetable patch was covered in small crosses bearing crucified beasts. Rasputin would have been jealous of the devious ways my shrew found of inflicting pain, its methods of skinning until the nerve ends of the victims were raw. It even found a way to debone a sparrow without killing the creature, so that it collapsed in a sickening splodge of feathers and flesh, and was left to perish slowly like a stranded jellyfish, eyes full of terror.

Towards the end there were genetic experiments going on outside in the wood and many was the time I was awoken to find a nightmare creature, part rat, part fish, part toad, flopping over my kitchen floor and mewling at me as if I were its devilish parent.

When the wicked shrew finally died of an overdose of heroin, I heaved a sigh of relief. The terrible creature's personality was beginning to affect even me: it was beginning to control my life too.

Thus Maurice-the-Unmentionable, as I had nicknamed him, went to Heaven, and as I now know, got in without a second glance at his stained and bloody soul. He slipped quietly beneath the hem of St Peter's garment and into the tranquil place beyond the gates. What I didn't know at the time was that God had updated his system and had a huge, powerful IBM with megabytes coming out of its ears. Not only were the archs putting the History of the World on to this monster, God had ordered them to put all spirits of the dead on it too – all, that is, except for the wrecking crew, down in the hot hole.

What happened, I'm sure, is that Maurice went into the archives with the rest of welkin's pure of heart, and the little bastard's soul became yea, as a software disease, which spread throughout the system and corrupted everything with which it came into contact.

Maurice is a computer virus, and that's why the world is coming to an end, with no hope of salvation for anyone, especially not me.

I hope Satan isn't into writing his own software yet. Some of those video games can be pretty frightening, and I'm sure he's got it all there, HUNT THE SINNER or BURN THE INIQUITOUS, one of those garage jobs which made twelve-year-olds into millionaires. I know, I know. Damn Maurice and his little black soul. Damn me, too.

I'm not without my problems down on Earth, either. Ever since Maurice crawled into a corner to die with a smile on his face, the woodland creatures have been gathering outside my house. I believe they want to be sure that his reign of terror is finally over, and won't believe it until they see the corpse. There are mice, voles, small birds, weasels, stoats, squirrels, even a fox and a couple of badgers out there, all burning holes in my house with their eyes. Maurice's intrigue and evil affected every creature in the parish. I guess I owe it to them to show them a carcass.

Maurice has dried out now, to a husk, the way small creatures do. Mummified, I suppose. I've got an empty Benson and Hedges cigarette packet, which is the nearest thing I can find to a bronze casket. I intend putting him in it and laying him out in state on the lawn. The animals and birds can file past and spit on his corpse, or whatever wild creatures do with their dictators. I feel like spitting on the arrogant little shit myself, but I'll let them have first shot.

It's the least I can do.